The Mystery of the Black Moriah

By
David A. Crossman

Down East Books

CAMDEN, MAINE

ISBN 0-89272-536-2
Library of Congress Control Number: 2002104555

Printed at Versa Press

1   3   5   4   2

DOWN EAST BOOKS / CAMDEN, MAINE
Book orders: 1-800-766-1670
www.downeastbooks.com

To the friends of my youth.
Thank you.

Contents

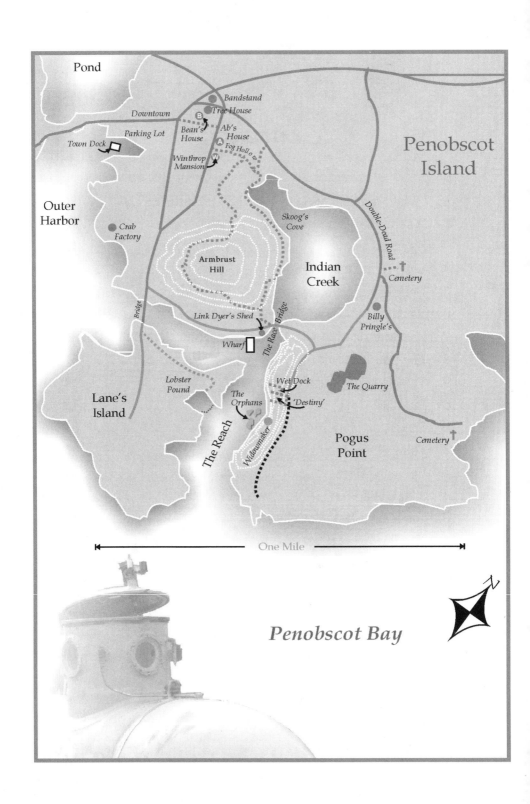

Pond

Bandstand
Tree House

Downtown

B Bean's House

Parking Lot

Ab's House

Town Dock

Winthrop Mansion

A

W Fog Hollow

Penobscot Island

Outer Harbor

Crab Factory

Skoog's Cove

Indian Creek

Double-Dead Road

Cemetery

Armbrust Hill

Bridge

Link Dyer's Shed

The Race Bridge

Billy Pringle's

Wharf

The Quarry

Lane's Island

Lobster Pound

Wet Dock

'Destiny'

The Orphans

The Reach

Widowmaker

Pogus Point

Cemetery

One Mile

Penobscot Bay

1

"What Trouble Can They Possibly Get Into?"

Spooky always looked as if he were standing in a pretty stiff breeze. As he burst into Bean's house, he might have just stepped out of a hurricane. His wispy red hair shot out in all directions like exclamation points, and his pale blue eyes danced with the excitement of the discovery he was bursting to make known.

"You'll never guess what I found washed up on the shore of Indian Creek!" he exclaimed as the screen door slammed behind him. "Sorry, Mrs. C."

"Oh, please," said Mrs. Carver, putting down the newspaper with the account of Bean and Ab's latest experience. "No more adventures. We're all exhausted."

Bean and Ab, however, having had a few days' rest, were ready for a little excitement.

"But you ain't gonna believe this!" said Spooky.

"We *aren't* going to believe this," Mrs. Carver corrected.

"You sure ain't," Spooky agreed, the grammar lesson whizzing over his head. "I was walkin' home 'round the east side of Armbrust Hill when I saw this big yellow thing floatin' under the bridge."

"What was it?" said Ab, her excitement rising.

Spooky's eyes sparkled with mischief. "I ain't tellin', 'cause you wouldn't believe me anyway. You an' Bean gotta come see for yourselves. An' we're gonna need a wrench."

"A wrench? What for?" Bean wanted to know.

Spooky just smiled. "For the thing," he said cryptically.

Bean cast a quick look of appeal at his mother. It was almost supper-time, and he knew she wouldn't be thrilled with the idea of his missing the family meal. "I'll be back in thirty minutes," he said.

Mrs. Carver looked at her husband, her eyebrows arched skeptically. "What do you think?"

Captain Carver shrugged. "I guess it won't hurt to hold dinner for half an hour."

1

"I suppose," his wife replied, a little hesitant. "We can find something to do in the meantime." She winked at her husband, who had just returned from three months of sea duty with the Coast Guard, in a way that Bean didn't understand. Besides, Spooky's announcement had Bean too wound up to think about it.

"So, we can go?"

"I doubt he could eat anyway, with another mystery hanging over his head," Captain Carver decided, tousling his son's hair. "There's an adjustable wrench in my toolbox out in the shed. But one thing—"

"We'll be careful!" the trio chimed as they ran out the door.

Mrs. Carver reflexively held up her hand. "And don't slam the—" *Slam.* "Door."

"Sorry!" Ab called behind her. In seconds they had grabbed the pipe wrench from the shed and thundered down the wooden walkway and up the sidewalk. The echo of their footsteps followed them toward Fog Hollow, the narrow dirt lane that led to Indian Creek.

"Thirty minutes," Mrs. Carver whispered, snuggling herself against her husband's shoulder.

"As far as Bean's concerned, thirty minutes might as well be an hour." He squeezed her around the waist. "Let's hope."

Mrs. Carver was silent for a moment. "You don't think they're in any danger, do you?"

"I wouldn't worry," said her husband. "What kind of trouble can they possibly get into in thirty minutes?"

Fog Hollow was named for the thick tendrils of mist that drift down the ragged slopes of Armbrust Hill like arms of a ghostly octopus whenever the southeast wind pushes the fog in from Penobscot Bay, as it was doing now. The fog collects in a thick blanket in the hollow between the hill and the shores of the creek.

As they raced through the narrow canyon formed by the Moses Webster House—the B and B where Ab and her folks were staying for the summer—and the brooding Winthrop mansion, Ab couldn't suppress a tingling shudder of fear. Only days before, she and Bean had nearly lost their lives in the secret tunnel they had found between the houses. Even though Bean always claimed that Ab didn't have any imagination, what little she had was having no trouble picturing dark, malevolent eyes watching them from the gaunt, gaping windows of the empty old house.

The same thought must have occurred to Bean, because he picked up his pace. Ab had all she could do to catch up.

"You know what this place makes me think of?" said Spooky, as if he'd been reading their thoughts.

"We know," said his companions in unison as they sped even faster from the scene of images that would haunt them forever.

Once they had put a safe distance between themselves and the mansion, they slowed to a trot. "So, what's this great secret?" said Ab. "What did you find?"

"You'll never guess," Spooky replied, lowering his voice to a mysterious moan. "Not in a million years."

For the next few minutes, Bean and Ab tried every trick they could think of to make Spooky divulge his secret. Ab even knocked him down and tickled him mercilessly. But for once the usually talkative Spooky was silent as the tomb.

The long, low wail of the ferry whistle wound its way through the fog.

"The last boat's comin' in," Spooky observed, standing up and brushing himself off.

For several seconds the lonely moan echoed from the trees and granite cliffs, weakening a little with each retelling. It was a melancholy sound, but one that Abby found oddly comforting. Despite the fact she had been born and raised in New York City, and spent most of her life amid the constant clamor of traffic, the wail of sirens, and the traipsing of countless thousands of feet, she was an island girl at heart. This was where her spirit was at home: swimming in the fresh, cold water of bottomless quarries, wading through fields of feathery golden grass, climbing heaped-up piles of granite slag, picking blueberries and blackberries on Lane's Island, spending idyllic hours on the shore digging for clams or searching the seaweed for crabs, or finding bits of colored glass that the ocean had worn to polished gems.

The last boat of the day meant Penobscot Island was sealed off from the rest of the world, like a castle with the drawbridge raised for the night.

Bean picked a piece of grass and, holding it between his thumbs in that special way Ab had yet to master, blew a shrill squeal in reply to the ferry horn.

It aggravated Abby no end that Bean could do things like that—skipping stones, making a musical instrument of a blade of grass or a tender shoot of alder. He tried to teach her, but she just couldn't get the hang of it. "You can't help it," he'd tease. "You're just a city girl."

Next to being called a "summer jerk," it was the worst thing he could say. She didn't like being reminded that, no matter how much time she spent on the island, she would probably never know what it was like in the fall, or winter, or spring. Only summer. She would always be an outsider.

No doubt about it, Bean knew how to get under her skin. But, truth be known—which it never would if she could help it—her summers on the island wouldn't be the same without him. He had a curious way of finding magic and mystery in ordinary things she wouldn't even notice under normal circumstances. For Bean, life was one big adventure. When she was with him, she felt part of all those possibilities, and she never knew what might happen next.

"Your turn," said Bean, handing her the soggy piece of grass he'd just blown spit all over.

"You're so immature," Ab retorted, tossing her hair back in a way that seemed to annoy him.

It worked. "If you keep shakin' your head like that, it's gonna pop right off the sprocket," he said flatly. Fact was, that particular gesture was one of many things about Ab that had changed since last summer, all of which made it hard to overlook the fact she was a girl—from head to foot—and it bothered him in ways he hadn't figured out yet.

Just a few days ago, when they'd found Minerva's grave, Ab had grabbed him and kissed him right on the lips, in front of everybody in town. He'd never been kissed before, except by his folks, or his grandmothers, and those kisses were different. Ab's kiss had shot through him as if she'd been hooked up to a twelve-volt battery. Then she'd just gone on as if nothing had happened, and he stood there gaping like a fish out of water, with his insides all twisted up. He didn't understand why. Not at all.

Not that it was a bad thing.

Failing in their efforts to get Spooky to share his secret, Bean and Ab had tried Twenty Questions. That didn't work either. By the time the trio arrived at the soggy little path that wound along the shore of Indian Creek,

Spooky declared that neither of them had come within a "billion light years" of guessing what he'd found.

"So," said Bean, stopping on a little spit of mud and seaweed that poked into the creek. "Where's this big yellow whatever it is?"

Spooky pushed by Ab on the path. "Over this way, in Skoog's Cove."

Skoog's Cove was no more than a dent in the shoreline where, years ago, a man named Gus Skoog had built and launched sailing dinghies. Nothing remained of the boat shed but a rectangle of square-cut granite stones that had formed the foundation. Over time, the cove had become hidden from view by thick vegetation.

"When it floated in under the bridge, I followed it—runnin' along the shore—an' this is where it washed up," Spooky announced as they stumbled through the undergrowth.

Bean saw it first, and he stopped in his tracks so fast that Abby ran into him, nearly knocking him over. But he didn't notice. All of his attention was fixed on the object floating in the water, its nose gently poking the seaweed, prodded by the persistent legion of little waves that assaulted the shore.

Abby had been just about to scold Bean for stopping so abruptly—and had inhaled a good lungful of air for the purpose—when she saw it, and the complaint died on her lips.

Spooky was right. They'd never have guessed in a million years.

"Told ya!" said Spooky, almost dancing with glee.

2
WHERE'S CAPTAIN NEMO?

"IT'S A SUBMARINE!" said Bean breathlessly, his heart suddenly racing with excitement.

"A yellow submarine!" Spooky announced proudly. "Just like the song."

"It's not real, is it?" said Abby, quickly jumping a series of stones to the head of the cove. "It's so small."

The awkward-looking vessel was about fifteen feet long and had a tower that stood about four feet above the waterline. "It's a one-man sub," proclaimed Spooky. "They use 'em for research. I read about 'em in *Popular Science*."

By this time all three kids were standing at the bow of the little vessel, and Bean ran his hand over the cold steel hull. "Who was in it? Did you see 'em get out?"

"There wasn't nobody. I stood right here and waited after it come ashore," Spooky explained. "But no one got out. It just laid there, thumpin' the rocks. So after a couple minutes I come down an' banged on it." He illustrated his point with a loud rap on the hull, which responded with a hollow, bell-like note. "Nothin' happened, so I looked in the windows on the conning tower—"

"Conning tower?" said Ab.

Bean explained. "That's the part that sticks up." He pointed to the cylindrical tower that rose from the hull.

"It's got windows on three sides," said Spooky. Climbing onto the hull, he pressed his face against the round Plexiglas porthole. "Can't see much, but it don't look like nobody's to home." He knocked on the conning tower for emphasis.

"That's like a quadruple negative," Ab said, thinking it was in Spooky's best interest to know how to speak properly.

Spooky didn't notice. Bean was too awestruck to care. "Did you open it?" he asked, crawling up beside his friend. He peered into the porthole, but due to the darkness within and the gathering gloom of the fog, he couldn't make out much more than the other portholes.

"I couldn't turn this wing nut," said Spooky, indicating the sealing latch that clamped the hatch shut. "That's why I wanted the wrench." He took the instrument from his back pocket and applied it to the nut.

Abby stood on the shore and held the bow of the sub with both hands to keep it from drifting off. The waves were no longer lapping at the mud. That meant the tide was turning and soon the saltwater fingers that pushed the sub ashore would be trying to pull it back out to sea. "What if somebody's in trouble?"

Bean looked up, his hair hanging in his eyes. "What do you mean?"

"I mean, what if whoever was in this fell overboard or something?"

"How do you fall overboard from a submarine?" said Spooky. He gave Bean a look that said, leave it to a girl to think of something like that.

Bean considered Ab's concern. He studied the conning tower. "It was sealed from the outside."

"So?"

"So," Bean explained patiently, and a little condescendingly, "he was outside the sub when he closed the hatch."

"Then he *could* have fallen off," said Ab, with just a trace of *I told you so* in her voice. Then she thought of another explanation, one that sent chills up her spine. "What if somebody *outside* wanted to lock somebody *inside*?"

Bean hadn't thought of that. "Then why don't he knock back to let us know he's in there?"

That's the part Ab especially didn't like. "What if he can't? What if he's tied up, or unconscious, or—"

"Dead?" said Bean.

Spooky suddenly stopped wrestling with the wrench. "Dead? You mean you think there might be a dead body in here?" All at once he wasn't so eager to loosen the bolt.

Bean collected his thoughts. "Well, we still have to open it an' find out. If there's somebody in there, he might need our help."

"If he's alive," Spooky reminded. "Here. You do it." He handed the wrench to Bean.

Bean looked at Ab in the hope she would be annoyingly practical, as always, and tell him to go get Constable Wruggles. That would give him an excuse not to open the sub. But all she said was, "If somebody needs us . . ."

He felt like saying, Big help *you* are, but he didn't.

Marshaling his resolve, Bean clamped the teeth of the wrench on the nut and gave it a sharp, downward tug. The nut held fast for a second or two—long enough to give Bean hope that he wouldn't be able to loosen it. Then, with a loud snap, it turned freely on the thread.

Spooky backed carefully off the sub and planted his feet on the shore. "I'm goin' to help Ab hold it still."

"Thanks a lot," said Bean sarcastically. He took a deep, steadying breath, unscrewed the nut until the bolt swung free of the latch, and stood up so he'd have leverage as he opened the hatch. He clamped his fingers around the lip of the cover and pulled.

The hatch squeaked open with unexpected ease. Bean, who had over-balanced against the expected resistance, nearly fell off the sub deck.

Reflexively, he dropped to his knees to steady himself. He looked at the hatch and realized why it had opened so easily: a heavy-duty spring was wound around the hinge bolt.

"What's inside?" Ab asked, just above a whisper.

Bean didn't really want to look. They'd already found one body that summer, and he didn't relish the thought of finding another. But, as his dad always said, there are some things you just have to do, whether you want to or not. He decided this was one of those things. Closing one eye and squinting with the other, as if that would somehow minimize the impact of whatever he was about to see, he bent over the open tower and looked inside.

"Hello?" he said.

No reply.

He opened both eyes. No body. He exhaled a long sigh of relief.

"Any dead bodies?" Spooky asked expectantly.

Bean didn't reply. He placed one hand on either side of the tower, then swung himself over the opening and down into the belly of the sub, feet first.

"No bodies, I guess," said Spooky with the slightest trace of disappointment. Reassured, he abandoned Ab to her chore and scrambled over the deck to the conning tower for a look inside.

Bean had already dropped to his bottom on the little iron and wood bench that spanned the hull.

"How cool is this!" said Spooky.

It was better than cool, Bean thought. This was no Disney World ride. It was real. He took a quick verbal inventory of the various controls, most of which were toggle switches. "Battery on/off. Forward and rear ballast tanks. Port and starboard thrusters." For the latter there was a little joystick, which he moved as he read the markers: "Forward, reverse, left, and right." His feet came to rest on metal pedals suspended on a bar just above the floor. "I bet this is the rudder." He pushed the pedals back and forth, and the sub's stern wiggled subtly in response. "Yup."

"What are you doing?" Ab called, her voice nearly muffled by the thick steel hull. Bean ignored her. All of his senses were focused on studying the controls.

"What's this, I wonder," he said, gently pulling a lever that rose from the floor on his right. There was a slight motion of the sub, as if something were tugging it from below.

"Do it again," said Spooky. He extracted himself from the hatch, then knelt on the deck and, with one hand on the conning tower for support, leaned over the side.

Bean repeated the process, and Spooky saw a narrow metal plate tilt up and down. The plate was affixed to the hull by a shiny stainless steel rod. "Stabilizers," he said, poking his head into the tower. "Push 'er forward and she goes down, pull 'er back and she'll come up."

In the bow, just in front of Bean's feet, was a large underwater porthole made of Plexiglas that would give the driver a clear view of the ocean floor. There was also a radio, tuned to a frequency that Bean didn't recognize.

"You got room in there for me?" said Spooky. Not waiting for a reply, he swung his legs through the opening. Bean squeezed himself as far forward and to the left as possible. In an instant, Spooky was wedged so tightly into the seat beside Bean that neither of them could move. "This ain't gonna work," Spooky decided.

"There's nowhere to go forward," said Bean. "What's aft?"

Spooky folded his skinny frame as tightly as possible and leaned back farther and farther until, suddenly unwedged, he tumbled into the aft compartment with a thud. "Ow!"

Once more free to move, Bean turned to see what had happened. Spooky was sprawled amidst a tangle of wires, tubes, and hoses. "You okay?"

Spooky rubbed his head, which had banged sharply against the cast-iron bracket holding a bank of batteries in place.

"What are you guys doing down there?" said Ab. In all the commotion they hadn't heard her crawling across the deck to the tower. Her hair was hanging down in Bean's eyes. He tried to brush it out of the way.

"Hey, this is a one-man sub!"

"Yeah, but you're just boys," Abby replied, then she shimmied through the narrow hatch and dropped down beside Bean on the seat formerly occupied by Spooky. "See? Perfect fit."

Abby was smaller than Spooky, so she didn't take up quite as much room. Besides, Bean didn't necessarily mind having her so close. "Who's holding us ashore?" he said.

"Nobody," said Ab. "The bow's in the mud. It's not going anywhere. What's this?"

Taped to the inside of the conning tower, just below eye level, was a piece of lined yellow paper. Bean lifted it up by the bottom edge, revealing a rough diagram in blue ink. "Looks like a map," he said.

"Of what?"

Bean lifted the edge a little farther, until the faint light from the starboard porthole made it somewhat more legible. "Here's Indian Creek," he said, tracing the outline with his finger. "There's Armbrust Hill and the bridge."

Ab shifted in her seat. "What's that?" she asked, pointing at a small X that had been marked in red.

"It's the Reach," said Bean, tilting the map slightly for a better perspective.

"Where's that?"

Spooky, who had twisted himself around so he was on his knees in the cramped compartment, stuck his freckled face between his companions' shoulders and studied the map. "It's out on the southwest end of Pogus Point. They call it Hurricane Reach 'cause it takes the worst of the weather. Some of the highest cliffs on the island are out there."

"Why would somebody mark it with an X?" Ab wondered aloud.

The answer was obvious to Spooky. "Treasure!" he said. "What else?"

"You've got treasure on the brain," said Bean. "Besides, you don't go lookin' for treasure in a submarine. I bet it has something to do with scientific research. That's what they use these subs for."

Abby fidgeted in the seat. "What kind of scientific research?"

Bean shrugged. "Marine biology an' stuff."

"But that doesn't explain how it got here," said Ab.

Bean theorized. "Most likely it was tied up somewhere an' just pulled free. Let's get out an' see if there's a line on the bow." He nudged Ab in the ribs. "You go first."

Abby reached up, grabbed the rim of the conning tower, and pulled herself halfway out, then stopped suddenly. "Uh-oh."

"What's the matter?" said Bean. "Climb out, will ya?"

Abby's legs disappeared up the tower, and her feet thudded to the deck. Bean was right behind her and immediately saw the problem.

Apparently the weight of all three of them moving about in the sub had rocked the bow free of the shore, and they had drifted out into the creek. At the same time, the fog—cold and clammy—had swept in with a vengeance, cutting visibility to no more than six or eight feet. "I thought you said the bow was in the mud!"

"Well, it was," Ab snapped. "If you hadn't been fiddling with the rudder . . ." It was a weak defense, and she knew it. "What are we going to do?"

"Hey!" Spooky complained from below. "Move, will ya? I can't get out."

"Not much point," said Bean, climbing out onto the deck. He stood opposite Ab, his hands holding the hatch door.

Spooky's head poked out of the tower. It didn't take him long to grasp the situation. "Uh-oh. Looks like we're in trouble again."

"Help!" Abby cried, but the fog sopped up her voice like a huge sponge.

"That won't do any good," said Bean. He knew how the fog played tricks with sound, making it seem to come from all directions at once. Anyone who heard the cry would never be able to tell where it was coming from.

"Well, we've got to do something!" Ab protested, desperation rising in her voice.

"Let me think," said Bean. "We can't be far from shore . . ."

"But which way is shore?" Ab wanted to know.

Bean had an idea. "Spook, get down below and find the compass."

Spooky's head popped out of sight. "Got it!" he said seconds later.

"Which way is east?" said Bean.

Spooky studied the gauge and reemerged. "That way," he said, pointing to the right.

"Then all we gotta do is find a paddle or something," said Bean, "and we can row ashore."

Once again Spooky disappeared from sight, but this time his search was fruitless. "There's nothin' that ain't screwed down."

There wasn't anything on deck either.

"Well, what now?" said Abby.

"We could swim 'er in," Bean replied, though it was clear from his tone of voice that he didn't hold much hope for that option.

"I'm not getting in that water!" said Ab. "Not when we can't even see where we're going. Besides, this thing's too heavy for me to paddle. I'm just a girl, you know."

"How convenient," said Bean. "Two of us could do it." He looked at Spooky.

"That'd be you and who else?"

"You," said Bean.

Spooky shook his head emphatically. "Your name must be José, 'cause there ain't no way."

Bean was a little relieved. Fact was, he didn't think it was a great idea. But Ab was right, they had to do something. "We'll have to crank 'er up," he said after a little thought.

Ab didn't think that was a good idea either. "You don't know how to drive a submarine."

"How hard can it be? Everything's marked," said Bean. With a quick warning to Spooky to get out of the way, he swung himself back down the hatch. "You get on the bow," he commanded Abby. "Watch for rocks and ledges."

Abby started to complain, but Bean cut her off. "The tide's goin' to take us back toward the bridge. If we get caught in that current . . ." He didn't know what might happen, but he was pretty sure it wouldn't be good. "Anyway, we gotta try to drive 'er ashore before we get there."

As Bean sank out of sight, Abby crawled toward the bow on her hands and knees. Despite her protests, she felt it was her fault they were in this mess, and if anyone could get them out of it, Bean could. She hoped.

Once back in the seat, with Spooky tucked out of the way in the aft compartment, Bean studied the instrumentation in earnest. "Okay," he said at last. "All we have to do is figure out how to turn these thrusters on."

"How 'bout that button by your left knee?" Spooky suggested.

"Which one?"

"The one that says Thrusters On."

Bean inhaled slowly, not sure what might happen, and flipped the switch. Nothing. "Maybe the batteries are dead," said Spooky.

That reminded Bean of another label he'd read. "Batteries," he said to himself. "Batteries. Here! Battery Power." He flipped the designated switch and instantly a faint crackling hiss surged through the wires.

"Now try it," Spooky urged.

Bean pinched the Thrusters On toggle between his fingers and, closing his eyes, flipped the switch. A deep electrical hum made the hull vibrate slightly, and the vessel surged forward.

"That's it!" Spooky proclaimed loudly. "You got it! She's movin'."

"Now all we need to do is figure out how to steer," said Bean under his breath. He pressed lightly on the right pedal, and the sub obediently turned in that direction. When he applied counterpressure to the left, it straightened out of the turn. "Hey, this is easy!"

"Let's dive!" Spooky suggested enthusiastically.

"I don't think Ab would like that much."

"Oh, yeah," said Spooky. "I forgot."

"Besides," said Bean, "the creek's only six to ten feet deep and the bottom's all mud. We'd get stuck."

"If we could get 'er out through the Race, we'd be in deep water. We could take 'er under there," he said, using the local word for a narrow opening where the tide flows swiftly from one body of water to another.

"All I care 'bout right now is gettin' 'er ashore," said Bean. He glanced at his watch. "I'm supposed to be home ten minutes ago."

"Watch out!"

3
SWEPT TO SEA

ABBY HAD BEEN STARING HOLES in the fog, but by the time she saw the rock it was too late. Half a second after her warning cry died away, the sub struck the ledge. She was nearly knocked overboard by the shock of the impact, but at the last possible moment she grabbed the rounded dome of one of the sub's lights and held on for dear life.

Bean and Spooky felt the shock, too. Suddenly, as the sub bounced off the rock, it began to shudder. Slowly at first, then faster and faster, it began to spin to the left. "We hit one of the thrusters!" said Bean, struggling with the pedals to regain control. He pressed the right-hand pedal to counteract the spin, and for a second it seemed to be working. Then the rudder dragged over the submerged part of the same ledge with a long, loud scrape and crunch. "Uh-oh."

All at once the pedals moved freely. Much too freely. The connection between the pedals and the rudder had snapped, a realization that made Bean feel sick to his stomach. Thinking quickly, he cut the power to the thrusters. Immediately the spinning stopped, as did the shuddering of the hull, and the sub bobbed silently in the water. "Ab!" he called. He jumped onto the seat and lifted himself up through the tower. Ab was flat on the deck, still clinging to the light. "You okay?"

For a moment, Ab didn't answer. Then, with careful effort, she pulled herself to a sitting position on deck. "What happened?"

"The port thruster hit the ledge. Why didn't you yell sooner?"

"I shouted as soon as I saw it," Ab protested angrily. "Why didn't you stop?"

"It was too late."

"Well, what are we going to do now?"

"We've still got the main motor," said Bean. "If I can get that goin', it'll push us ahead. Then all I need to do is use the starboard thruster to steer."

"Then do it," Abby snapped, her voice tinged with genuine fear.

"Trouble is, I don't know which way we're headed anymore." He bobbed out of sight to consult the compass.

Abby, meanwhile, heard a rushing, rumbling sound straight ahead in the distance. It made her heart sink. "Bean?" she said weakly. The sound was growing steadily louder, and all of a sudden, she knew what it was. "Bean!" she screamed.

Bean popped out of the hatch. "Did you say something?"

"Listen!"

He listened, his eyes widening and his pulse quickening as the realization dawned that they were just about to be sucked into the roiling vortex of the Race, where the waters of the tidal inlet called Indian Creek thundered under the bridge into the Reach.

"I'm goin' to try to get 'er to come about, Ab. I might be able to slow down enough so you can grab the bridge as we go under." He called down below. "Spooky! Get up here, quick!" Bean climbed out of the tower to make room as Spooky pulled himself onto the deck.

"What's up?" he said, but the words weren't out of his mouth before he heard the rush of the water. Despite the fog, he could tell they were being siphoned rapidly toward the Race. "Abandon ship?" he suggested unsurely.

Bean knew that Ab could probably outswim the current. There was a chance he could, too, as long as he stayed underwater. Just a chance. But Spooky was no swimmer. "No. It's too risky," he said. Quickly he outlined his plan.

"If you can get a good grip on the bridge, you can hand-over-hand yourselves to shore."

"What about you?" said Ab.

"I'm goin' to ride 'er through," said Bean. Before his companions could protest, he swung back down into the tower and stood on the seat with his head and shoulders above the rim. "You got one chance. Don't fart around. When you see the bridge, grab it."

Without another word, Bean grabbed the hatch lid and pulled it shut after him. Ab and Spooky heard the bolt twist.

"This stinks," said Spooky. "Big-time."

Abby agreed, but she didn't say so. There was no time. Often, she and Bean had sat on the little wooden bridge that straddled the Race and played Pooh Sticks in the rushing tide, tossing in branches or tin cans or anything that would float to see whose would be first through the Race. She'd seen logs and wooden lobster traps smashed to pieces on the rocks on the far side—a fate she and Spooky would share if they failed to get a good grip on the bridge as it passed overhead. She held even less hope for Bean, trapped in the submarine as the rushing waves threw it against the jagged boulders.

There was nothing she could do. She braced herself and waited, the roar of the water rising in her ears. Spooky did likewise.

Despite the growing darkness, Bean was able to find the battery that powered the main motor. He turned it on, and it crackled to life. "At least we've got power," he said to himself. A lever near his right shoulder indicated that the motor could run in either forward or reverse. Given his experience with outboards, he doubted that reverse would generate enough thrust to slow them down in the Race. Before he engaged the main propeller, he'd have to see if the starboard thruster was strong enough to turn the sub around.

Acting quickly, he engaged the thruster and applied full throttle. At first, the sub didn't seem to respond. Then, ever so slowly, she began to come about.

Soon the sub was broadside to the current, with the waters of the creek piling up to push it through the Race. The little thruster whined and trembled, but it was no match for that much pressure. Leaving the throttle wide open, Bean unsnapped the hatch and threw the lid back. "Spooky, reach over the stern and grab the rudder, if it's still there. When I bang on the hull, hold it over to starboard."

On all fours, Spooky crept to the rear of the sub, where a large horizontal fin that he hadn't noticed before projected over the propeller just below the waterline. He stuck his feet into the frigid water and, bracing them on the fin, seized the broken rudder with both hands. "Got it!" he cried. "Go!"

"As soon as she's headed into the current, straighten 'er out as much as you can. Then you guys jump for the bridge," Bean commanded. Once again, with a quick, meaningful glance at Ab—who was clutching the tower and looking terrified, tears flowing freely from her eyes—Bean disappeared into the sub. He slammed the hatch and sealed it shut.

Bean had no more alighted on the seat than he banged on the hull with his pocketknife. As soon as he heard the rudder pivot on its spindle, he engaged the main motor and applied the throttle. At once the sub swung smoothly into the current. "Good job, Spook!" he said to himself.

The sub had begun to pitch up and down as the water heaped up in waves in its headlong rush toward the open ocean. Bean knew they were getting close to the bridge. Now he had to buy them time. If they swept through the Race at the speed of the current, Ab and Spooky would never be able to get hold of the bridge. He had to slow down the sub as much as possible. He quickly disengaged the starboard thruster, then pushed the main engine throttle as far as it would go. He prayed that the little motor would hold its own against the tide, even for a few seconds, and that the rudder would hold, and that the battery would have enough power, and that Spook and Ab would see the bridge before it was too late.

Out on deck, the maelstrom of the Race had risen to such a pitch that Ab and Spooky had to yell at each other to be heard, even though they were less than three feet apart.

The waves were tumbling over one another, gathering in a swift-moving funnel as they surged toward the Race. Ab knew they were getting close, but she still couldn't make out the lines of the bridge in the blinding fog.

"I don't see it yet!" she yelled, turning to Spooky.

Spooky shook his head. "Me neither."

"Are you ready?"

"Ready as I'll ever be," Spooky replied. Then, his eyes widening suddenly, he yelled, "Look out!"

In an instant the hulking, horizontal beams of the decaying old bridge materialized from the fog. Ab swung around just in time to duck. As she threw her arms up to protect her head, her fingers seized almost by accident on the rusted iron lip of the low I beam. Before she knew what was happening, she was swinging by her fingertips, her feet dragging in the stinging cascade of froth and foam that seemed to grab her and pull her down. A wave of sheer panic gave her strength she never thought she had; after three attempts, she managed to swing her waterlogged feet up high enough so her sneakers caught on the lower edge of the beam, and she hung there like a trussed pig.

"You okay?" Spooky bellowed.

Ab looked in the direction of the voice to see her companion suspended in the same fashion from the struts on the other side of the bridge. Had he jumped half a second later, he'd never have made it. Beyond and below him—in the brief instant before it disappeared in the fog—she saw the submarine being tossed around like a pot buoy in the brief, tumultuous calamity of waters.

There was nothing she could do for Bean now. She had to save herself.

"This way!" Spooky shouted. Already he was shinnying along the beam toward the granite pilings on the Armbrust Hill side of the bridge. Summoning all her strength, Ab followed suit.

By the time she'd gone three feet, Spooky had already gained a foothold on the pilings and was pulling himself to the shore through the slippery webbing of seaweed.

Meanwhile, Abby had come up against an obstacle; a hundred years of salt and wind had eaten away at the beam to which she had entrusted her life and, for a space of two to three feet directly ahead, had worn it to a brittle membrane of rust that obviously wouldn't hold her. A quick look over her shoulder told her she couldn't go back; it was too far. Already the strength that adrenaline and fear had sent coursing through her veins was ebbing. "Spooky!" she cried with all the breath she could muster. "I'm stuck!"

17

She couldn't see where he'd gone, and apparently he couldn't hear her. She had no choice but to press on, and pray that the paper-thin iron would hold. She shimmied another eighteen inches with her hands and, bunched up like an inchworm, prepared to move her feet to the weakened section of the beam. "Okay, Lord," she whispered. "It's up to you."

Tentatively, she slid her feet along the beam until she was fully extended, then slowly shifted her weight to the delicate, almost transparent tracery of metal she gripped with her knees. For a second it seemed as if it were going to hold. Then, without warning, it gave way.

As if in slow motion, she watched her feet—still clinging to the jagged section of beam—swing down toward the water. With all that weight suspended from her fingers, they could not sustain their tenuous grasp. But her reflex had overcome her reason and she couldn't let go of the beam. In a heartbeat, it would all be over. She pictured the jagged rocks at the foot of the falls.

Suddenly she felt something grasp her wrist like a vise. The shock brought her to her senses enough that she finally released the remains of the beam between her knees. No sooner had it fallen into the seething water than she felt herself being pulled up onto the bridge. For what seemed like an eternity she hung in midair, her legs flailing for purchase on something. Anything. Then, before she knew what had happened, she was kneeling on the surface of the bridge, and Spooky had collapsed beside her.

"You're a lot heavier than you look," he sputtered, breathless.

He'd saved her life. She could ignore the fact that he'd scraped her up pretty badly in the process. She was about to fall on him in a heartfelt embrace of relief and thanks when she remembered the submarine.

"Bean!" she cried, clambering to her feet. She raced to the other side of the bridge and squinted into the fog just as it parted in a teasing veil, revealing the little yellow submarine lying on its side, wedged between a nasty cluster of rocks and seaweed. Then the fog closed in again, obscuring the sub from view.

"The sub's down on the rocks!" she said, returning to the still-prostrate Spooky. "We've got to get help!"

Spooky would rather have lain where he was, at least long enough to catch his breath. Ab would never know how much effort it had taken—

18

how much sheer force of will—to pull her onto the bridge, or how close he had come to dropping her as she thrashed about. However, realizing his best friend was still in trouble, he thrust aside his personal pains and jumped to his feet. "We've got to go tell his dad. He'll know what to do."

"You go," said Ab. "I'll stay and watch the sub."

"Watch what?" Spooky objected. "You can't see anything."

"Go!" Ab commanded. "Someone's got to stay here. You're faster than I am."

There was no time for argument. Spooky quickly tied his shoelaces, which normally flapped in the breeze, then set off at a gallop toward the mountain path that circled the east side of Armbrust Hill. In a moment he was out of sight, and Ab was left alone with the thunder of the falls, the frantic beating of her heart, and the horrible feeling that Bean was unconscious, or worse.

"What a stupid thing to do!" she screamed, the tears flowing again as desperate fear overwhelmed her. "What a stupid, stupid thing to do. We should have just gone and told Constable Wruggles. But no . . ." She kicked at the spiny, dried remains of a sea urchin that some seagull had probably had for lunch long ago. "What a stupid, stupid thing to do!"

She was right. But fussing about it would do no good now.

"I've got to get closer," she said aloud. She ran to the end of the bridge and tumbled down the rocks as close to the Race as she dared. "Bean!" she called into the cold, thick mist. "Bean!"

Over the roar of the waves, she thought she heard a creak of metal. At once she imagined the poor little sub breaking to pieces on the rocks. "Bean!" she screamed again, and again heard only the sound of twisting metal in reply.

Then the vapors parted again ever so briefly. Her glimpse was enough to see that the waves had pushed the sub free of its resting place. Once again in deep water, it had righted itself and was bobbing in the pull of the current that was sweeping it out Hurricane Reach toward the open ocean.

As it had before, the curtain of fog closed on the scene, leaving only the memory of the frightful image embedded in her brain.

"You're an idiot, Bean!" she cried in impotent fury. "If you die out there, I'll . . . I'll never speak to you again!"

She fell sobbing to her knees. What she was saying was, I love you, Bean. But she didn't know it.

Ages seemed to pass before she heard the crunch of tires on the gravel road leading to the bridge. She scurried up the rocks and arrived at the old blue Chevy truck just as Bean's dad and Spooky were climbing out.

"Captain Carver, I'm so sorry!" she said, falling into his arms. He squeezed her reassuringly for a moment, then held her at arm's length.

"Alvin told me everything," he said, using Spooky's Christian name. "I've called Constable Wruggles, and he's having the harbormaster come up the Reach in his boat. Where's the submarine?"

Abby pointed into the fog in the direction of the eastern bay. "It came off the rocks. He's drifting out that way."

A look of increasing concern crossed Captain Carver's brow. "That's bad. He doesn't have much control, I take it."

"I guess not," Abby said, shrugging. She cast a questioning glance at Spooky.

"He can't turn," Spooky explained. "Only in circles. Like I said, the rudder's broken, and the port thruster's toasted."

Left unsaid was the possibility that Bean might not have survived the headlong plunge of the submarine onto the rocks. Abby was reassured by Captain Carver's presence. Bean had often recounted his father's adventures as a navy Seal, and during years with the Coast Guard he'd faced many grim situations. He'd know what to do.

"What are we going to do?" she asked.

"I don't have a clue," Captain Carver replied.

Abby's heart sank.

"Let me think." So saying, Captain Carver walked to the shore and climbed down the rocks.

"We're in so much trouble," said Spooky as they watched him descend out of sight in the fog.

"I'm not worried about us," said Abby. She grabbed Spooky's elbow and squeezed hard. "Isn't there something we can do?"

Spooky shook his head and bit his lip, but he didn't say anything.

Abby was just about to start crying again when the earsplitting blast of a boat horn pierced the fog.

"That's Hutch Swenson," said Spooky, who was familiar with the distinctive sound of the harbormaster's whistle. "He'll be pullin' up to Link Dyer's wharf. This way!"

Apparently Captain Carver had the same idea. He emerged from the fog on the run, passing the kids as they turned toward the wharf. By the time they arrived, he'd already jumped aboard the distinctive red and white rescue vessel and was about to push off.

"Can we come?" Abby called from the top of the ramp.

Captain Carver beckoned them sharply. "Hurry up!" he said. They tumbled down onto the float, and he lifted them aboard and cast off in a single, self-assured motion. "You kids get in the bow," he ordered. "Watch for ledges, and holler if you see anything of the sub."

Obediently, the kids huddled at the bow and leaned over the rail. "You watch ahead," said Spooky. "I'll keep an eye out for ledges."

Abby did as she was told but was unable to see anything in the fog, which seemed thicker than ever. To make matters worse, it was getting dark. She glanced at her watch. The sun would be down in another forty minutes.

The boat crept through the dangerous shallows at an agonizingly slow pace as Spooky, using his hands to gesture left or right, guided Hutch Swenson through the shoals at the foot of the falls. It was a masterful performance, and soon the boat broke through to open water. "We're clear!" Spooky yelled. "Clear!"

Instantly, Hutch applied more throttle and the boat surged forward, its narrow bow gracefully parting the waves like a knife.

4
BEAN RUNS OUT OF TIME

FOR THE NEXT HOUR, the rugged craft crisscrossed Hurricane Reach, beginning close to the falls and, by degrees, making its way toward open ocean. By that time several lobster boats, which Hutch had summoned to the search on the marine radio, were tracing and retracing the broadening expanse of water. Using radar, GPS, and foghorns, they kept out of one another's way, their running lights making dim halos of red and green in the rising mist.

When the fog finally lifted, it was pitch dark. Searchlights and flashlights from the various vessels swept the Reach with dizzying shafts of light, but there was no sign of the little submarine. Nevertheless, the searchers kept on with grim determination.

Spooky and Ab, huddled by the steering console in survival jackets Hutch had given them to keep warm, watched helplessly and listened to the constant chatter of the rescuers on the radio.

"Hey!" said Spooky, jumping to his feet. "I just remembered something!"

"What is it?" Captain Carver asked. Abby was shocked by how tired and worn his eyes seemed in the feeble glow of the console lights.

"He's got a radio!"

"Who does?" said Hutch.

"Bean! There's a radio in the sub."

The men exchanged worried glances. "That's not good," said Hutch.

"Why?" Abby asked, her anxiety amplified by the look on their faces.

Captain Carver stared straight ahead. "Because if he's got a radio, and he hasn't used it to contact us, it means . . ."

Abby didn't want to know what it meant. "Maybe it's broken," she suggested.

"No," said Spooky, wedging himself excitedly between the Captain and Hutch at the console. He tapped the radio. "It's set on a weird frequency."

"What was it?" Captain Carver demanded, grabbing Spooky by the shoulders.

"I don't remember," said Spooky, wracking his brain, trying to visualize what he had seen in the sub. "It was twenty something . . . I think."

"Twenty something?" said Hutch skeptically. "That don't make any sense. Nobody 'round here monitors those channels except the Coast Guard."

"It's a carrier frequency," Captain Carver said, hope rising in his voice. "Of course, I should have known. That's what a sub would need to broadcast underwater. Quick!" He pushed Spooky out of the way and grabbed the handset. "Turn to twenty-three kilohertz."

Hutch complied.

"Bean!" Captain Carver yelled into the handset. "Bean, do you copy?"

For a moment the annoying hiss of the radio continued unchanged. Then suddenly a faint voice responded. "Dad, is that you?"

"Bean!" his father cried, tears welling in his eyes. "Where are you?"

The reply was weak, the words barely loud enough to break through the white noise of the electronics.

"Shut her down," Captain Carver commanded. Hutch cut the engine. A massive silence fell over the open boat as all ears focused on the little radio speaker. "Bean, say again," Captain Carver barked into the handset. He released the talk button and listened. Once again the familiar voice crackled through the ether. It was still weak and distant, seeming to come from another universe or another time, but, in the absence of the over-riding throb of the boat engine, the words were discernible.

"Dad, I'm okay."

"Where are you?"

"On the bottom," said Bean.

"Sounds like his batteries are weak," said Hutch.

"Shh!" said Captain Carver. "Bean," he snapped into the radio, "can you tell where you are? How deep?"

"Twenty feet," came the reply. "I blew the ballast by mistake. I think I musta hit the lever with my knee when she went up on 'er side."

Abby had been listening with her heart in her throat. She didn't like the sound of Bean's voice; it was weak and unsure.

The same thought must have occurred to Captain Carver. "Bean, do you have air?"

Again, there was a maddening delay before the reply. "Some, I guess. Not much."

"Are you tired? Dizzy?"

"Yeah," said Bean. "Dizzy."

Captain Carver shot a glance at Hutch. "I was afraid of that. He's running out of oxygen."

"See if you can get a fix on 'im—find out where he is," said Hutch. "I'll call Mosey Brown and get 'im to bring his salvage barge over here. He's got a crane that can bring 'er up, if we can just get some idea where he is.

Mosey's a diver, too." Hutch pulled a cell phone from his pocket and made the call.

"Bean, we need to get a fix on your location."

"I don't know how," said Bean.

Abby spoke up. "Twenty feet isn't that deep, is it? Can't he just open the hatch and swim out?"

"Even at twenty feet, the pressure would be too much," Captain Carver replied. "Especially if he's as weak as he sounds. I need someone who knows submarines."

"Just a minute," Hutch said into the phone. He lobbed a hopeful glance at Captain Carver. "I know a man over in South Thomaston who builds the things. Ten to one he built that one. His name's Kittredge. Retired navy man. I'll get through to 'im."

Hutch finished giving orders to Mosey Brown and rang off. "Mosey's on his way. It'll take a good half hour." Hutch punched another series of buttons on the number pad, got the number from directory assistance, and called Captain Kittredge.

Bean's dad, meanwhile, continued to talk reassuringly to Bean, not just to keep his hopes up but to keep him alive. "Help's on the way, Bean," he said with a calmness that belied the worried look in his eyes. "But you've got to stay awake. Hear me? Stay awake. Do you copy?"

"Copy," came the drowsy reply. "I'll try."

"You've got to do more than try, son. Breathe slowly. Hold each breath as long as you can to conserve air. Copy?"

"Roger that," said Bean.

"Do you have light? Press your talk button twice for yes, once for no."

Two distinct clicks crackled over the air.

"Good."

Hutch handed Captain Carver the cell phone. "Captain Kittredge is on the line. I brought 'im up to speed. He says the sub is one of his. It was rented 'bout a week ago by a marine biologist and hasn't been seen since."

"Captain Kittredge, Captain Carver here," he said. "Thanks for your help."

"No problem," said Captain Kittredge. "Listen, Captain, it's going to be all right. The sub has redundant safety systems for situations like this. She's a tough little fish."

24

It must be, thought Captain Carver, to have survived the falls intact. "I can't tell you how glad I am to hear it. But time is running out, I'm afraid. His air's low."

"First things first, then," said Kittredge. "We've got to get the boy some oxygen. You're in radio contact, right?"

"Roger that."

"Good. Now, tell him to find the little red-handled lever under the seat, more or less to starboard."

Captain Carver repeated the instructions to Bean. "Click twice when you've got it."

Almost immediately the reassuring clicks followed.

"He's got it," Captain Carver said into the phone.

"Good," Captain Kittredge said calmly. "It should be in the down position. Have him push it forward as far as possible. That will release air from the dive tanks into the sub."

Bean followed his father's instructions and was instantly rewarded with the hiss of life-giving air as it filled the compartment. Almost immediately his head felt clearer. Although he was still a little nauseated, relief coursed through him as he breathed deeply.

"Got it, Dad," he said, his voice much stronger.

"That sounds more like my Bean!" Abby cried, jumping to her feet. For the first time, she felt hope. Things were going to be all right.

Captain Carver held up his hand to quiet her. He placed the phone next to his ear. "What next?"

"There are two things we can try," said Kittredge. "First, once he's got all the air he needs, have him push the lever aft as far as it will go. That will release air into the ballast chambers and should bring her up. If there's enough air, that is."

"And if there isn't?"

"If that doesn't work, he can release the lead ballast. That'll bring him up for sure, as long as he's not caught on anything."

Bean listened carefully to his father's commands. Once he was breathing comfortably, he eased the lever back. Almost at once, the little sub responded. The nose lifted slightly, then the stern, until the sub floated free of the mud.

A tense minute later, while those in the launch waited breathlessly, there was a chorus of horns and whistles from boats a quarter mile up the Reach as the sub gently broke the surface amidst a glaring network of searchlights.

No sooner had the hull breached the waves than the hatch on the conning tower flew open and Bean popped out like a jack-in-the-box, waving and smiling. But he was in trouble and he knew it. He'd probably be grounded for life, but at least he had a life to be grounded for.

Abby waited her turn while Bean was hauled aboard the launch. His father took him in his strong arms and held him so tightly he could hardly breathe, while Hutch and Spooky alternately slapped him on the back.

"What am I going to do with you, boy?" said Captain Carver at last, holding his son at arm's length.

Bean shrugged. "Feed me, I hope," he said. "I'm starvin'."

Everyone laughed the tenuous laughter of relief. Only then did Abby realize she'd been crying again.

"Hey, Ab," said Bean, freeing himself from his father's grasp. He intended to give her a pat on the head or something, but before he could act she threw herself into his arms, dampening his shirt with her tears.

"Too bad, you come this far without even gettin' wet," said Spooky with a chuckle, "and now she's gonna drown ya."

Next morning, once again, the misadventures of Bean, Ab, and Spooky were the talk of the town.

"Yessa," said Drew Meescham, owner of the hardware store, as he emptied a box of twelve-penny nails into a metal bin. "A midget submarine, they call it. Built right over in South Thomaston. They sell 'em all over the world, they do, to marine researchers and whatnot."

"You mean to say them kids took 'er out of Indian Creek through the Race when the tide was runnin'?" said Oakey Miller in disbelief. "It's a wonder they wasn't stove to pieces on them rocks."

"That ain't the half of it," said P. MacPhearson, helping himself to a Tootsie Roll. "Mosey Brown got 'er up on his barge and says there's hardly any damage. Port thruster's about as much use as a howdy in a hurricane, and the rudder's pretty near off the gimbals, but them things can be fixed easy enough."

"Got to admit," said Oakey, "that ain't a bad piece of sailin'."

"Takes after his dad, I'd say," Meescham hypothesized. "What I can't figure, though," he added, settling himself in his favorite chair, "is where did it come from? Who had it out here in the first place without anyone knowin'? That's what I want to know. And what was they doin' with it?"

"And where are they now?" said MacPhearson ominously.

A similar conversation was taking place between a group of women on the sidewalk outside the Paper Store, though the emphasis was more on the kids than the technology.

"I've never seen such a couple for trouble as that Bean and Ab." The speaker was Merilyn Feathers, what Bean's mom would call a "substantial" lady, with curly blue hair and a tongue that never ran out of words. "If I was Missy Carver, I'd lock that boy in his room 'til you-know-what froze over, or he was old enough to know better, whichever come first."

"Now, you can't do that," said Edna Maclain, another member of the cluster. She had a special fondness for Bean, who mowed her lawn every other week. "Kids will be kids. If it wasn't for them, they'd never have found where poor Minerva Webster was buried."

Several other customers agreed this was so. Bean and Ab's last adventure had been quite a coup.

"Well, that's one thing," retorted Merilyn, as if Edna had proved her point. "But I ask you, whatever possessed them to get in that submarine? Whoever heard of such foolishness as that?"

Millicent Fenwick felt it was time to put in her two cents. "All I know," she said, "is that them kids have turned the whole town upside down more than once this summer, what with one thing and another, and somehow their folks better get a handle on 'em before someone gets hurt." She lowered her head and leveled a telling expression over the top of her glasses. "I mean really hurt."

As they spoke, the women's eyes were constantly on the move, inspecting the new load of tourists who had disembarked from the ferry and were thronging Main Street, peering into shop windows, ordering crab rolls from the take-out, stopping traffic as they wandered aimlessly up the middle of the road, and generally getting underfoot.

Among the new arrivals, most of whom were dressed in as little as possible, owing to the warmth of the day, was an older couple, probably in their late sixties or early seventies. The man was not remarkable except that he wore a coat and tie, which was unheard of on the island on any day other than Sunday unless there was a wedding or a funeral, and sported a mop of pure white hair that sat on his head like some misplaced alien being. His companion, presumably his wife, was a veritable feast of peculiarities—so many, in fact, that the women didn't know which to comment on first.

Nearly as wide as she was tall, the woman wore a huge pink bonnet with a broad brim that flapped in the gentle breeze. Large, transparent globes of glass or plastic hung like pendulums from her ears, which peeked out of a mass of tightly curled orange hair. Adding to the effect were several strands of multicolored beads draped haphazardly around her neck, and a long, flowing dress—the design of which incorporated every color known to man, and some that weren't—which enfolded her ample form like a tent. Over the dress she wore a massive scarlet cape clasped at the breast with a thick gold chain. The whole ensemble swung hypnotically back and forth as she walked.

In one hand she clutched a brace of large books. In the other was a canvas bag overflowing with objects impossible to identify.

"Seems like someone don't know if it's Easter or Halloween," said Merilyn Feathers, her attention diverted, for the moment, from the problem of Bean and Ab.

"Just when you think you seen it all," Millicent chirped. "Anyone havin' a costume party that you know of, Edna?"

Edna laughed into her hand, which she'd clapped over her mouth in disbelief. "Well," she said philosophically, "it's a cheerful outfit."

"There's a difference between cheerful and hilarious," Merilyn opined. As the curious couple drew abreast, the women turned toward the Paper Store and pretended to be reading posters in the window, but they were really watching the reflections of the duo as they passed by.

"I feel the vibrations," the colorful woman was saying. "Can't you feel them, Harold? We're surrounded by ghosts! Isn't it wonderful?"

Whether or not he thought it wonderful, Harold didn't say. With his head slightly bowed, he trudged purposefully onward, his brows bent in concentration. "We'll have no trouble finding her this time, I'm sure," the woman continued enthusiastically. Her monologue droned on, but because they had gone beyond the radar of the little group of women, the words and their meaning were lost.

"Well, what do you make of that?" Millicent huffed, making question marks of her eyebrows. "Vibrations, did she say?"

"And ghosts," Merilyn recalled.

Millicent Fenwick gathered herself together. "Well, she needn't fear anything like ghosts in that outfit," she said. "No self-respecting spook would be caught dead within a hundred yards of it. I feel dizzy just looking at her."

The old man and his colorful wife soon swept the length of Main Street, blissfully unaware of the commotion they were causing, and came to a stop at the sidewalk's end.

"Where now, Harold?" said the colorful woman, readjusting her armload of books.

Harold absentmindedly withdrew a dog-eared piece of paper from his inside coat pocket and consulted it.

"No need, Harold," said the colorful woman suddenly. "That must be the Moses Webster House. I can feel its vibrations."

Harold's eyes followed to where she was pointing—across the street, beyond the fountain, beyond the huge forsythia and the row house where Bean lived, to the old Victorian mansion, now a B and B, where Ab and her folks spent the summer months. He finally saw the connection between his wife's vibrations and her directions. "Why, I believe you're right, Mrs. P." He took her by the elbow and, with a careful glance to the left and right, tugged her gently across the street.

The old sidewalk, overgrown by grass on either side and cracked and creased along its length, led straight to the Moses Webster House. As they approached the massive old structure, with its three-story tower overlooking the town, Mrs. Prinderby vibrated with increasing intensity. "Could this be it, Harold, after all these years? I believe it is," she whispered reverently, massaging the granite gatepost as they climbed the steps. "Oooh," she quivered. "Ooh, the vibrations!" Her body shook like an overgrown Gummy Bear.

5
Dark Deeds Before Dawn

EARLIER THAT MORNING, Abby had awakened with a start. The sun wasn't up yet, but its eventual arrival was promised by the thin pinkish veil streaking the eastern sky. The night before, after their safe return from the submarine adventure, Mr. and Mrs. Peterson had had a Long Talk with their daughter, which pretty much boiled down to what she already knew, namely, how Foolish and Irresponsible she and Bean and Spooky had been, and how they were not to do anything so Thoughtless and Dangerous again. The words had not been wasted. They still rang in Ab's ears as she disentangled herself from the sheets and pulled herself to a sitting position.

But there was something else in the room: the persistent echo of a question that had come to her in her dreams. She struggled to banish the cobweb of sleep from her brain. "Focus!" she said. What was it her subconscious was trying to say?

Then it came to her.

"The map!" She swung her feet to the floor. That was it. If anything could tell them what had happened to the man who had rented the submarine and what he'd been up to, it was the piece of lined yellow paper that had been taped to the inside of the hull.

That presented a problem. She knew the submarine had been taken aboard Mosey Brown's salvage scow, which would be tied up at the public landing for the night. Most likely, no one would have bothered to inspect it, because it was so late by the time they brought it in. But at first light, Constable Wruggles and, no doubt, half the people in town would be crawling all over the little sub like "ugly on an octopus," as Bean would say.

What if, in the process, something happened to the map? Important evidence could be lost forever.

That was the noble kind of thing she was telling herself in the silence of her room, but the fact was she knew the authorities would comprehend the significance of the document, and she and Bean would never see it again. Which meant they wouldn't be the ones to solve the riddle of its meaning. They'd be left out of their own adventure. Who knew what that map might signify?

She jumped out of bed and put on her blue jeans, T-shirt, and sweat-shirt, grabbed a pencil and her journal from the bedside table, and crept quietly from her room and down the back stairs. Long before Mrs. Proverb would be getting things ready for breakfast, Ab was through the kitchen and out the back door.

The night air was cool and damp, thick with the smells of spruce and sea, into which were woven the heady fragrance of roses and new-mown grass. She ran toward Main Street, careful to keep just off the sidewalk so her footsteps wouldn't echo. The last thing she wanted was to draw attention to herself.

On Main Street, everything was quiet. The only sign of life was the lights in the rear windows of the cafe, which meant Johnny Philbrook was getting his usual early start on preparations for breakfast. Soon the lob-stermen would be filing in for their morning ration of bacon, eggs, and home fries. Already she could smell the coffee, dark and strong.

Ab didn't like coffee—it was too bitter—but she loved the smell.

Otherwise, apart from the occasional passing truck, the town was all hers.

It was mid-tide when she arrived at the public landing, so the ramp leading to the float angled downward. There, tied loosely to the chocks from bow and stern, was the salvage scow. Sitting amidships, having been lifted into position by the powerful crane, was the sub. Its port thruster drooped like a broken wing. Someone had strapped the rudder more or less into place with duct tape. There were quite a few scrapes in the bright yellow paint, and the bottom was covered with mud, but other-wise she seemed unscathed.

Before descending the ramp, Ab reconnoitered carefully. There was no one in sight. Quickly and quietly, suspending most of her weight from the railings to lessen the shock of her footfalls, she made her way down the ramp to the float. Somewhere in the distance she heard the sound of oars pivoting in their locks. Some lobsterman on the way to his boat, she thought. She studied the harbor and, though the lights on one or two of the boats were on—indicating owners eager to get a jump on the day while the sea was calm—nothing moved.

A fiberglass and aluminum ladder hanging from the side of the scow made easy work of the climb to the deck. Getting onto the sub was a little harder, because there was no ladder or any footholds. But eventually she managed to make her way to the conning tower, where, with her feet braced on either side of the hull, she lifted the hatch.

The hinge squealed loudly, the sound bouncing off the boats and the buildings. Startled, she almost dropped the hatch cover, the crash of which would have ripped through the village like a cannon shot, but she caught it at the last second. She held her breath for a moment. Then, satisfied that no one had heard, she lifted the cover slowly until it came to rest against the stop.

Emboldened by her success thus far, she placed her hands on either side of the conning tower, as she'd seen Bean do, and swung her legs down inside. Her feet hit against something soft. "Ow!" said a voice within.

Abby shot out of the tower like a rocket and had tumbled loudly onto the metal deck of the scow before she realized there was something familiar about the voice. Very familiar. "Bean?" she whispered sharply, the words nearly getting caught on the knot in her throat. "Is that you?"

Bean's head appeared slowly from the tower. "Ab?" he said tentatively. "Is that you?"

Reflexively, Abby put her hands to her chest and let out a low moan. "What are you doing? You scared me to death!"

Bean held up a piece of lined yellow paper and waved it weakly. "The map," he said. "I guess you had the same idea."

"Great minds think alike," said Abby, climbing up the side of the sub until her eyes were level with his.

"Yeah, and so do ours," Bean said with a smile. He handed her the sheet of paper. "Here, take it while I get out."

"We can't take it," Abby objected. "It belongs to somebody."

"Well, what were you goin' to do?" Bean asked snidely. "Memorize it?"

Abby dug the pencil and her journal out of her pocket. "Copy it," she said.

Bean was impressed. That never would have occurred to him. "Not a bad idea," he allowed. "There's a flashlight down below. Come on in so we can see what we're doin'."

Seconds later they were huddled shoulder to shoulder in the sub. Bean held the flashlight while Ab copied the map. "There!" she announced at last. "Done."

"Good. Let's get out of here."

Abby was about to tape the paper back into place when Bean caught it in the shaft of light. "Hey, wait a second. There's something on the other side."

Abby turned it over. "It's a poem," she said.

"A poem?" said Bean, disappointed.

"I think so," said Ab. She began reading aloud.

> *Three score and four, nor scarcely more*
> *One gets there by degrees*
> *Then nought and twice times six and seven*
> *Count minutes o'er the seas*
> *Three score and eight the bosun's mate*
> *Shouts fathoms to the shore*
> *Then eight and half of eight and four*
> *And one completes the lore*
> *A cave, a stone, my mark alone*
> *And none remain to save*
> *For hoard, and men and secrets keep*
> *Forever in their grave*
> *A cave, a stone, my mark alone*
> *And none remain to tell*
> *But follow these and you shall find*
> *Thy treasure, Anabel.*

"Well," said Bean when Ab had finished reading. "At least we got the map."

"Don't be thick," Abby said, exasperated. "This isn't just a poem, it's a puzzle. A riddle."

"A riddle?"

"Must be," said Abby. "Because it makes no sense."

"Well, it sounds like gibberish to me," said Bean. "But copy it down anyway."

Abby was already writing, and within two minutes had completed her task. "Got it," she said, taping the original back in place. "Now, let's get out of here before everyone and his grandfather shows up."

Bean clicked off the flashlight. Ab was halfway out of the conning tower when, once again, she heard the distinct chafing of oarlocks, only this time they weren't distant. She folded herself hastily back into the compartment, nearly sitting on Bean's head.

"Hey! What're you—"

"Shh!" Abby hissed sharply. "Somebody's coming."

Her announcement was followed immediately by a hollow *tunk* against the steel hull of the scow. A breathless second later, they heard someone climbing up the side of the sub. Bean fell backward amidst the hoses and wires in the rear of the compartment pulling Ab with him. Scarcely had they come to rest when they saw a dark silhouette etched upon the little circle of gray sky visible at the mouth of the tower. They held their breath.

It was clear from the furtive actions of the intruder that he wasn't supposed to be there any more than they were. The question was, what would he do when he discovered he wasn't alone?

Fortunately they never found out. Instead of climbing into the sub, which would have made it *way* too crowded, the stranger simply reached in and peeled the lined yellow paper from the wall. "Got it," he said in a low, raspy voice. Evidently he was unaccustomed to rowing, because he seemed short of breath. He tucked the paper into the pocket of his black pea coat, then withdrew from the hatch and climbed down from the sub, leaving Bean and Ab trembling in spite of themselves.

A moment later, they heard the dinghy push off, then the rhythmic chatter of oarlocks as the unknown visitor rowed away.

"He's gone," said Bean under his breath. Still, neither of them moved for nearly a full minute.

"Did you recognize him?"

Bean shook his head in the dark. "No. Did you?"

"No. I couldn't see his face."

"Me neither."

"The voice wasn't familiar?"

"No," said Bean, playing back the intruder's voice in his mind. "Could've been anybody. He didn't say much."

"Well," said Ab, unbunching herself from Bean's lap, where she had landed, "whoever it was, he knew about that paper and right where to find it." She pulled herself onto the seat and stood up with her head sticking out of the conning tower. She scanned the harbor.

"See anything?" Bean asked, wedging himself up beside her.

Abby pointed to a small white inflatable dinghy that was pulling past the crab factory on the far side of the harbor toward Lane's Island. "Over there."

Though the sky was much brighter, the sun still wouldn't be up for a while, so there wasn't enough light to see who was rowing. Bean doubted they could make him out under the best of conditions at that distance.

"Do you think he's the one who rented the sub?" Ab asked, climbing out of the sub and down onto the deck of the scow.

Bean was right behind her. "Who else? We gotta follow 'im."

"How?" Ab wanted to know. "He's got a heck of a head start."

"He must be headed under the Lane's Island bridge and out toward Indian Creek. We can beat 'im there on the Blue Moose."

"Oh, no," said Ab, slowing her footsteps as they headed up Main Street toward Bean's house. "My bottom hasn't recovered from the last time."

"Don't be a weeny," Bean said, laughing over his shoulder. "She rides like a Lexus."

"Easy for you to say," said Ab, catching up to him. "You get the padded seat."

The Blue Moose was a rickety old moped that Bean's Uncle Phil had given him—and his mother had let him keep because she was sure he'd never get it running. She underestimated his determination. Not only had he gotten it running, he and Ab had become a fixture zipping through town in a cloud of oily blue smoke to the irregular throb of the one-cylinder engine.

The one drawback to this mode of conveyance—of which Ab was acutely aware—was that the Blue Moose had only one seat. Which meant she had to ride on the luggage rack over the rear wheel. Although neither of them really minded too much that the only way she could stay on was to put her arms tightly around Bean's waist, he had an uncanny knack for hitting every pothole they came to, and there were a lot of potholes on the island. "Maybe I'll just walk," she said as Bean rolled the moped out of the shed behind his house and wheeled it out to the street, where the sound of the engine sputtering to life wouldn't wake his parents.

"What a wuss," said Bean, straddling the moped.

"If you were a gentleman, you'd let me drive," Ab replied.

"Yeah, right. If I was a gentleman with no brains."

Despite her protestations, Ab untied her sweatshirt from around her waist and folded it to sit on. Climbing on behind him, she tried to think of something clever to say. She put her arms around him and threaded her fingers together as he turned the key to the on position and pumped the starter pedal vigorously. Instantly, the little engine sputtered to life.

"If the guy we're chasing," said Ab when they were under way, "is the one who rented the sub in the first place, why doesn't he just come forward and claim it? What's up with sneaking around before dawn? That makes no sense."

"Good point," said Bean, swerving to miss a pothole. "Do you think there's somebody else?"

"What do you mean?"

"I dunno," Bean said, shrugging. "Maybe there were two of 'em."

"Like, partners?"

"Yeah," said Bean, thinking aloud. "What if only one of 'em knew how to operate the sub, an' he was, I don't know, in an accident or something."

"Or something," said Ab. "What if they had a fight, and the guy in the dinghy murdered his partner?"

Bean slowed down. It was one thing to follow someone who stole pieces of paper, but it was something else to be chasing a murderer. "Maybe we should get Constable Wruggles," he said. The Blue Moose rolled to a stop, and he formed a buttress with his outstretched legs.

"We won't have much to tell him unless we find out who this guy is," said Abby, shifting a little on her seat. "Or at least where he's going."

Bean deliberated.

"And if we lose him now, we might never know," Ab prodded.

That was all the incentive Bean required. He twisted the throttle, and seconds later the Blue Moose was hurtling down the road toward Lane's Island.

At the top of the hill overlooking the bridge, Bean cut off the engine and coasted the rest of the way. After drifting to a stop at the crab factory, they hopped off and Bean propped the bike against an outbuilding.

"Which way?" Abby whispered.

"I doubt he's gonna pull up here," said Bean. "Too many houses. I bet he's goin' under the bridge, either to Lane's Island or Pogus Point."

"Near where we found the sub," Ab observed.

Bean nodded. "Come on," he said, and they were off toward the shore, the gravel crunching under their feet. "Watch out for the—"

His warning came too late. Ab stepped on a shard of broken glass, and it sank into her sneaker.

"Did it go all the way through?" Bean asked with genuine concern.

Steadying herself with one hand on Bean's shoulder, Ab lifted her foot and looked at the sole of her sneaker. "I don't think so."

"Then what'd you say 'ow' for?"

"Just in case," said Ab curtly. "Can you take it out?"

Bean was surprised how deeply embedded the glass was. Ab was lucky. It left a long, deep gash in the rubber when he took it out. He tossed it into the water. "The operation was a success. Dr. Carver triumphs again."

"Oh, please," said Ab, drawing her foot from Bean's grasp.

Arriving at the bridge, Bean held up a cautionary hand and stopped. "Listen."

Abby, who had been looking the other way and didn't see the cautionary hand, ran smack into Bean and nearly knocked him overboard. "Sorry," she said with a giggle as he regained his balance. She was on the verge of laughing out loud when they heard the rhythmic tick of oarlocks. She grabbed Bean by the elbow and pulled him down behind a clump of beach roses. "There he is!" she whispered sharply. An opening in the leaves framed the solitary figure in the inflatable dinghy as he rowed under the bridge. The sun was just coming up now, so the furtive individual was clearly visible. But he was still unidentifiable, because a hooded jacket cast a shadow on his face.

"He's not from the island," said Bean into Ab's ear.

"How do you know?"

"Look at the way he rows: little strokes with one oar an' then the other. I don't know anyone who rows like that except summer . . ." He was going to say summer jerks, but he edited himself for Ab's sake. "Summer people." He quickly appraised the situation. "We'll have to split up."

"Why?" Abby demanded.

"Because we can't tell where he's goin'. If he ends up on Lane's Island an' we get stuck on Pogus Point, or vice versa, there won't be any way to keep an eye on 'im. Which way do you want to go?"

Ab was not thrilled with the idea of being alone as she followed the stranger, and one who might be a murderer at that. But Bean was right, they had to split up. "I'll take Lane's Island."

"Okay," said Bean. "There's a path along the shore," he said, pointing across the channel toward a cove on the Lane's Island side. "But you have to stay off it."

"Obviously," Ab replied condescendingly. It was apparent that the only way she could follow without being seen would be to keep to the woods.

"All you have to do is find out where he's goin' an' what he's up to," Bean cautioned. "Don't go doin' anything foolish."

"Like what?" Ab retorted haughtily. "Getting caught in a submarine?"

The jab found its mark, but Bean chose to ignore it for the time being. "All I'm sayin' is this guy could be dangerous. Once we find out what he's up to, we can tell Constable Wruggles and let him take over." Keeping an eye on the dinghy, which was already twenty yards beyond the bridge despite the stranger's unconventional method of rowing, Bean stood up slowly. "Let's get goin', before we lose 'im."

"Meet here in thirty minutes?" Ab suggested.

Bean looked at his watch. "Okay. Thirty minutes."

He waited to see if Ab would make it across the Lane's Island bridge without being seen by the man in the rowboat. Much to his surprise, she strode boldly across, sometimes whistling, sometimes humming loudly, as she picked up jagged bits of gravel and dropped them into the water. The man, after an initial glance, paid her no attention.

"She's pretty smart, for a girl," Bean said to himself. Behaving normally, Ab had made herself part of the scenery, not a suspicious-looking individual skulking in the shadows, which would surely have roused the rower's curiosity. Why should he care about a kid crossing a bridge?

Apparently he didn't. The stranger, turning now and then to see that he was on course, otherwise kept his head bent toward his hands as he rowed steadily on.

6
Bubbles, Bubbles, Toils and Troubles

BEAN ADOPTED A MORE stealthy approach. Whereas Ab would have the cover of trees once she was on Lane's Island, the only thing blocking the rower's view of him was the row of small waterfront houses and lobster shacks that stood between the road and Hurricane Reach.

Cautiously, Bean made his way from building to shed to shack, sometimes darting across wide stretches of open yard where he was exposed to view for several seconds. But there was nothing in the attitude of the rower to suggest he'd noticed Bean's movements.

By the time Bean arrived at Indian Creek, it was evident the stranger was headed for Pogus Point. Bean was sure that Ab would realize this before long and head back toward their rendezvous point. He was relieved to know she was out of danger. But now he encountered the biggest obstacle to his surveillance—the little bridge over the Race.

The difficulty was that the man in the rubber dinghy was heading out the Reach, which meant—because rowers sat facing the stern—he would be looking directly at the bridge. Bean stood behind Link Dyer's weathered old shed just above the Race and considered his options.

There were none.

The bridge offered no cover. No trees. No fence. Nothing. He couldn't even get *to* the bridge without being seen. He had only two choices: He could run all the way around the creek, which would give the stranger enough time to row to Bermuda and back, or he could follow Ab's example.

Not much of a choice.

He crossed the road and went in among the trees far enough so that, when he emerged on the path a little farther down, any observer would think he had just come around Armbrust Hill.

He strode casually into the clearing where the path met the road and plucked a handful of little green apples from a tree that overgrew the path, then strolled toward the bridge. On the way, he stopped and threw one of the apples out toward the Reach in a high arc, pretending to watch with interest as it splashed into the water and bobbed immediately to the surface. What he was actually doing was getting a fix on the skiff as it rowed toward the cliffs of Pogus Point.

The rower—only a dark silhouette against the bright ocean and the rising sun—suddenly stopped pulling at the oars. The skiff slowly drifted to a halt, its zipperlike wake dissolving behind it.

Bean had absorbed all this in a fraction of a second. As he turned toward the bridge, he could feel the eyes of the stranger like lasers on the back of his head.

Once on the bridge, Bean stopped again and leaned on the lichen-covered rail facing Indian Creek, so his back was to the rower. He dropped a couple of apples into the Race as it surged toward the ocean, as he and Ab had done countless thousands of times, then he ran to the other side to see which would come out first. He knelt on the planks and bent over as far as he could to watch the perilous journey. One apple was far ahead of the other. "That one's mine," he said. Which meant, of course, that the other was Ab's.

His apple emerged triumphant from the shadows of the bridge. He stood up, raised his hands, and did a little victory dance to the sound of his own cheers.

The stranger resumed rowing. Apparently he had decided Bean was harmless.

"Way to go, Bean!" he congratulated himself. Ab's apple, which had apparently hung up on some seaweed, finally tumbled out into the falls. "Poor Ab," he said, "you lose again."

He continued to play his way across the bridge and onto the grass and gravel shore on the opposite side, always keeping the dinghy in sight. Finally, a high outcropping of granite slag concealed each from the other's view. He made a hasty appraisal of his situation. There was no way he could follow the shore; on that side of the bridge, it consisted only of high slag mounds overgrown with raspberry and juniper bushes, none of which was tall enough to conceal him.

Bean broke into a run up the path to where it dead-ended on a paved road. Later that day, the warm midsummer sun would soften the tar, forming hot little asphalt bubbles, which he loved to squish with a stick. Now, though, it was firm underfoot, and his sneakers slapped loudly as he turned right and sped downhill toward Pogus Point.

Farther ahead, the road dropped sharply through a swampy area of poison sumac and cat-o'-nine-tails, then rose just as quickly through granite crags to spruce-covered heights. They overlooked Hurricane Reach and the inner harbor to the west, and endless open ocean to the south. The official name of this area of jagged cliffs and thick, tangled forest was Pogus Point, but islanders called it simply the Point.

Bean dodged off the road and scrambled up a nearly invisible path through tangled undergrowth. Then he climbed a windswept granite slope to a clearing on the summit from which he could gaze directly down to the Reach—and the dinghy—a hundred feet below.

The stranger had pulled to within twenty feet of the shore and was rowing slowly, skirting the base of the cliffs, at which he was staring intently. Now and then he stopped rowing, crossed the oars in his lap, and consulted the lined yellow paper.

"What's he lookin' for?" Bean wondered aloud, and wished he had Ab's copy handy. It might tell him something.

Frequently the man would interrupt his scrutiny of the shoreline with surreptitious glances up and down the Reach. Whatever his chore, though, he kept at it. For the better part of half an hour, Bean watched from the cliff top as the stranger continued his inspection.

At the top of one cliff, the ledge jutted out a few feet, obscuring the skiff from view. Not wanting to cast a shadow that might be seen below, Bean lay flat on his belly and pulled himself onto the ledge across jagged chips of granite, which clawed at his clothing. Ignoring the discomfort, he crawled to the edge of the cliff and peeked over the side.

The inflatable was just disappearing into a narrow cleft in the rock. Bean knew there were caves along this coast, many of which were completely hidden at high tide. That was why his father had warned him not to go near them. Bean still remembered, word for word, a chilling story his father had told. "When I was a kid, a man went into one of those caves on a bet. I guess he figured he could get out when the tide turned, but he figured wrong. Any kind of wind at all, and the waves slam into those caves like ramrods, making it impossible to get out. Then the tide comes in and does the rest."

That was all he'd had to say. Bean could imagine all too vividly being trapped in one of those caves, the only exit sealed by thundering walls of water as the tide turned and began to rise. In no time at all it would surge across the cave floor, so he'd have to start climbing. The waterline would follow him up the rocks, higher and higher, until there was nowhere left to go. And still the water would rise. He shivered involuntarily, and in physically shaking the image from his mind he accidentally knocked a small avalanche of stone chips over the edge. He held his breath as he watched them fall just as the dinghy drifted into view.

Most of the chips fell harmlessly into the ocean, but the little chorus of splashes—percussive and musical in the early morning stillness—drew the rower's attention instantly to the cliff top. Bean jerked his head back from the edge, but he was sure he'd been seen. He rolled over on his back and lay there, cursing himself for his carelessness, and waited to see what the stranger would do. He looked at his watch and decided to let two minutes go by, but after a minute and a half his patience ran out.

Cautiously, he rolled onto his stomach and poked his head over the edge.

There was no sign of the dinghy. He waited a long time, thinking the man may have pulled up on one of the beaches of crushed rock and seashells cradled between the rugged granite battlements to continue his investigations on foot.

What if he'd gone into one of the caves? Bean looked for the low-water line along the shore. Already it was six inches under. The tide was rising. The wind had begun to pick up, too, as it always did when the warm rays of the morning sun hit the cold surface of the ocean. What if the stranger didn't know what kind of danger he was in?

Bean stood up abruptly. No matter what the man had done, or what he was up to, he didn't deserve to drown in one of those caves, his flesh and bones crushed by the churning waves.

The question was, how to save him?

The most obvious choice was to climb straight down. Bean looked over the edge. The cliff face was jagged, pocked with plenty of places he could put his hands and feet. Of course, one misstep and he'd be lunch for the seagulls. Besides, if the beach below was the wrong beach, the only way he could get around the granite escarpment to the next beach—if there was one—was to swim. The other option—climbing back up—would be a lot harder than climbing down. Bad idea.

He'd need a boat. He looked across the Reach to where a number of small skiffs and dories lay bottom up in the thick grass along the shore. With no time to waste, he slid, tumbled, and skidded down the hill and ran back the way he had come.

Link Dyer was in his fish house mending nets. The door to the little shack by the shore stood open, and as Bean approached he could hear the tinny sound of country music blaring from a cheap radio and smell the smoke from the lobsterman's ever-present pipe.

"Link!" cried Bean with what remained of his breath. He rapped loudly on the doorpost.

The old man turned his sad-looking, sea-worn face toward the disturbance. Seeing Bean in the doorway, he shut off the radio. "Bean Carver, ain't it?" he said, his thickly accented drawl tinged with just the mildest curiosity. "Come on in. Been runnin', have ya?"

Bean entered the shack and was immediately embraced by a potion of smells that Link Dyer and the passing years had concocted. Equal parts man and nature. Tobacco, sea salt, paint, spruce, turpentine, gasoline, and sawdust—it was a pleasant perfume that seemed to tell a story just beyond hearing.

"I was wonderin' if I could borrow your rowboat for a few minutes." Bean leaned against a paint-stained workbench and folded his arms, trying to catch his breath and make the request seem as natural as possible.

"Sure ya can," Link said without hesitation. "Mine's the white one with the blue bottom out there. She's all yours."

"Thanks!" said Bean. "I'll bring it back . . . soon."

"No hurry," said Link. "If the tide's up, just tie 'er to the float."

"Okay," said Bean. He turned to leave, thankful that Link hadn't asked what he wanted the boat for.

"So, whaddaya want it for?"

The words halted Bean halfway out the door. He turned around. "Oh, I just want to give someone a hand with something," he said, praying silently that Link would be satisfied with such meager information.

Apparently he was. "Well, take care, now. There's a life jacket under the bow seat. You put that on, hear?"

"Okay," said Bean. "I will."

Bean flipped the skiff over on the grass and slid it down to the shore, across the wrack and over the slippery gravel, until the stern floated free in the clear green water. He untied the oars from the gunwales, put in the oarlocks, and, true to his word, put on the moldy old life jacket.

For a moment, he thought about going back to the rendezvous point to find Ab and tell her what he was up to, but that would take precious time the stranger might not have. He also thought about telling Link, and asking him to call his dad and Constable Wruggles. This thought made him cringe. What if the stranger had simply rowed up the Reach, which he could easily have done without Bean being able to see from the top of the cliffs. The town had already been turned inside out several times on his account, and he had no desire to call attention to himself again. Besides, all he was going to do was row across the Reach and check out the caves, just to make sure. What could possibly go wrong?

With a backward glance at Link, who was standing on the stone steps outside his shack thumping the old tobacco from his pipe against the heel of his hand, Bean pushed off. Once the oars were fixed in the locks, he waved casually. Link returned the wave and went back inside. Moments later the sound of badly distorted country music filled the air as Link cranked up the volume.

The skiff, a narrow wooden lapstrake that Link had built himself, was both solid and fast. She rode high in the water, cleaving the waves with her sharp bow and making a neat wake as Bean pulled expertly at the oars. In less than three minutes he had crossed the Reach and pulled up under the cliff from which he'd dropped the gravel.

As he suspected, there was a narrow wedge of beach, consisting mostly of pulverized seashells and granite chips, between the towering fingers of granite—like the webbing of a duck's foot—but it was piled with driftwood and seaweed, which had already begun to undulate in the rising tide. The beach showed no signs of recent visitation.

A little farther along, the cleft into which he'd seen the inflatable disappear wasn't deep enough to warrant further investigation. It was evident there was no dinghy there now.

Bean lifted his oars out of the water and let the boat drift with the tide, pulling leisurely only now and then against the rising waves that would have pushed him ashore.

Although the cliff face was pocked with numerous caves, only three were big enough to accommodate a rowboat, and all would be completely underwater at high tide. Bean made a quick survey of sea and sky.

He decided to go into the smallest cave first, because it would be underwater soon and therefore inaccessible. As it was, even though the tide had risen no more than a foot, he had to ship the oars and, ducking as low as he could, pull himself into the cave by his fingertips.

Once inside, he saw that the ceiling was not much higher than the mouth, giving him just enough room to sit up for a proper look around. Not that there was much to see. The cave was about twenty feet across and wedge shaped, with no tunnels branching off the main cavern. A narrow crescent of beach on the opposite side had been scraped by a keel since the last tide, indicating that the stranger had indeed been here. But he wasn't here now.

Bean gripped the porous ceiling with his fingers and, pulling himself through the entrance, was surprised that he could sense the tide rising unnaturally fast. The waves were taller and more aggressive as they surged through the shrinking opening. His final pull through the exit had to be timed to coincide with the trough between waves; otherwise, the boat would have scraped against the jagged opening, and Link Dyer wouldn't think much of that.

The entrance to the next cave, about an eighth of a mile up the coast, was much like the first in shape, though considerably larger. By the time Bean got to it, the waves had kicked up a good bit and he had to work to keep the boat away from the rocks. He turned stern first toward the shore and, plying the oars to keep even with the opening, stared at the cave with rising apprehension. It was deep and dark and filled with foaming waves that rose like shark's teeth in sharp ranks, snapping at the skiff as if to chew it to pieces. Immediately his dad's warning echoed through his brain, and, for a moment, he almost heeded it.

But there was something else calling him, drawing him like the Sirens he'd read about in the *Odyssey*. Those ghostly mermaids had lured sailors to their doom with songs of enchantment. It was the irresistible seduction of the unknown. Before his common sense could prevail, Bean guided the boat into the cave's mouth. In that brief moment when the waves seemed like an angry mob, passing him hand over hand as they crowded through the opening, he wondered if they'd ever found the bones of the man who had entered the caves on a dare.

Confined to the cavern, the energy of the waves was quickly spent, and the small vessel bobbed calmly on an inky sea. Bean sat up. This cave was a lot bigger than the first, and what little light was afforded by the small opening was quickly lost in darkness that had been undisturbed for eons.

"Hello?" he called. "Are you here?" He wanted to specify that he was looking for one individual in particular, and if anyone or any*thing* else was there, he didn't want to know it. He held his breath and listened, but all he could hear was the rhythmic sloshing of the sea against the stone walls, like the sound of a huge, thirsty dog lapping its water dish. "I can't believe I didn't bring a flashlight," he chided himself.

His eyes were wide with trying to see in the darkness, and his imagination was outdoing itself, peopling the bottomless shadows with a host of the dead and dying in varying stages of decay, reaching for him, their eyes evil and hungry. Wasn't that an arm, there just beyond the edge of the light? Of course not. Common sense told him it was just a floating branch. But the voice of reason had fallen to a whisper, and not a very comforting one at that. Besides, weren't those fingers—stretching, opening, and closing with the push and pull of the waves?

What if he'd entered a world in which common sense no longer applied? A world where there was no death, only the endless act of dying. Life's blood perpetually oozing from the pores, flesh rotting on the bones and falling off in fetid clumps, food for the fish.

"That does it," he said aloud, the sound of his voice somehow reassuring as it echoed from the walls. "No more Stephen King novels."

Bean wanted nothing more than to leave. A glance at the mouth of the cave told him there was still plenty of time. Having come this far to help the stranger in case he was in trouble, Bean couldn't bring himself to leave until he had checked thoroughly. After all, the dinghy could be back there somewhere, floating in the darkness, and the man could be incapacitated somehow. A heart attack, maybe, or an accident. What if he had knocked himself out or fallen overboard?

Wrestling mightily against his instinct for survival, Bean sat down, dipped the oars in the water, and pulled lightly. The skiff drifted easily across the water and almost immediately thudded to a stop against a wall. The cave wasn't that big after all, just a little deeper than the daylight seeping through its mouth could reach. Nevertheless, he made a quick sweep of the periphery on his way back to the opening and, by the time he emerged into the welcoming light of day, was satisfied that the man with the map—wherever he might be—was definitely not here.

"One more," Bean said to himself as he continued up the coast toward the cave that local fishermen had dubbed Widowmaker. He'd never wondered why. Could it be the cave the man died in?

He felt like Goldilocks, going from one to the other until he found the one that was just right.

As he rowed, he searched the Lane's Island shore for Ab, but he didn't see her. "She must be waiting at the rendezvous," he reasoned aloud. He was already long overdue. What had she done when he hadn't shown up? He didn't like to think what his dad would say if he had to come looking for him . . . again.

Bean looked up the Reach toward the Widowmaker and did some quick figuring. Five minutes getting there. Another five to check it out—providing the man wasn't there, or in trouble—then ten to fifteen minutes back to Link's. "Hold on just a little longer, Ab," he said out loud.

The Widowmaker was partially concealed by three spires of rock that an ancient glacier had carved from the cliff eons ago. These were called the Orphans. At one time they must have been quite tall, judging from the debris that countless years of wind and tide had whittled from their tops and deposited around their bases. Still, at fifteen to thirty feet in height, they were impressive.

In the time it had taken Bean to row to the Widowmaker, the wind had freshened considerably and the sea was crashing ominously against the Orphans. If Bean got caught in those waves, Link's beautiful skiff would be chewed to driftwood in no time.

The mouth of the Widowmaker, just visible in the lee of the spires, was wide, low, and jagged. At that particular moment, it looked like the gaping maw of some hideous demon from the deep, gulping at the ocean.

Bean would have to time his attack perfectly, surfing the trough between waves all the way to the opening. A little too early or too late, and the sea would push the boat against the cliff, probably tipping it over in the process.

He worked his arms feverishly, trying to maintain his position as he waited for the perfect moment. At last it came, a deep sluice that, in two seconds' time, would be perfectly positioned to carry him into the cave. He steadied the oars in their locks. The muscles of his arms and legs were tense and burning in anticipation of the one mighty thrust that would either take him safely into the Widowmaker, or not.

He cast a quick glance up at the Orphans, which loomed almost close enough to touch with the tip of his oar. Instinct told him it was now or never. He was just about to apply all his strength to the oars when, amid the chaotic breaking of the waves, he thought he heard a voice. He held his position. "Hello!" he yelled at the cave, for that was where the sound seemed to have come from.

The reply, though distant and echoing, was distinct. "Hello, you there! Help! I'm trapped!"

7
CHEATING DEATH

ABBY WAS A GIRL OF LITTLE PATIENCE. When it became evident that the man with the map was not rowing to Lane's Island, she returned to the rendezvous point and waited for what seemed like forever. It was, in fact, only about ten minutes. When Bean didn't show up, she decided she had to do something. But what?

She thought a moment. She doubted Bean was in trouble; he was just a lousy judge of time. More likely, he had followed the man to wherever he was going and had already discovered his secret. The idea that Bean was having an adventure all on his own was more than she could bear. No sooner had this occurred to her than she was hurtling along the mountain road with all the speed she could muster.

Just before the ancient bridge that spanned the Race, she stopped to reconnoiter. A quick sweep of Indian Creek and the Reach turned up no sign of either the stranger or Bean. Somewhere behind her, near the shore, a door closed. She turned to see Link Dyer emerging from his weather-beaten fish house. He saw her at the same time. "Ah, I should've known you wouldn't be far behind," he said with a smile. He was tall and lean and as worn as the shingles on his fish house, but his eyes were light blue and full of good humor. He tossed a toolbox in the back of his ancient green pickup truck. "Lookin' for young Mr. Carver, I expect?"

"Hi, Mr. Dyer," Ab said, joining him at the truck. "Yes, I am. Have you seen him?"

"Done better than that," said Link, securing the handle of his toolbox with a bungee cord. "Talked to 'im. Lent 'im one've my boats."

"A rowboat?"

"Yup."

"Did he say what he wanted it for?" Ab asked.

Link rubbed his fingers thoughtfully across his chin. "Said he wanted to help somebody. Didn't say who or what." He opened the truck door and climbed into the cab.

"Did you happen to see which way he went?"

"Seemed he was headed out the Reach at first," Link replied, "but I looked out the window not long ago and couldn't see hide n'r hair've him, so I figured he must've turned up 'round the east side of Lane's Island outta sight somewhere." He looked doubtfully out over the water. "Bean's a pretty good rower, but he should be comin' in soon the way the sea's kickin' up. You'd prob'ly be best off waitin' right here. I don't guess it'll be long." He looked at his watch. "I gotta get down to the ferry." He slammed the truck door and rolled down the window. "You want to get out of the wind or anything while you're waitin', just go on in the shop. She's open."

"Thanks, Mr. Dyer," said Ab. She knew that, as a rule, adults on the island preferred to be called by their first names rather than Mr. or Mrs., but with a lifetime's indoctrination in city manners, she couldn't bring herself to do it. A thought occurred to her. "Do you have a boat I could borrow?"

Link started up the truck. "I got plenty of boats," he said, giving her a skeptical once-over. "But I don't think it'd be a good idea your settin' out in risin' seas."

"But I'm a good rower," Ab protested.

"Oh, I don't doubt you do fine," he said. Ab could tell from his tone of voice that he was thinking "for a city girl" but was too polite to say so. "But in risin' seas like this," he continued, "even Bean's gonna wear himself pretty thin fightin' back up the Reach. No, I think it's best you just stay put and wait."

It was sound advice, and Abby knew it. But she didn't like it.

"Okay," she said dejectedly.

Link was determined that no amount of female pouting was going to have any effect on his resolve. Like everyone else on the island, he knew all about Bean and Ab's recent adventures—and how close they'd come to death—and he didn't want to have their next brush with the Grim Reaper on his conscience. Nor did he relish the notion of facing Ab's parents with the news that he had loaned her a skiff so she could put off in a rising tide. He looked warily out over the Reach. "There's a pair of binoculars in the shop. You keep an eye out for him. He'll turn up soon."

The old boatbuilder and part-time lobsterman hoped it wasn't just wishful thinking. Suddenly he wondered if it was such a good idea to have loaned Bean the skiff in the first place. He waved good-bye and backed up the gravel drive to the asphalt, then he ground the truck into first gear and drove off toward town.

Inside the shop, Abby felt like an intruder. This was the portal to a man's world, and it wasn't hard to believe she was the first female ever to cross the threshold. Everything was in disarray. Tools, paint cans, nets, wire, engine parts, pieces of wood, and lengths of rope with fraying ends lay where they had last been used. It was a strange and mysterious place, and she couldn't imagine how anything got done amidst such chaos. Yet even she, summer girl though she was, knew Link Dyer's reputation for building the finest wooden boats on the Maine coast. Ships from his shop—not this one, which was little more than a shed, really, but his big boat shop down on Sands Cove—plied the oceans of the world and were the envy of all who saw them.

On the wall was a calendar with a picture of a woman in a bikini holding a huge wrench. Men must find the combination appealing, Abby thought, but she couldn't imagine why. She remembered seeing something similar at Peaselee's garage and in the stockroom down at the hardware store. Other than the calendar, the only concession to decor was a bunch of dusty plastic flowers stuck in green Styrofoam that had been discarded in a dark corner at some point in the distant past.

The smell of the fish house was like nothing else on earth and, because of its strangeness, at first made her wrinkle her nose. After a few minutes, though, she became accustomed to it and was able to identify the individual ingredients in that curious perfume. There was nothing remotely feminine about it. It wasn't bad, she decided after a while, but it was different, and strange.

She fought back an overwhelming urge to straighten things as she rummaged around for the binoculars that Link seemed confident were there somewhere. Finally she found them hanging from a hook behind the door.

The window over the bench was wide and low and afforded a panoramic view of Hurricane Reach and Lane's Island. Abby bent slightly at the waist and propped her elbows on the bench, pressed her eyes against the rubber cups of the field glasses, and drew the scene slowly into focus through the wavering panes of old glass.

For a while, still unable to find Bean anywhere, she entertained herself with a general survey of flora and fauna in the area, eventually focusing her attention on a blue heron that stood still as a statue among the low green rushes of the marsh on Lane's Island. It stood so still for so long that she had just about convinced herself it *was* a statue, perhaps placed there by some whimsical island artist for the purpose of deceiving gullible summer people like herself. Then, with a suddenness that startled her, the bird's head shot beneath the waves like an arrow and, in the next instant, emerged with a large silver fish gripped tightly in its thin, pointed beak. The heron thrashed its prey violently back and forth a few times, rendering the fish senseless. Then it tipped its head back quickly and swallowed. Ab watched in fascination as the lump that was the fish slid slowly down the long, down-covered throat of the regal bird.

"Burp," she said. Bean would have burped for real, but she couldn't do that. Not that she would if she could, of course.

Just offshore, a seagull had been preening and washing itself. Its morning ablutions completed to its apparent satisfaction, it leapt almost effortlessly into the air and headed across the Reach as Ab struggled to keep it in view through the glasses.

The gull came to rest gracefully upon the highest of three granite spires that protruded from the water like dragon's teeth not ten feet from shore on Pogus Point. The bird seemed to be watching something below with interest. Following its line of sight, she spotted a little white skiff bobbing violently in the waves. It was empty. Judging from the line extending tautly from its bow, it was anchored precariously between the spires and the cliff.

Suddenly, as she was watching, two struggling figures burst from the water, grabbing frantically for the gunwale of the boat. Ab took a deep breath to steady the glasses in her hands and squinted into the lenses. There was no doubt: one of the swimmers was Bean. He had his arm around the chest of the other man, in the rescue position, and now seemed to be trying to push him up into the boat.

He succeeded, but once in the boat, the man turned on Bean, who was struggling to get over the side himself. As Abby watched in helpless disbelief, the man pushed Bean back into the water and began slapping at him with an oar.

"Bean!" Ab screamed. She ran from the shack, binoculars in hand, and began jumping and waving frantically. "Hey! You stop that! Bean! Bean!"

She clapped the glasses to her eyes. Clearly they were much too far away to hear her. By this time Bean had let go of the boat and swum clear of the oar. The man was using it to push himself between the cliff and the spires and out to open water. Ab ignored him. All her attention was on Bean, who was clearly in trouble. "Dive!" she screamed. "Dive!" On the surface, Bean was a gawky and ungainly swimmer, and if he stayed there, at the mercy of the waves, he'd be thrown against the jagged rocks in seconds. Underwater, however, he could outswim a halibut and would be able to get clear of the shore. "Dive!" she yelled again.

As if he heard her, Bean suddenly disappeared beneath the waves.

Abby held her breath and counted the seconds, waiting for him to reappear. She got to thirty and was beginning to get worried when Bean's head finally broke the surface. She fixed him in the binoculars. He'd made it a good fifty feet from shore. Though he was no longer in any immediate danger of the cliffs, the waves were high and he was clearly having difficulty getting a breath. Worse yet, the sea was pushing him back toward the rocks. All he'd managed to do was buy a little time.

The man in the boat, meanwhile, was rowing madly up the Reach. He apparently had not seen Bean resurface but didn't seem troubled by the idea that he might have drowned.

There was no time to get help. If anyone was going to rescue Bean, it had to be Ab. She considered her options. There were several rowboats upended on the shore, but it would take her too long to get them into the water—assuming she had the strength to get them that far—and row halfway out the Reach. She glanced at the float, which was empty. The nearest motorboat, an outboard, was moored thirty feet offshore, near the middle of the narrow channel.

Kicking off her shoes almost in midair, Abby ran and dove into the water, which embraced her with cold so shocking that she nearly lost her breath. But she had Bean to worry about, so she ignored the cold. The channel was protected from the wind, so Ab didn't have much in the way of waves to contend with when she came to the surface not ten feet from the motorboat. She put that distance behind her in no time, competitive swimmer that she was.

The sides of the boat were too far above her to reach with anything but the very tips of her fingers, which weren't strong enough to lift her clear of the water. She swam around to the stern and placed her feet on the stanchion of the outboard motor, which she used as a ladder to climb into the boat. No sooner had she righted herself than she gave the bulb on the fuel line a few quick squeezes, checked to see that the gear lever was in neutral, and gave a mighty tug on the starter rope. The motor sputtered noncommittally, as if it had been awakened from a nap. Flipping the hair out of her eyes, she pulled again. This time her effort produced a few chugs, a little cloud of blue smoke, and a spit of saltwater from the exhaust. Overeager, she pulled again before the rope had reset. Because it was as good as unconnected, she went flying backward, tripping over the seat and crashing to the bottom of the boat in two inches of oily rainwater.

The rope, flying from her hands as she fell, had snapped back into position. She gathered herself together and braced her feet for the next pull. This time the engine came to life, idling quietly as she rushed to the bow to untie the line from the mooring buoy.

As she slipped the engine into gear and headed out the channel, she couldn't help but wish Spooky was in the bow to guide her between the rocks. More than once she felt the control stick shudder as the prop grazed a submerged boulder or ledge, but this was no time to be overly cautious. She cranked the throttle wide open, and the boat shot from the mouth of the channel into the open water of the Reach.

In order to see over the bow, Abby steered standing up, as she had often seen fishermen do. But the force of the heavy seas knocked her to her seat. At first she was taking the breaking waves sidelong, which, at her present speed, tossed curtains of salt spray into her face and threatened to overturn the boat. Remembering something Bean had told her, she turned the bow directly into the waves. The spraying stopped at once as the bow sliced neatly through the breakers.

As the boat surged forward, Abby got her bearings. The only landmark she could recognize, a quarter mile ahead and to port, were the three granite spires. Wishing she had thought to bring the binoculars, she scanned the water for a sign of Bean. At first it seemed hopeless. The sea was so agitated that she even failed to see several brightly painted lobster buoys until she was almost on top of them. Thirty times in as many seconds she thought she saw Bean's head or arms poking above the waves, but each time it turned out to be either driftwood, or a seabird, or a trick of the eye.

Cheating to the Lane's Island side of the Reach, for fear of running over Bean, put too much distance between Abby and the stone spires to see much of anything clearly. It was a catch-22 situation: Should she head straight across the Reach—side to the waves—and risk either capsizing the boat or possibly hitting Bean, or should she stay on course, head upwind, make a quick turn, and come back down the Reach with the waves on the Pogus Point side, by which time he might drown?

Bean would be exhausted by now, too tired to dive again should the sea push him back toward the rocks. She glanced toward the tall granite teeth that seemed to be chewing up the waves, and that's when she saw him, his head bobbing helplessly between the whitecaps as the surf pushed him toward the cliff. He wasn't fighting. It probably took all this strength just to stay afloat.

"Bean!" she screamed, but he didn't hear her. Or if he did, he was too tired to respond. He was facing away, toward the rocks, watching the closing chapter of his fate.

The choice was made for her. She pushed the control stick sharply to starboard, swinging the bow toward the spires. At once the sea began pouring over the gunwales in a shimmering cascade. Countless freezing needles stung her face, arms, and legs. She hardly noticed. All her attention was focused on keeping Bean in view. Several times she lost sight of him beneath a wave, but with concentration sharpened by desperation, she managed to locate him again each time.

She yelled his name repeatedly at the top of her lungs as she raced across the Reach, but still he didn't hear. Nor did he respond to the sound of the motor. Evidently the roar of the breakers crashing against the rocks drowned out everything else.

By the time she got close enough to be of any use, it was almost too late. Bean was less than fifteen feet from the rocks and surfing helplessly toward them with alarming speed. Abby had no time to think, only to react: She had to get between Bean and the rocks.

If she headed upwind and turned down with the tide, the stern would be facing the waves, and the boat would be swamped as the sea poured into the engine well. Instead, she turned quickly downwind, then jackknifed back into it, driving the boat like a wedge between the spires and Bean.

Fearful of hitting him, she pressed too close to the rocks. As she pulled back the throttle, the gunwale began pounding against the center spire with sickening thuds. Abby, however, was heedless. Her attention was riveted on Bean. All that remained above water was a soggy mass of brown hair that was just about to drift under the stern of the boat when she reached down and grabbed it, pulling his head clear of the water.

"Bean!" she cried. With an almost superhuman strength that seemed to pulse suddenly through her veins, she grabbed him under the arms and pulled him up the side of the boat until he was hanging by his armpits over the gunwale.

Holding a fistful of Bean's T-shirt with one hand and grabbing the control stick with the other, Abby pointed the bow toward open ocean and gave the throttle half a turn. The boat plowed into the waves as if glad to be free of the rocks. She was just about to breathe a sigh of relief when she realized Bean wasn't out of trouble yet. Waves were slapping his dragging body with such force that they threatened to suck him back into the water. Somehow, Abby had to get him into the boat.

Having put all the distance between themselves and the ledges she felt she could afford, she cut the throttle to idle and stood up. She placed one foot in the engine well and rested the opposite knee on the seat. It was important she keep her center of gravity as low as possible as she attempted to tug Bean into the boat, or the wild pitching of the sea could knock her overboard as well.

She leaned over the side as far as she dared and wrapped her fingers around Bean's belt. With all the desperate strength of the moment, she stood up quickly and leaned back, letting her falling weight pull him into the boat. No one could have been more amazed than she when, half a second later, she found herself buried beneath a damp mass of arms and legs that was Bean. It had worked!

Snatching a hasty glance at the rocks—during the rescue operation the boat had once again drifted ominously close—Ab clawed her way out from under Bean and crawled up onto the seat. With barely a second to spare, she twisted the throttle hard to the left. The boat leapt forward, the prop wash mingling with the spume of the waves as they shattered against the spires.

8
THE ONE THAT GOT AWAY

IT WAS PROBABLY the compression of his chest as he was dragged over the side that got Bean breathing again. By the time Ab had steered the boat to the relative safety of open water, he had begun to come to and was coughing up prodigious amounts of foul-tasting seawater. From her station by the motor, she looked at him with thankful tears in her eyes. "Bean, are you okay?"

Bean choked and coughed and sputtered for a while, then slowly propped himself up on his elbow and looked back toward the Orphans. He muttered something Abby couldn't make out.

"What?"

"I said I got a wicked wedgy." As he rectified the situation, it slowly dawned on him how close he had been to death. As he looked at Ab, his eyes widened with unalloyed amazement as he began to realize what she had done. "You saved my life," he said. Although she couldn't hear all the words, she could fill in the blanks by reading his lips.

"Somebody had to," she said, wiping tears from her eyes and hoping he would think it was just sea spray. She tried to laugh but ended up sobbing unreservedly.

Bean pulled himself to her side, took the throttle in his expert hand, and cradled her with the other. She cried all the way back to Link Dyer's dock, and he let her, simply squeezing her arm now and then.

Back at the float, Bean wrung out his wet shirt and they lay side by side on the warm, weathered boards, too exhausted to move, and let the sun dry them. The channel was calm, shielded from the wind by the evergreen forest on Lane's Island, and above them seagulls spun in wide, lazy circles against a brilliant blue sky.

Bean spoke first, as the last of Ab's tears trailed away. "How did you find me?"

"I prayed," she said. No doubt she had done that several times in the last few minutes—silently and fervently—in semiconscious fragments that leapt from her heart to heaven on wings of hope and fear. She told her story, and Bean listened with all his ears.

"Wow!" he said when she had finished. He propped himself up on one elbow and looked down at her face. "You did all that for me?"

Her eyes had been closed. Detecting something unusual in his voice, she opened them and looked at his silhouette, shadowed against the sun. She shielded her eyes with her hand. "Of course I did. Wouldn't you do the same for me." It wasn't a question; it was a statement. She had no doubt he would.

He hoped he would be as brave as she had been.

Then the most unexpected thing happened. Bean bent down and kissed her, right on the lips. It wasn't a quick, see you next summer kind of kiss at all, but a real I mean to kiss you and I don't care who knows it kiss that lasted several seconds. All of a sudden Ab forgot she was wet and miserable and cold and had come close to crashing against the rocks and falling overboard. Oddly enough, her feet tingled. So did the hairs on the back of her neck. Although something in her wanted to push him away and say, What do you think you're doing, Beanbag, something stronger was sort of melting in a warm, fuzzy cloud where there didn't seem to be any up or down or left or right.

A moment later, it was over and neither of them knew what to do about it. "That was for savin' my life," Bean stammered, trying to uncurl his toes.

"Well," said Abby, propping her elbows behind her. "I sure won't make that mistake again." She made a show of wiping her mouth with the back of her hand.

There was just enough levity in the comment to allow both of them to pretend nothing serious had happened. Before they knew it, and without any particular reason, they erupted into spontaneous laughter. When its last echo had died away among the trees across the channel, they were sitting cross-legged, facing each other. "What happened out there, Bean?" Ab asked at last.

Bean told her his story up to the point where he was just about to enter the Widowmaker. "That's when I heard him shout."

"Who shouted? The man with the map?"

Bean nodded. "He told me to come get 'im, 'cause his boat was all stove up in there. Well, I figured maybe Link's boat stood a better chance than that inflatable, but in that extra few seconds it took for us to yell at each other, I saw a coupla waves totally obliterate the cave."

"Obliterate?" Ab echoed.

"Yeah, it means, like, cover up, or wipe out."

"Thank you, Mr. Webster," said Ab, a little haughtily. "I knew that." She tossed her hair in a way that aggravated him, but it was so wet and stringy it just fell in her face. "Carry on."

Bean almost laughed, but at the last second decided it would be better not to and just sort of choked a little instead. "Anyways, I knew it'd be a miracle if I got in between the breakers, and even more of a miracle if I got out, which meant there was only one thing to do."

"Go and get help," Ab suggested reasonably, which is what she would have done if she had been there.

"I *was* the help," Bean argued. "There wasn't time to get anyone else. The tide was risin' and that guy was trapped in there with nowhere to go. If I'd gone to get help, it would've been too late by the time we got back."

"That's why you didn't come get me?"

"Well, sort of," said Bean. "I was followin' him. If I'd broken off to go back to the rendezvous, I'd've lost 'im."

"It might have been better if you had."

Bean shrugged. "I wanted to find out what he was up to."

Abby could understand that. "So, I take it you decided to swim in and get him."

"Yup." Bean took a scrap of seaweed out of his shirt pocket and tossed it back into the ocean.

"I don't think that was a very good idea."

"What else could I do?" said Bean. "I had to do something. The guy was drownin' for all I knew."

Abby wanted to remind him that he hardly swam well enough to keep himself afloat, much less a drowning man, but she refrained. They both knew it.

"I tucked the bow up under one of the Orphans as much as I could," Bean continued.

"Orphans?"

Bean explained. "So that kept it a little out of the sea. Then I dropped anchor and, when just the right moment came, I dove in."

Abby was impressed. Of course she had braved the water herself, but in the relative calm of the shallow channel, and she was an expert swimmer with six red ribbons, numerous trophies, and a Red Cross lifesaving badge to show for it. Bean, on the other hand, poor swimmer that he was, had put himself at risk by jumping into crashing seas and forcing himself through a low, jagged opening into an unknown cave.

And she liked his kiss.

Where did that thought come from? she wondered to herself, and shook her head suddenly as if to sift the memory into the further reaches of her brain. "What were you saying?"

"Ain't you listenin'?"

"*Aren't* you listening," Ab corrected. "And no, I wasn't, I just . . . zoned out for a second."

Realizing she'd been through a lot, Bean repeated himself. "As I was goin' in, my feet hit bottom a couple times, whenever the waves let me down. Just inside the cave there was this drop-off, like a pool, and I sorta spilled into that. It was kinda deep, but the life jacket brought me up pretty quick."

"What life jacket? You weren't wearing one when I found you."

"I'll get to that in a minute," said Bean. "Anyways, the first thing I saw when I come up—"

"Came up," said Ab.

Bean cocked an eyebrow. "You gonna give me an English lesson or let me tell the story?"

"There's no rule that says you can't tell the story and speak properly," said Ab with an upward tilt of the chin. "You may proceed."

Bean sighed and shook his head. "Anyways, the first thing I saw, even though it was pretty dark in there, was the dinghy. She'd been tore up pretty good, prob'ly on the jagged rocks comin' into the cave, an' was flappin' up against the ledges like a big ol' pancake.

"The man spoke up. I swam toward his voice an' pretty soon found him clingin' to a ledge just outta the water. I told 'im to come on in an' I'd help 'im get out of the cave, but he said he couldn't swim."

"So you gave him your life jacket," Ab concluded.

"Had to, didn't I?" Bean replied.

Ab had nothing to say.

"Anyways," Bean continued, "I got that on him an' pulled him down into the water. He was scared to death an' started grabbin' me 'round the neck 'til I thought he was gonna drown me. Then I thought of how you showed me how lifeguards rescue people in the water. Remember? Up at the quarry?"

She remembered. The amazing thing, thought Ab, was that *he* remembered. With a distinct flush of pride, she nodded.

"So, I did what you told me. I dove under to get out of his grip, then came up behind 'im an' threw my arm around his neck."

"You're supposed to put your arm around his chest, not his neck."

Bean considered this. "Really? Well, all I knew was I was s'posed to keep his head above water, so that's what I did. An' it worked.

"We got across the pool to the ledge where the waves were comin' in pretty fierce by that time, an' the cave was fillin' up fast. Then I noticed that as each wave started to pile up between the Orphans an' the cliff, there was this trough just outside the cave an', for just a second or two, water poured from the Widowmaker into the trough. I figured if we could ride into the trough an' get hold of the boat before the next wave come—"

Ab cleared her throat.

"Came crashin' down on our heads, we'd have half a chance. Well, it turned out I didn't have much to say about it. We were right at the entrance when this huge roller come smashin' in an' sent us halfway back across the pool, then it pulled back for the next wave to pile up, an' pulled us right up over the lip like a vacuum.

"Next thing I knew, I was lookin' down at the trough an' just sorta threw myself at it, with my arm still around the guy's neck. So down we went—six to eight feet, I bet—an' the boat was in the same trough. We grabbed the rails an', when we started to ride up the other side of the wave, I pushed 'im up over the side. That's when you came to get me."

"I guess your guardian angel was taking a break."

Bean looked at her and smiled. "I don't think so," he said.

"Did you see his face?" said Ab, squirming with a curious discomfort under Bean's close scrutiny. "Who was it?"

"It was too dark in the cave," Bean said with a shrug, "an' after that I was too busy tryin' not to drown to notice much." He took off his shirt and lay down again, surrendering himself to the warm embrace of the midsummer sun.

Ab was jealous. She almost always wore her bathing suit under her clothes while on the island, but for some reason she hadn't put it on this morning. Of all days. "Figures," she said aloud in response to her own thoughts.

"What?"

"Oh, nothing," said Ab. "I didn't see where he went, did you?"

"Nope. Like you saw, I had other things on my mind."

Ab untucked her shirt and tied it in a knot around her stomach. "What was he doing out there?"

"Lookin' for whatever's on the map," Bean reasoned.

"What do you think it is?"

Bean shrugged. "Don't know. Must be something valuable for 'im to go to all the trouble he's been up to. Maybe some kind've treasure, like Spook said."

Abby doubted it. "There are lots of things besides treasure that are valuable," she said, looking down at Bean. He looked so warm and peaceful and self-satisfied that she wanted to get a bucket of water and toss it on him. She fought back the urge.

"Like what?" said Bean, blissfully unaware of the battle raging in Ab's mind.

"Like secrets," she said.

"Secrets?"

"Sure. Remember how your mom told us that people will do almost anything for love?"

"Yeah, so?"

"Well, they'll do almost anything to keep secrets, too."

Bean allowed this was so. "But what's secret about the Widowmaker? And," he said as another thought occurred to him, "is he someone who's tryin' to keep a secret of his own, or is he tryin' to find out somebody else's secret?"

"I'd say he's trying to find out someone else's secret," Ab replied thoughtfully. "I bet that map he has is a copy, and the original is really old."

"What makes you think so?"

"The poem," said Abby. "It sounded old-fashioned."

"So, we're talkin' about an old secret. How old?"

It was Abby's turn to shrug. "I don't know. Really old. Not as old as Shakespeare or anything, 'cause there weren't any *thee*s or *thou*s in the poem. But it's old."

"Then whosever secret it is, is dead."

"I think so."

"Then why is he skulkin' around like he is? An' why would anyone care? I mean, I could understand if you was tryin' to find out somebody's secret an' they was still alive, you'd have to be careful they didn't find out what you was up to. But if you're just tryin' to dig up something about somebody who's been dead forever, who cares? That ain't a secret, that's just history."

"I know," said Abby, whose attention was drawn to a Styrofoam cup that drifted against the float. Stealthily, she reached over and lifted it, half full, from the water. "What if it's a secret so bad that someone's come back from the dead to protect it?" She made a shrill, ghostly sound. Just as Bean was about to open his eyes, she dumped the water on his stomach.

Bean jumped up as if he'd been electrified, but Ab had already dropped the cup and sprinted halfway up the ramp. He dipped the cup quickly into the ocean and ran after her. By the time he caught up, though, all but a few drops had either spilled or leaked out, and these didn't produce much more than a little squeal as he flung them at her. Not very satisfying.

"What are we going to do?" Ab wondered aloud as they stopped to pick some early blueberries from a roadside patch. "Our folks are going to freak when they find out what's happened."

Bean's thoughts hadn't been that practical. He'd been thinking about what Abby had said about the dead rising from the grave to protect a secret. It was a silly thought, he knew, but somehow he couldn't shake it from his mind.

"We won't tell 'em," he said. Before Abby could protest, he added, "not right away. We'll tell Constable Wruggles first, an' let him decide what to do."

9
THE MAN WHO WASN'T THERE

"YOU SAY THE LAST YOU SAW of this fella he was rowin' up the Reach?" said Constable Wruggles, staring down at the Orphans from the cliff where he'd parked his SUV. If not for the fact that the kids had proven themselves pretty astute detectives over the years, he'd have been skeptical about Bean's story of the man with the map. It sounded a little far-fetched even for Bean, who was known to embellish the truth from time to time. The fact that Abby, no-nonsense girl that she was, attested to it gave it extra weight.

Bean perceived the constable's doubt. "I could prove it if we'd go out in a boat, like I said."

Wruggles shuddered. He preferred to stay out of boats, if at all possible. "I got better things to do than chuck Ma Wruggles's good cookin' overboard, thank you very much. I can see fine from here."

"But you can't see in the cave," Bean objected. "An' that's where you'll find what's left of the rubber dinghy."

"Well, leftovers of a rubber dinghy wouldn't go far convincin' somebody if they was of a doubtful turn of mind," said Wruggles, tucking his thumbs into his belt loops. "Things like that wash up all the time."

Bean was just about to protest when Wruggles held up his hand. "I'll tell you what. I'll poke around the point an' see if I can turn up something of Link's skiff. If I find it, I'll let you know. I expect that if it turns up, we can find some evidence. Maybe fingerprints that match the ones we found in the submarine. That'll give us a startin' place, at least.

"In the meantime, keep all this to yourselves. Town's still wound up enough 'bout you findin' ol' Minerva's grave. 'Sides, if word got out that we're lookin' for this fella, he'd go to ground an' we might never find out what he's up to. Meanwhile, see if you can't stay out of trouble for a few hours, will ya?

"Here." He rummaged through the pockets of his khaki pants and produced two rumpled dollar bills. "Getchyerselves some ice cream. Chill out. That's what kids say, ain't it?"

"You mean," said Abby hopefully, "we shouldn't tell our parents?"

Wruggles thought carefully. "Well, I don't see there's much to be gained by puttin' 'em to all that worry, 'specially after all they been through. Maybe if I turn up something concrete, well, we'll cross that bridge when we come to it. For now, why don't you just go home an' watch TV or play video games like normal kids do."

Bean had never seen anything on television that was even the pale equal of his own active imagination, and Ab, having grown up without a TV in the house, couldn't imagine a bigger waste of time. As for video games, Spooky had told them that he read somewhere that a kid lost ten billion brain cells for every hour playing a video game. Not sure how many brain cells he had to spare, Spooky swore off the games, dubbing them "brain eaters." Bean followed suit, donating his Game Boy to the medical center rummage sale. Abby never liked video games in the first place.

"Thanks," said Bean, pocketing the bills. "We'll stay outta trouble."

Wruggles watched after them doubtfully as they ran down the hill, both talking at once, their excited voices echoing off the towering, tree-covered slag heaps. "Famous last words," said Wruggles as he climbed into his Jeep.

At the top of the rise, Bean, who was several steps ahead of Ab, darted unexpectedly off the road, down a little overgrown path of soft, sweet grass through overhanging trees. "Where are you going?" Abby called, but before she could catch up, she heard a loud splash. The multiple echo that followed told her he had jumped into the quarry. A moment later, she burst through the underbrush and skidded to a halt three inches short of the edge.

Although her feet had stopped, the upper half of her body had too much forward momentum, and with nothing but air to hold onto, she started to topple forward. She was looking down at Bean, his snow-white shoulders and copper-colored hair accented by a bright circle of golden sunlight against the bottomless green depths of the water. He was laughing.

"I'll get you for this!" she yelled, almost laughing herself as she flailed about in a futile attempt to regain her balance, but it was too late and she was too close to the edge.

Gleefully, Bean witnessed her surrender to the inevitable forces of physics as she plummeted toward him as if in slow motion, trying to right herself for impact.

"I just got halfway dry!" she screamed, her words chorusing from outcroppings and ledges around the quarry.

No sooner had she managed to twist herself into a more or less vertical position than her feet struck the surface, momentarily swamping Bean beneath the short-lived tsunami that followed. As the waves settled, he peered into the depths, where she had shot out of sight like an arrow amidst an explosive trail of bubbles.

"She's gonna be ripped," Bean said, giggling mischievously.

"What's the big idea?" she sputtered when she broke the surface several seconds later, spitting and flipping stringy strands of hair from her eyes.

"Your folks are gonna ask how you got your clothes wet," said Bean slyly. "Now all you have to say is I tricked you into the quarry."

"That's not the truth," said Ab.

"Sure it is. You're in the quarry, ain't ya?"

"But the only reason we're here is to hide the fact that I was wet already, from swimming out to rescue you."

"Which is just what we don't want anyone to know, right?" Bean reasoned. "Now, if anyone asks, you have an answer, an' it's the truth."

"You know what it is," Ab objected. "It's disingenuous."

Bean didn't even pretend to understand. "What the heck's that mean?"

"It means using a little truth to hide the whole truth," said Ab, who wasn't sure that was what it meant, but she figured it was pretty close. Besides, it sounded good.

"Well, that's good, ain't it, if you don't want someone to know the whole truth?"

Ab stared at Bean with a knitted brow. She was genuinely disappointed, though she couldn't define her reasons. She hated to think Bean would ever be less than honest with her. Or had he been already? She swam across the cove toward the shallow ledges.

"What? Where are you goin'?"

"Home," said Ab. "And if Mom, or Dad, or the Proverbs ask why I'm wet, I'm going to tell them the truth . . . the whole truth."

"An' nothin' but the truth," said Bean to himself as he watched her climb angrily up the ledges in her soggy sneakers. "Come on, Ab!" he yelled. She gave her hair one disdainful toss for good measure as, without a word, she disappeared into the trees at the quarry's edge.

"Darn," said Bean. He dove underwater and swam to shore.

"Hey, Ab!" he called from the top of the hill by the ball ground. "Wait up!" He was surprised she hadn't gotten farther in the time it had taken him to climb the ledges and retrieve the T-shirt and blue jeans he had tossed off before plunging into the quarry. He would have been even more surprised if he'd known she had walked slowly on purpose, so he'd have time to catch up to her.

Both kids had a lousy, sick feeling in the pit of their stomachs, and although neither knew what it was exactly, they both had a pretty good idea it had something to do with their argument.

Ab stopped and waited.

"I don't wanna fight," said Bean as he came alongside.

"Me neither."

"Good," said Bean with his winningest smile. "Then why don't you just apologize, an' we'll get over it."

Abby laughed in spite of herself. "I'm not the one who needs to apologize," she said, slapping his shoulder. "You are."

Bean hung his head thoughtfully as they resumed walking. "So, you don't think it's a good idea, that . . . whatever you said the word was."

"Disingenuous. And it's not a good idea. It's dishonest. And if you're willing to be dishonest with your parents, how can I trust you to be honest with me?"

Bean hadn't thought of it that way. To him skirting the truth was kind of like telling a story, and frankly he did it quite often.

"How would you like it if your mom and dad weren't truthful with you?" said Ab. After a little hesitation, she added, "What if I wasn't honest with you? What if you could never be sure that what I said was completely true?"

He wouldn't like it at all. He just assumed everyone was honest with him.

Ab decided to let the notion ferment in Bean's brain. By the time they reached the bandstand, he'd arrived at a conclusion. "You're right, Ab. I'm sorry."

Ab took his hand and gave it a quick squeeze. "I've got to go change. I'll meet you down by the fountain in ten minutes."

"Okay," said Bean, watching her run across the Mitchells' lawn toward the back door of the Moses Webster House. "Where the heck does she find these words?" he said under his breath. "Disingenuous." He decided to look it up when he got home.

"Hello!" said Ab as the back door slammed behind her. "Anybody home?" She half hoped everyone was out. That way she could go quietly upstairs and change without having to explain herself to anyone.

"Well, here's the kitten that fell in the millpond," said an unfamiliar voice behind her. She spun around and found herself face-to-face with Mrs. Prinderby, Easter bonnet and all. "You must be Abigail."

"Yes," Abby replied as politely as possible, given the fact she was trying to keep from laughing.

"I'm Amelia Prinderby," said Mrs. Prinderby, shuffling an armload of unidentifiable objects to the crook of her left arm so she could shake hands. "Harold and I are your new housemates."

The curious woman shook hands with such vigor that her whole body seemed to quiver. With effort, Abby retrieved her hand. "Harold?" she said.

"My husband, the professor," Mrs. Prinderby explained. "He's come to the island to see if he can't find out what old Twing was up to." She bustled into the kitchen and deposited her burden on the table. Among the objects Abby could now make out were a crystal ball and a Ouija board. "And I've come in hopes that Anabel will have the good grace to present herself at last."

The name caught Ab's attention. "Anabel, did you say?"

"Yes, Twing's wife. He left her in Halifax when he sailed off as a privateer," said Mrs. Prinderby, as if simply reminding Ab of something she should know. She cast a distracted eye around the room. "The vibrations are excellent here."

"Vibrations?"

"Very good indeed. I think the professor's onto it this time. Of course, it's the map, you see. Made all the difference in the world." Mrs. Prinderby began rummaging through the cabinets. "Would you like some tea?" She produced two cups and saucers and placed them gingerly on the granite counter.

"Yes, please," said Ab. She didn't really want any tea, especially because she had to pee so badly, but her curiosity was so aroused by the apparition of Mrs. Prinderby that she couldn't refuse the chance to spend a few minutes with her. "Is anyone else home?"

"Oh, my . . . I was supposed to tell you something," Mrs. Prinderby said, patting her chest with a meaty hand as if to dislodge the memory. "Now, let me get this right. Your mother and father have gone to a place called Shore Acres for the day to visit some people whose names I don't recall . . ."

"The Kingsburys?" Ab suggested helpfully. They were the only people her folks were likely to visit at Shore Acres.

Mrs. Prinderby ruminated as she turned on the burner under the teakettle. "Could be," she said at last. "Of course, it could be Hepplewhite or the Brothers Cherible for all I know." She leaned confidentially close. "I'm terrible with the names of the living," she explained. "The dead I can recite like poetry!" She righted herself abruptly as water began to crackle in the kettle. "It's a gift. In any event, they will be back before supper. I'm referring to your parents," she clarified, "not to the dead. They aren't as perspicuous as one would wish."

Perspicuous. Ab filed it away in her mental index. There's one she'd have to look up so she could impress Bean with it.

"Meanwhile," Mrs. Prinderby continued, "Mr. Proverb has gone somewhere to get something fixed, and Mrs. Proverb is somewhere else doing something or other. Which reminds me, you're damp."

"Oh, yes, I am," said Ab, having difficulty following Mrs. Prinderby's logic. "I've been . . . swimming."

Mrs. Prinderby handed her a steaming cup of tea. "Well, this will warm you. Here, sit down," she said, patting the back of a chair. "I'll join you as soon as mine's ready."

Ab sat and added milk and a spoonful of sugar to her cup. "You mentioned a map," she said tentatively, trying to sound mildly curious but not too interested.

"Twing's map," said Mrs. Prinderby as she pulled out a chair and subsided into it, taking special effort not to spill her tea. "My husband found it last fall among some papers in the Halifax Historical Society."

"Who is Twing?" She wanted to know if the Prinderbys' map had any connection with the one she and Bean had found, but thought it best to take the unknowns in order.

"Twing?" said Mrs. Prinderby, surprised. "You don't know Twing?"

Abby shook her head.

"My goodness." She stared a moment at the linoleum. "I thought everyone knew Twing." She rearranged her bonnet. "Abnezar Twing was a privateer in the early 1800s."

"Privateer?" Ab repeated. "I don't know what that means."

"Pirate, my dear," Mrs. Prinderby explained.

Ab's heart skipped a beat. Bean should be here. For as long as she'd known him, he'd been trying to convince her there was pirate treasure buried on the island. She waited politely as Mrs. Prinderby sipped her tea.

"He was from Prince Edward Island, son of a well-to-do islander. Every fall after the year 1819, when Abnezar was seven, his father sent him down to Halifax aboard a ship with a load of fruit and produce for the market there. This went on until Abnezar was twenty or so, when he fell in with a bad lot, the worst of whom was a Scottish scoundrel named Athred Morrison.

"The two of 'em recruited a crew from the dregs of the waterfront. They stole a ship called *Privilege* and began their career as pirates." She leaned close, and her eyes widened through the steam of her tea, "A more bloodthirsty captain and crew never terrorized the seven seas."

She took another long sip of tea while Ab waited, not quite as patiently this time.

"Well, time came when Twing and Morrison decided they were rich enough to get out of the pirating business. They sailed for home in two ships, the *Privilege* and one called *Destiny*, which they'd captured in the Caribbean. They put in at Portland, where they paid off the crew—all but twelve that were needed to sail the ships—and headed up the coast."

"What happened to the original passengers and crew of the *Destiny*?" Ab asked. "Did they get off in Portland, too? Why didn't they contact the authorities and have Twing arrested?"

Mrs. Prinderby sat back and laughed. "They say questions come in threes, and answers in twos," she said. "But I've got one answer to satisfy 'em all." She grew suddenly solemn. "Twing and Morrison weren't in the habit of leaving witnesses. Everyone went over the side in the shark-infested waters of the Caribbean."

"The whole crew?" said Abby, aghast.

"And the passengers. Women, children—anything that couldn't be sold was consigned to the deep."

Abby's romantic notion of pirates as swashbuckling adventurers underwent a sudden and radical revision. "That's hideous."

Mrs. Prinderby agreed. "This is where things get interesting," she said as she began rocking subtly, rhythmically back and forth. "Most of the ships Twing and Morrison had looted were British, you see—despite the fact that, as Canadians, they were subjects of the Crown—so the Royal Navy put a pretty hefty bounty on them. Well, not a day out of Portland, an English man-o'-war called *Dauntless* got them in its sights and gave chase.

"According to the ship's log . . ." Mrs. Prinderby interrupted herself. "You know what a ship's log is, don't you, dear?"

"It's a kind of diary that the captain keeps," said Ab, "with information about cargo and weather and ports of call and stuff like that."

"Stuff exactly like that," said Mrs. Prinderby, satisfied. "Very good. Well, according to the log of the British ship, Twing and Morrison put in among a group of islands in Penobscot Bay. The captain of the *Dauntless*, fearing it was a trap, steered clear and waited, circling the island like a fox at a mouse hole.

"Three days later, it was just coming evening and the *Dauntless* had dropped anchor for the night when they heard a great explosion somewhere in the islands. Next morning, before dawn, the watchman spied the *Privilege* striking out under full sail.

"Now he had a dilemma, you see. He could give chase to the *Privilege* and run the risk that the *Destiny* was waiting for him to do just that very thing so she could come up behind him. Then the *Privilege* would turn on him, and the *Dauntless* would be trapped between the two. On the other hand, if he waited too long, the *Privilege* could make its escape."

"Or it could have been a distraction," Ab joined in excitedly.

"Pardon?"

"A diversion," Ab explained. "What if the crew of the *Privilege* stayed aboard just long enough to set sail and make sure she was under way, then went over the sides in longboats. In a steady wind, the *Privilege* would have held its course, with the *Dauntless* following after. Meanwhile, the *Destiny* could have made her escape in the opposite direction."

Mrs. Prinderby sat up and blinked tightly a couple of times, as if trying to absorb the notion. "Why, I don't think Mr. P. ever considered that possibility."

"What happened?" said Ab, eager to test her theory. "Did the *Dauntless* ever catch the *Privilege*?"

"No. The captain of the *Dauntless,* leaving some sailors behind in a longboat to keep an eye out for the *Destiny,* gave chase. Some hours later, the *Dauntless* was just closing on the pirate when a storm struck with such force that it was all they could do to keep afloat. Mr. Prinderby supposes it was a hurricane, given the description in the ship's log and the time of year—August, I believe it was. At any rate, by the time the storm cleared, there was no sign of the *Privilege*.

"The captain of the *Dauntless*, feeling he had a better than even chance against one ship, returned to the islands and recovered the crew in the longboat, then went in search of the *Destiny*, but—"

"Never found it!" Ab concluded, triumphant. "It *was* a diversion." She shifted to the edge of her seat. "With no one to man her during the storm, the *Privilege* went to the bottom, while the *Destiny* made her escape."

Mrs. Prinderby furrowed her brows in thoughtful consternation. "Dear, dear. I don't believe that would accommodate Mr. P's hypothesis. Not at all."

"Which is?"

"Well, much as I'd like to tell you, I'm afraid that's confidential, my dear. You know how academics are about their little theories."

Ab wasn't sure what an academic was. She'd look that up, too.

"As for this business of a diversion, I shall have to consult Anabel," she said, stroking the pointer on her Ouija board absentmindedly. "She couldn't have known in life, of course, but in death who knows what one may know?"

Anabel. There was that name again. "You said they were married?"

"Yes, dear. You find that surprising?"

"Well, yes. I mean, you don't think of pirates having families. At least, I don't."

"Oh, they did. Often they would put to sea for years at a time, leaving family and friends with the impression that they were simply conducting trade like countless other seafarers. Then they'd come home for a bit, having sold whatever booty they'd stolen, and live like gentlemen, often respected citizens and churchgoers.

"Then the blood lust and greed would overcome them, and they'd put to sea again."

"How horrible for his wife to find out what kind of man he was, and all he'd done," said Ab, her heart welling with compassion for the young woman. She was left alone for years at a time to raise her children, all the while thinking her husband was an honest merchant seaman.

Mrs. Prinderby smiled. "Not so horrible that it kept her from spending the rest of her life searching for his treasure."

"Treasure?"

"What good is a pirate story without it?" said Mrs. Prinderby.

"And that's why your husband is here? To find the treasure?"

"Mr. P. is a historian, my dear. A true historian. He cares as little for treasure as that." She snapped her fingers. "The Holy Grail for him is to prove his theory about what happened to the *Destiny* and her crew. It is his opinion that the ship was scuttled here among the islands."

There was a sudden, impatient pounding at the front door. Reluctantly, Ab went to answer it.

10
PIRATES?

"ARE YOU COMIN'?" Bean asked a little more sharply than necessary. "I been waitin' an hour."

Ab looked at her watch, then at Bean. "You've been waiting ten minutes," she said, her hand on her hip.

"Well," said Bean, shuffling his feet and studying his fingernails. "Seems like an hour. Anyway, what's takin' so long?"

Ab held up a quieting hand and stepped out onto the porch, pulling the door softly shut behind her. "I just met this lady named Mrs. Prinderby."

"Never heard that name before," Bean observed.

"Me neither. She and her husband are staying here. He's a history professor."

Bean cringed inwardly. He hated history. To him it was nothing more than a forgettable list of names and dates.

"She's the most . . . the most . . . ah . . . unusual person I've ever seen. You have to meet her," she reopened the door and held it open for him. "Come on, it'll just take a minute. Then we'll go get ice cream and I'll tell you what she told me, and what her husband is doing here."

Bean, who was no student of fashion, saw nothing particularly odd in Mrs. Prinderby's appearance or apparel, though it struck even him that the hat might be a little out of place. When Ab introduced him, he took the hand the woman offered and squeezed it lightly. "Hi," he said. "Pleased to meet you."

"Bean, you say?" Mrs. Prinderby repeated when Ab had completed the introductions. "I like that. Distinctive."

"It's a nickname, actually," Ab explained, lest there be any doubt.

"You don't say," Mrs. Prinderby replied with a slight smile. "Well, what does it signify?"

Bean shrugged. "Nothin', so far as I know. My uncle Phil started callin' me Bean when I was a kid. I guess it just kinda stuck."

"And what's your real name, then?"

"Arthur," Ab answered. "Like King Arthur."

"Oh! King Arthur!" Mrs. Prinderby cried. "My favorite." She leaned forward and absorbed the two of them with a wide-eyed stare. "I've never gotten through to him, try as I might. Even on Tintagel; that's the old ruin on the coast of Cornwall in England that's supposed to be Camelot itself," she explained.

Bean was beginning to see what Ab had meant about Mrs. Prinderby. He raised his eyebrows involuntarily. "What do you mean 'call 'em up'? You mean, like at a seance?"

Mrs. Prinderby sat back and sighed theatrically. "Something to that effect, yes. I'm a medium. It's my burden to have the gift of communicating with the dead."

Bean leaned close to Ab's ear. "I don't think this medium's too well done," he whispered.

Ab stifled a laugh. "Go on, Mrs. Prinderby. You mean, you can actually talk to ghosts?"

"Oh, don't call them ghosts," said Mrs. Prinderby, glancing quickly to the right and left as if someone might be listening. "They don't like to be reminded they're dead. Worst thing you can do. Makes them feel inconsequential. I call them guests. And yes, I talk to them; rather, they talk through me."

"But you haven't talked to King Arthur?" said Bean, teasing her along. Ab stepped on his foot.

"No, unfortunately. You see, one can communicate only with those . . . guests who are in limbo. The others, those who've gone on to their reward, for better or worse, are beyond the cares of this world. Utterly beyond contact."

"Then who do you communicate with?" Bean wanted to know.

"The unsettled ones," Mrs. Prinderby replied, crossing her hands on her chest and sighing deeply. "Quite often those who died untimely deaths, or harbored terrible secrets and can't come to grips with their fate. They keep trying to come back to settle things, but their only windows to this world are mediums."

"Like you," said Bean skeptically.

Mrs. Prinderby nodded gravely. "As I said, it is both a gift and a great burden."

"Must be," said Bean. "Talked to anyone we know lately?" Ab kicked his shins. "Ow!" he said. "What? I just want to know."

"As a matter of fact, for the past several years, since my husband began his research into Abnezar Twing, I have been overcome any number of times with the feeling that someone involved with him is trying to get through to me. I believe it's his wife, Anabel."

"Hey, that's the same name as—" Ab poked him with her elbow.

Before he could complain, Ab whispered, "I'll tell you about it later."

The front door swung open with its distinctive squeak. "Anybody home?"

"Sounds like Leeman Russell," said Bean as he followed Ab through the dining room to the entrance hall, where Leeman was standing with his hand on the doorknob.

"Hi, Ab. Bean," said Leeman. He was about to ask a question, but something about Ab caught his eye. "A little soggy, ain't ya?"

"I've been swimming," said Ab. "I haven't had time to change."

"Oh, you're practically dry," Bean chided. "No big deal."

Leeman absorbed this information matter-of-factly. Kids on the island spent most of the summer wet. "The Proverbs to home?"

"No, they're out running errands, I think," said Ab. "Anything I can do?"

"Well, I don't know," said Leeman, stroking his chin. "I picked up this fella down to the boat who says he's got a room booked here."

"That's easy to check," said Ab. She opened the register that lay on the phone stand in the corner of the hall. "What's his name?"

Leeman consulted the palm of his left hand, where he'd written the name in blue ink. "Daltry Lawson," he read.

Ab looked at the register. "Yup, here it is. He just called last night to book a room." She ran her finger across the page to the column on the right where the Proverbs listed the names of the rooms assigned to guests. "The Blue Room," she said. "That's downstairs, just through the living room. Why don't you send him on in, and we'll help him get settled."

"Well, that could be a little difficult," said Leeman. "He's in a wheelchair."

"Oh, I was wondering why Mrs. Proverb put him in the Blue Room. She usually lets guests use that as a reading room. That explains it. Do you want us to help you get him up the steps?"

"Can if you want," said Leeman, by which he meant, yes, I sure do.

The kids went out to Leeman's car and helped the new arrival out of the passenger seat while Leeman extracted the wheelchair from the trunk.

Daltry Lawson was heftily built, with light brown hair and green eyes. He was wearing a light yellow sweater, despite the warmth of the day, and blue jeans and white sneakers. As they helped him into the wheelchair, Bean noticed a fresh scrape on the man's left wrist.

"I'm sorry to be such a nuisance," said Lawson.

Bean and Leeman, taking opposite sides of the wheelchair, walked it up the three granite steps to the walkway. "No problem," said Leeman, puffing a little. "You ain't heavy as you look, anyways." Ab took up the rear, carrying Lawson's suitcase.

Ab handed Leeman the suitcase and pushed the wheelchair up the walk toward the short set of steps leading to the front porch. She introduced herself and Bean. "The Proverbs will be back to check you in properly, but we can show you where your room is."

"That's very nice of you," said Lawson. "Do you live here?"

"My parents and I are guests here, but we come every summer, so it feels like home. Here we are." They had arrived at the steps. Bean and Leeman took up their positions once more and lifted the wheelchair clear of the steps. "You'll be able to go out the back door without much help. There's just one little step."

Leeman slapped his forehead with the heel of his hand. "Shoot. Why didn't I think of that? I could've gone 'round back and brought him in that way."

"You gonna be here long?" Bean asked as they wheeled the new guest into the foyer.

Lawson replied without looking at Bean. "I'm not sure. I have some work to complete, and I need some peace and quiet, so—"

"What kind of work do you do?" Ab asked.

Leeman interrupted. "I guess you two can take it from here. I've got to go see Walter."

Bean and Ab glanced at each other and smiled. It was Leeman's day off. That meant he and Walter Franklin would spend most of the day sitting on the plastic deck chairs down by the take-out, drinking coffee and watching the summer folk come and go, especially the women. Leeman and Walter, both bachelors, would rate the women for marriageability on a scale of one to five. It was a game they'd played for years. Apparently none of the prospects had ever rated the highest mark, because Leeman and Walter, both well into middle age now, were still single.

"I think we've got it," said Ab.

"Thank you, Mr. Russell," said Lawson. With difficulty, he raised himself off the seat enough so he could retrieve the billfold from his rear pocket. "What do I owe you?"

"Oh, nothin'," said Leeman. "Island hospitality, you know." He laughed.

The man thanked him heartily and replaced his wallet.

"In answer to your question, I'm a writer," said Lawson as they watched Leeman bound down the steps toward his car.

"Oh, I've always wanted to be a writer," said Ab. "I love mysteries. Is that what you write?"

Lawson figeted a little in his seat. "I'm afraid nothing as romantic as that. I write textbooks, mostly postgraduate studies in cultural anthropology."

Just the sound of Lawson's profession was making Bean drowsy. He took the handles of the wheelchair and turned it toward the Blue Room.

"I don't know what that means," said Ab.

Lawson thought how best to put it. "It's the study of people groups and their relation to the world around them."

"Sounds interesting."

Bean silently mouthed the words *sounds boring.*

"Are you studying people on the island?" Ab asked.

"No. I've already got my work, in here," he said, patting the briefcase in his lap. "I just need solitude and quiet to do the writing."

"There's a fire escape with a little ramp on it just off the livin' room," said Bean. "I guess you can get down there by yourself if you need to."

Lawson slapped the wheels of his chair. "Don't worry about me. I've had plenty of practice."

"Been in that long?" Bean asked offhandedly, ignoring the disapproving look he got from Ab.

"Three years," said Lawson, avoiding direct eye contact with Bean. He didn't seem to have the same problem with Ab.

"Long time," said Bean.

Lawson nodded. "A long time. Automobile accident," he said, and that was all. "Thank you, kids. I appreciate your help."

Mr. Proverb returned just as Bean and Ab entered the kitchen. Mrs. Prinderby evidently had either returned to her room or gone out, for there was no sign of her or her psychic paraphernalia. Ab explained about Mr. Lawson, and Mr. Proverb left to introduce himself. Then Ab went to change her clothes.

"Anything strike you as strange about Mr. Lawson?" Bean asked as they headed down the sidewalk toward Main Street.

"Strange? No. He seemed pretty normal to me."

"Not to me," said Bean. He plucked a piece of grass and stuck it between his teeth.

It annoyed Ab that Bean was a lot more observant than she was. "Why?" she demanded.

"First of all, did you see the bottoms of his sneakers?"

"How could I? What am I supposed to do, ask him to lift his feet?"

"I saw 'em when he swung out of Leeman's car. They're worn, just like anyone's."

Ab saw the problem. If Lawson was confined to a wheelchair, how did he manage to wear out his sneakers? "Maybe he got them secondhand," she postulated. "Or maybe they're an old pair he had before his accident."

"I thought of that," said Bean, who hadn't. "But what about his wallet?"

"What about it?"

"He sits on it. Did you see what he had to go through when he tried to pay Leeman? If I was in a wheelchair, I wouldn't keep my wallet in my back pocket. I'd put it in my shirt pocket, or rig up a fanny pack or something on one of the arms of the chair."

They stopped by the fountain at the end of the sidewalk, leaned on the edge, and ran their fingers mindlessly through the sparkling water as it splashed from a lion's mouth. "That doesn't prove anything," said Ab, though inwardly she thought it was a good point. "Is that all?"

"Nope," said Bean. "His hands."

"What about them?"

"He had fresh blisters. I saw 'em when he reached for his wallet."

"So? He would, wouldn't he, from pushing himself around in the wheelchair?"

"That's what I thought. But these were new blisters—brand new. And there were no calluses, which there would've been if he'd been in a wheelchair all that time. And he had a scrape on his left wrist."

Ab had noticed none of this. "Still doesn't prove anything."

"Proves he's mighty active for someone in a wheelchair," said Bean.

From frustration, and without warning, Ab dipped both hands in the fountain and splashed Bean in the face. "You're it!" By the time Bean responded with a counterattack, Ab was gone. Having timed her assault to coincide with a break in the traffic, she was already across the street. Bean had to wait for a truck, two cars, and a motorcycle, by which time Ab was in line at the take-out window of the Harbor Gawker.

Bean came up behind her and pretended nothing had happened, knowing it would drive her crazy. "What kind are you gettin'?"

"Same as always," said Ab.

"Why don't you try something different for a change?"

"I like mint chocolate chip."

"Yeah, but you might like some other kind, too, 'cept you'll never know 'cause you never tried it."

"If I don't know what I'm missing," Ab reasoned, "I won't miss it. Besides, you're getting chocolate. You always do."

True. He always did. Always would. As far as he was concerned, all the other exotic flavors on the chalkboard by the window might as well not even be there. "Double chocolate in a sugar cone," he said to Millie, the girl behind the counter, who handed it to him before the words were out of his mouth.

"Saw you in line," Millie said. "Figured I'd have it ready for ya."

Ab laughed and danced down the sidewalk toward the millrace, threading her way through other pedestrians and spinning in circles as she licked her ice cream. "Told you!" she sang.

As they leaned over the bridge eating their ice cream, Ab told Bean what Mrs. Prinderby had said.

"You think it's the same map we found?" said Bean.

"Don't know," said Ab. "But it's sure a weird coincidence."

Bean's fevered brain was spinning a hundred miles an hour. "Pirates," he said. "Spooky was right! There's a treasure buried on Pogus Point, maybe in the Widowmaker, and the guy that tried to drown me this mornin' was lookin' for it."

"But who is he, and where did he go?"

Bean looked out over Carver's Harbor, tossing the remains of his cone to the seagulls. "I don't know," he said. "But I'm gonna find out."

Ab ate the last of her cone. "*We're* going to find out," she declared.

11
THE BLACK MORIAH

BETTY LOU AREY was not a superstitious woman. Countless hundreds of nights after closing up the Pizza Pit, she had walked the two miles from town to her home near the turnoff to Pogus Point. Cemetery Road, as it was called, had been well named. It was the kind of road kids would dare one another to walk from one end to the other on a moonless night. Sparsely populated, the road was a pleasant, peaceful walk on a sunny day. But after the sun went down and long, dark shadows spilled into its hollows, it became a place of disquiet where it was easy to imagine evil specters among the trees to the right and left, hungrily ticking off on fleshless fingers the final heartbeats of passersby. There were only two streetlights along the entire stretch of road, and on foggy nights they kept their light to themselves, small smudges of illumination that seemed afraid of the dark.

In the distant past, some islander had nicknamed it Double-Dead Road, because it led to two cemeteries. The name had stuck.

All this meant nothing to Betty Lou, a no-nonsense, cherub-faced girl of eighteen, recently graduated from high school. In the fall she was off to college in Bangor to become an accountant. She thought like an accountant; if she couldn't see it, taste it, touch it, smell it, or hear it, it didn't exist.

Bean would have said that Betty Lou had no imagination, and he would have been right. Which made what happened that night all the more terrifying.

Betty Lou had just rounded the corner by the Dickys' old horse barn and was beginning the descent into Lawrey's Hollow, which was filled with a thick, chilling fog. On the far side of the hollow, above the low-lying mist, she could see the lights in the windows of her house: yellow rectangles of welcome embedded in the night. Just at the crest of the hill, she saw the bright, cyclopic eye of the lone streetlight.

The night was rich with the smells of salt and evergreen laced with the damp, sweet redolence of beach roses and decomposing vegetation. As Betty Lou walked down the hill, she was musing on the wonders of double-entry bookkeeping and scarcely noticed as the fog closed about her in a clammy embrace.

A long-dead apple tree marked the lowest point in the hollow. She saw its gnarled, lifeless branches—white as bones against the darkness— emerge slowly from the misty gloom and knew the road was about to rise. It was at that moment she heard footsteps other than her own. They were coming in the opposite direction. She slowed somewhat, wondering who could possibly be heading toward town at this time of night.

"Hello!" she said. The footsteps stopped and she anticipated a reply, but there was none.

"Hello!" she repeated. "Mo, is that you?" She thought Mo Phillips might be on his way to work the night shift at the crab factory, though she couldn't imagine he'd walk rather than take his pickup truck. "It's me, Betty Lou."

Still, there was no response. She slowed almost to a standstill. Suddenly she felt distinctly uncomfortable, and a little shiver of apprehension shimmied up her spine. All at once her senses were open to the world around her. It was cold in the fog. Drops of mist condensed on leaves and branches, forming raindrops that plunged to earth in a chorus of irregular splatters all around her. The crickets up by Martin's Cemetery were singing their familiar, single-note songs, a symphony she usually found comforting. Tonight, though, it seemed ominous, as if it were trying to warn her of something.

As she stood there, the footsteps started again. They were slower now, and coming directly toward her. Judging from the sound, the person was wearing hard-soled shoes that clip-clopped on the pavement.

The steps drew closer, but in the thickness of the fog it was no longer possible to tell exactly where they were coming from. Betty Lou turned slowly, trying to get a fix on where she might expect to see someone emerge from the murkiness. That's when she saw it—a hooded figure dressed in black. It was so dark, it seemed to be cut from the night.

"Hello?" she said with a mounting sense of foreboding. The figure stopped in its tracks, surrounded by tendrils of mist. It was very tall and thin, bent slightly from the waist at an unnatural angle, and seemed to be studying her. She thought she could hear its breathing, raspy and wheezy, with a mucousy click at the back of the throat each time it drew a breath.

At first she decided it was someone trying to play a trick on her, and she would have none of it. "Listen, whoever you are, if you think you're going to scare me, you'd better think again." She took a belligerent step toward the specter, but it didn't move. Instead, one of its arms rose slowly, and, though she couldn't see its fingers, it seemed to be pointing at her. For the first time in her life, she began to feel genuinely afraid, and all she could think to do was run. At the same time, she realized she didn't know which way to go. The apple tree, which had marked her approximate location, was no longer visible. And having turned around several times, she had no idea which way was home. Had the specter come up from behind or in front of her? She didn't know. "Who are you?" she said, backing slowly away from the creature.

The reply grated across the miasma with a low, strangled moan. "Fear," it said, the end of the word trailing off in a raspy breath and a long hiss that hung in the air. All at once, Betty Lou was overcome by the unmistakable stench of death emanating from the phantasm. Nearly choking, she spun on her heels and began to run, her hands groping blindly through the fog. The sharp clip-clop of footsteps, like cloven hooves, followed behind and was getting closer. Betty Lou screamed at the top of her lungs.

An instant later, she burst from the mist. Its vagrant fingers clung briefly to her sweater before dissolving in the clear night. The footsteps stopped. Turning around to get her bearings, Betty Lou realized she was back where she had started, on the wrong side of the hollow. On the hill opposite, the lights still glowed warmly in the windows of her house, and the streetlight still watched the world around it with complete indifference.

Between herself and safety was the hollow, filled with fog that smoldered like a witch's brew in a boiling cauldron, reeking of decay and evil.

All at once she heard distant footsteps of a very different kind and looked up to see people running toward her from the house. Her parents. Her father was carrying a flashlight, which swung in wild arcs of alarm as he ran. Clearly they had heard her scream. "Betty Lou!" her father called. "Betty Lou!"

"I'm here, Daddy!" she cried from the dark side of the hollow.

They stopped at the edge of the fog and her father trapped her in the beam of his flashlight. He was startled by the fear in her voice; she hadn't called him "Daddy" since she was three years old. "Was it you who screamed?" he asked.

Betty Lou was embarrassed. But still overcome by fear, she started to cry pitifully. In response, her folks plunged into the fog. "Don't, Daddy! Don't go down there!"

It was too late. They were soon out of sight, and all she could see were dull, intermittent smudges of light marking their progress through the thick, low-lying cloud.

A moment later, as she watched breathlessly, her father emerged from the fog and shined the light in her eyes. "What is it, girl? You look like you've seen a ghost."

"Where's Mom?" she asked, searching the fog in wide-eyed terror. No sooner were the words out of her mouth than her mother appeared like an apparition from the mists. Betty Lou fell into her father's arms, pressed her head against his chest, and, between sobs, told them what she had seen.

Betty Lou's parents exchanged worried glances over her head.

"After all these years?" said Mrs. Arey, her words lightly accented with the lilt of her native Scandinavian tongue. "Is it possible he's back?"

Betty Lou lifted her head from her father's chest and looked at her mother. "Back? Who's back?"

The parents, clearly shaken by some unspoken dread, looked silently at each other for a moment, until Betty Lou impatiently repeated the question.

"The Black Moriah," said Mr. Swanson at last.

The little family stood at the edge of the hollow, staring into the cauldron of fog.

That was the night Betty Lou got an imagination.

The next day, for the first time in a long time, the exploits of Bean and Ab were not the chief topic of conversation in town. That was just as well, as far as they were concerned. Instead, the name Black Moriah was on everyone's mind. Whereas younger people spoke of it with the kind of morbid curiosity born of ignorance, older people whispered it with genuine dread. But the oldest people wouldn't speak the name at all; they merely looked at one another with fear-filled eyes.

Hutch Swenson, who had business at the other end of the island, had asked Bean's Uncle Phil to meet the morning ferry. Captain Kittredge was coming to the island to repair his submarine and take it back to the mainland. He'd be staying at the Tidewater, Uncle Phil's motel, and because the captain was getting on in years, Hutch thought he could do with a lift. Uncle Phil was happy to comply. Bean and Ab had come along for the ride.

"So, what's the Black Moriah?" asked Bean as they waited at the ferry landing for the whistle announcing the boat's arrival.

"Old island legend," Phil replied, running his hand through his thick salt-and-pepper hair. "Pretty much died out since I was a kid, but we used to hear it all the time, years ago. 'Course, it's kinda hard to tell where fact leaves off and fancy takes over with old stories like that."

"Tell us what you remember," Ab urged.

Uncle Phil leaned his head against the back of the seat and stared up at the bare metal roof of his old yellow truck. "It started back in the late twenties or early thirties," he began. "Fella named Pitch Huggins lived in a little shack up by the fork in Double-Dead Road—same place Billy Pringle lives now, only a different house. The original place burned down.

"Anyway, seems Pitch was a strange old bird; told people he was a demon. From what I gather, his personality didn't make it too hard to believe. He took to killin' people's pets that wandered up that way and hangin' the corpses from the pole he had in his front yard."

"That's sick!" said Ab, shocked. "Didn't anyone do anything?"

"Oh, they tried a couple of times, but he'd come bargin' out've that shack of his wavin' a pitchfork or an ax and screamin' like a banshee that he was gonna steal people's children and sell 'em to the devil, things like that. Folks realized they were dealin' with someone who didn't have both oars in the water. No tellin' what he might do. So they took to keepin' their pets indoors at night and lettin' ol' Pitch be."

"But?" said Bean, knowing there was more to the story. Just then the boat whistle blew.

"Boat's comin'," said Uncle Phil, casting a weary eye toward the mouth of the harbor where the ferry was just throttling back after its hour-long run across the bay.

"It'll be five minutes before they dock and unload," said Bean. "Tell us the rest of the story."

Phil leaned his head back again and collected his thoughts. "Well, one day one've the island girls named Cassy Flagg went missin'. Last anyone saw of her, she was headed up Double-Dead Road toward Pogus Point."

"Where Pitch lived," said Ab.

Uncle Phil nodded. "I guess the island folks put two and two together and figured Pitch had made good on his promise, or next best thing. The whole town was fevered up over it. A lot of angry talk got started, and when Cassy still didn't turn up next day, some folks took it in their heads to get up a kind of posse and go drag ol' Pitch out by the collar and have him up on charges.

"'Course, there wasn't any proof of anything. Just suspicion. Anyway, they tried to put the plan into motion, but Pitch put up more of a fight than they expected. In the process, somebody knocked over an old oil lamp and caught the place on fire. 'Course, the fellas in the posse ran outside and waited for Pitch to do the same, but he never came. They got as close as they dared and hollered and called, but that was all she wrote."

Bean was incredulous. How could he have lived on the island all his life and never have heard this story? "You mean, he burned to death in the fire?"

Uncle Phil shrugged. "That's what people figured. The men ran to get help, of course, but by the time they got back with the fire brigade, the place was pretty much leveled. There was no sign of Pitch."

86

"Did they ever find Cassy?" Ab wanted to know.

"Yup," said Uncle Phil stoically. "Her folks got a letter from her about a week or two later, from down in Philadelphia."

"Philadelphia?" said Ab.

Phil nodded. "Seems she'd run away with this guy who'd come to the island sellin' encyclopedias or something."

"So, Pitch was innocent," Bean conjectured.

Phil didn't say anything.

"That's a sad story," said Ab. "But what's it got to do with the Black Moriah?"

There was a long, loud squeak as the ferry nudged into its slip.

"Not long after that, people started seein' something up at that end of the island. They all described pretty much the same thing—a man draped in black, smellin' of smoke an' death, who'd follow folks who ventured up that way late at night, mostly women. 'Course, soon as someone suggested it was the ghost of Pitch Huggins come back to get his revenge on the town that had killed him, the notion caught on like wildfire. That's when they started callin' him the Black Moriah. I'm not sure where the name came from, or what it means."

The low whine of the winch motor indicated that the ramp was being lowered onto the deck. Soon the cars would be driving off the ferry and the foot passengers would follow behind them. Phil finished his story: "After that, anytime something bad happened, the Black Moriah got the blame. Mind you, there were a couple of pretty grisly things that couldn't be explained any other way."

"Things like what?" the kids said in chorus.

There was curious concern in the slow look Uncle Phil gave them. "The kinds of things you don't go repeatin' to kids," he said enigmatically. "You guys climb in back so Captain Kittredge can have the front seat."

Bean and Ab scrambled out of the cab and up over the sides of the truck bed, where they sat on the wheel wells and stared questioningly at each other.

"This is spooky," Ab said at last.

Bean said nothing. An island legend safely confined to the past and to old people's faded memories was fun and exciting, but an evil phantom wandering the back roads of Penobscot Island in the present was something else.

"What does Captain Kittredge look like?" Bean asked through the sliding back window as he watched passengers come off the boat.

"I'm not sure," said Uncle Phil. "All he said was he'd be carryin' an orange toolbox."

As the last of the passengers strode up the ramp, the only one answering the description was a tall, thin, elderly man who stood at the edge of the parking lot and seemed to be looking for someone. "Is that him?" Bean asked, incredulous.

"Must be," said Phil, looking at the bright orange toolbox the man carried effortlessly.

"He's old," Ab observed.

Uncle Phil opened his door. "I'm goin' to go give him a hand."

"Need some help?" Bean asked. He hopped over the side in an easy motion and fell in behind his uncle.

"Captain Kittredge?" said Uncle Phil as they approached.

The man put down his duffel bag and greeted Phil with a handshake. "Yes," Captain Kittredge replied. His searching eyes made a quick survey of Uncle Phil. "You're the harbormaster?" he asked.

Uncle Phil smiled and laughed in his easy way as he picked up the duffel. "Nope. Call me Phil. Hutch had some other business and asked me to pick you up. I own the motel where you'll be stayin'."

Captain Kittredge nodded. "I see." He looked at Bean. "And who's your helper?"

"Oh, he's no help," said Phil wryly. "He's my nephew Arthur. You can call him Bean."

"Pleased to meet you, Bean," said Kittredge, shaking his hand firmly. His white hair was cut short and flat on top in military fashion, and his smile was sincere, but Bean was mildly shocked by the penetrating intensity of the captain's bright blue eyes.

"You built that submarine?" Bean asked, making no attempt to conceal his awe.

"That I did," said the captain. Then suddenly his eyes brightened. "Ah! You wouldn't be the young man who took it for a test-drive!"

Bean felt the blood rise in his cheeks.

"He's the one," said Uncle Phil. "Take this, Bean," he said, thrusting the toolbox into Bean's hand.

The box was unexpectedly heavy and nearly pulled Bean's arm out of its socket. "Can you handle that all right?" the captain asked.

"Sure," said Bean, holding the metal handle with both hands and counterbalancing the weight by leaning as far as possible in the opposite direction. "No problem." He followed the men to the truck, where he and Ab wrestled the toolbox over the side and into the bed.

As they drove to town, the kids leaned through the sliding window and Bean introduced Ab.

"So, you're the girlfriend of this young pirate," said the captain with an unseen wink at Uncle Phil.

"Girlfriend!" said Ab, blushing. "Oh, no. We're just—"

"*Pirate*?" said Bean.

"Well, what else do you call someone who steals a boat?" said the captain over his shoulder.

"Bean didn't steal it," Ab defended. "He saved it."

Kittredge raised his eyebrows. "Did he indeed?"

The kids hurriedly explained about finding the sub washed up on the beach, and their opinion that, had Bean not been in it when it went through the Race, it probably would have drifted out to sea and sunk without anyone being the wiser.

"Well," said the captain as Uncle Phil turned into the motel parking lot, "you've made a good point. Which leaves us with a question: What happened to Steerforth?"

"Who's Steerforth?" asked Bean.

"The man who rented the sub last week. Said he was a marine biologist who was going to study the migratory patterns of lobsters on the ocean floor. I gave him lessons for the better part of a day," the captain continued as he got out of the cab and lifted the toolbox effortlessly from the truck bed, "then he put out into the bay. Said he'd have her back in three days. That's the last I saw of it."

"Steerforth," said Bean. "Was he about medium height? Kinda slim, with light brown hair?"

"Why, how could you know that, young man?"

Ab was about to blab the whole story when Bean grabbed her around the neck and slapped his salty hand over her mouth. "Shh," he said sharply. "You're gonna get me in trouble."

He felt Ab relax and let her go. "Sorry," she said. "I forgot nobody was supposed to know."

"Well, this is beginning to sound interesting," said the captain as Uncle Phil returned from the lobby with the captain's room key. "Why don't you come into my room and tell me all about it."

Bean and Ab exchanged unsure glances.

"It is my submarine, after all," said the captain. "Don't you think I have a right to know?"

"Know what?" said Uncle Phil.

Bean flushed suddenly. "Oh, nothing. The captain just wants to know what's happened since we found the submarine."

"Hmm. Well, I've got some errands to run," said Uncle Phil, excusing himself. "Captain, if you need anything, just pick up the phone in the lobby. It rings up at the house, and my wife will answer. See you guys later," he said, mussing Ab's hair. "Think you can stay out of trouble for ten or fifteen minutes?"

Why did people always say that? Ab wondered. It's not as if they were in trouble *all* the time.

Captain Kittredge's room had a deck overlooking the harbor, where they could sit in the warm sunshine. After swearing the captain to secrecy, the kids told him about Bean's misadventure at the Widowmaker.

When they finished, the captain stared at them for some time, making them squirm in their seats. "You shouldn't have sworn me to secrecy," he said at last. "Your parents should know what happened."

Both the kids knew that was true, but at the same time they had the unspoken fear that if their parents thought they'd gotten themselves in another dangerous situation, they'd separate them, as they had after they discovered the secret of the missing grave. Neither of them could stand that.

"Well," said Captain Kittredge, slapping his knees as he stood, "at least the constable knows. See that you leave it to him. Now, where's my sub?"

"Right over there," said Bean, pointing to the barge tied to the public landing, just off the town parking lot.

"So it is," said the captain, squinting. "Well, I'd best get at it."

"Are you gonna drive it back to the mainland, or ferry it?" asked Bean.

"Depends on the damage," said the captain. They reentered the motel room, where he picked up his toolbox without so much as a groan and ushered them out the front door. "It'll save me a few dollars in transport fees if she can make the trip on her own. We'll see." He sensed a hesitation on Bean's part. "What is it, young man?"

"I was wonderin' if . . . I'd like to go for a ride in it, if you get it fixed. I mean, go down and look around."

"You've been down once already, as I understand it," said the captain dryly.

"Yeah, but that wasn't on purpose. I mean, I'd love to go down and look around and see what it's like on the bottom."

The captain smiled. "Well, let me have a look at the damage. If I can fix it, and you can get your parents to give you the okay, we'll see. Least I can do since you 'saved' her." He winked at Ab. "I don't suppose you'd like to go as well?"

"No, thanks," said Ab adamantly. "I've had enough of submarines to last a lifetime."

The kids said their good-byes with promises to stop by the barge later to check on the captain's progress.

The captain watched them cross the street. "Something tells me the trouble's just begun for those two."

12
THINGS LONG DEAD

"OH, NO, MY DEAR, YOU'RE MISTAKEN," said Professor Prinderby, for whom details were very important. He and his wife were sitting with Bean and Ab on the porch of the Moses Webster House. "Twing didn't drown in the wreck. He survived—the only one of his crew who did, in fact. He was picked up by a merchantman just off Halifax the next morning."

"Did they arrest him?" Bean wanted to know.

"No. There was nothing to arrest him for," said the professor. "In fact, at that point, there wasn't even any suspicion. He was embraced by one and all as an honest merchant who had suffered a shipwreck. He returned to his wife and children on Prince Edward Island, where he discovered that his father had died, leaving the estate to him, his only son. Abnezar sold the estate, which made him a rich man even without his pirate treasure, and he moved his family to Halifax, where he became a respected member of the community."

"Didn't his wife know what he'd been up to all that time?" Ab asked, incredulous.

The professor smiled. "I expect she simply assumed, like everyone else, that he was a merchant. Those were different times, my dear. It wasn't at all unusual for a woman to have no clear concept of her husband's profession."

"Weird," said Abby.

"Simply different," said the professor philosophically. "At any rate, it was in Halifax that Twing made his greatest mistake. One day, while attending a meeting of the town fathers, he was recognized by the captain of a ship that had recently put into port. Seems this fellow had been a seaman on one of the ships Twing and Morrison had commandeered in the Indian Ocean. Like everyone else aboard, he'd been made to 'walk the plank,' as they say. Only he had survived, and he remembered Twing, identifying him by a deep scar across the brow, which Twing had gotten as a boy.

"Of course, nobody believed it at first. But the captain, motivated by his hatred for Twing, soon proved that the wreck Twing had been rescued from was the *Privilege,* known to the British navy as a pirate ship.

"One thing led to another, and the story of his misdeeds was made known. Before the month was out, the populace turned on Twing and he tried to run away."

Ab interrupted. "What about his wife and children?"

"I'm afraid," said the professor, "they were not his foremost concerns at the time. But be that as it may, Twing was captured, tried, and sentenced to hang by the neck until dead."

The professor lit his pipe, and soon a sweet, stuffy cloud of blue smoke lay suspended in the air. "The captain of the *Dauntless* had heard that Twing was in jail, and he sailed to Nova Scotia to interrogate him as to the whereabouts of his suspected treasure, but Twing just laughed. They say he taunted his interrogators, swearing that the treasure he had amassed would beggar King Solomon and was in the keeping of the dead. Nothing the captain could say or do would induce him to give up the secret. Twing said it would die with him."

"What a dreadful, dreadful man," said Mrs. Prinderby, who had been crocheting furiously as her husband related the tale.

"I agree, my dear," her husband nodded. "A most unpleasant individual. For all intents and purposes, he seemed to have made good on his promise to take his secret to the grave. He was eventually hanged, and that, as far as anyone was concerned at the time, was that.

"What most people didn't know, however, was that on one of his wife's visits to his cell in the days before his execution, he had slipped her a piece of paper that contained a clue to the whereabouts of the treasure. Aware that the paper could fall into the hands of the authorities, he had coded the message as a poem."

"Which is what you found in the historical society in Halifax," said Ab.

The Prinderbys both nodded. "Just so."

That evening, Bean and Ab sat in the bandstand talking until past ten o'clock. Mostly, they had questions. Who was Steerforth, the man who had rented Captain Kittredge's submarine, and why had he abandoned it? According to the description Captain Kittredge had given, it had to be the same man Bean had rescued from the Widowmaker. Why had he tried to drown Bean? Last but not least, was there a pirate treasure buried somewhere on Pogus Point?

They found no satisfactory answers to their questions, and started walking slowly home. As they passed Double-Dead Road, Bean looked down it. A thin veil of mist, eerily illuminated by a distant street lamp, hung in a little hollow at the bottom of Ballground Hill. "You think there really is something up there?" he asked, almost to himself.

Ab followed his eyes. "The Black Moriah," she said theatrically, widening her eyes and holding her arms out in front of her like a zombie. She made a long, low moan. The whole little pantomime had been meant to dispel the shadow of genuine fear that threatened to grip them, but it didn't work. Instead, the mention of the specter's name seemed to make it all the more real. And dangerous.

Early the next morning, Ab showed up at Bean's house. She was eager to continue their investigation, but he had to mow the lawn first. She sat on the fence and watched as he pushed the ancient old Lawn Boy back and forth through the tall grass. It would have been easier if he'd waited until the sun dried out the heavy dew the night had left behind, but Bean was anxious to move onto more interesting things. By the time he finished, he'd worked up a good sweat, and his sneakers, which had been more or less white, were stained bright green by the grass.

Abby helped him put the mower back in the shed. They were just closing the door when Spooky came running down the driveway. "Did you hear what happened last night?" he hollered without even saying hello. He had been down at the fish factory since six o'clock that morning, so he had the early edition of local gossip. "They saw it again!"

"Who saw what?" Ab demanded.

"Calm down, Spook," said Bean, who knew it was hard to get any clear information from Spooky when he was wound up. "Take a deep breath."

Spooky inhaled deeply. "They saw the Black Moriah again," he said on the exhale.

"Who did?" Bean demanded sharply. "Where?"

"Two people," Spooky replied after gulping down another lung full of air. "Megan Littlefield saw it up by her house about ten o'clock."

The Littlefields lived in a gray-shingled house just before the cemetery on Double-Dead Road, not a hundred yards from where Betty Lou had seen the apparition. "Who else?"

"Pommy Webster," said Spooky. "He was walkin' down the field to his rowboat on Indian Creek this mornin', and he seen it over by the slag heaps just past the bridge."

"What happened?" Ab asked anxiously.

As Spooky talked, the trio walked across the street to the galamander, the massive wooden wagon with nine-foot rear wheels that had been used to carry granite and now was a monument to the bygone days of stone quarrying. They climbed to the driver's seat and made themselves comfortable.

"Megan went to the back door to call the cat," said Spooky. "It usually comes right in, but not last night. So she went out into the backyard in her robe an' slippers, callin' up the trees an' under the shed an' around the woodpile, you know.

"There's this old apple tree in the backyard that she ties one end of her clothesline to. That's where she was, she said, when she got this feelin' all of a sudden like somebody was watchin' her. She looks up an', sure enough, there he was, not thirty feet away."

"What did she do?" Ab asked worriedly.

"Run like heck!" said Spooky, who thought it was a pretty good plan. "She'd heard all 'bout Betty Lou an' everything, so when she saw it just standin' there, well, she didn't let the grass grow under 'er feet."

Bean was skeptical. "It was prob'ly just shadows or something. Prob'ly she was half expectin' to see something, so she did—all in her head."

"Could be," Spooky allowed, "but I don't think so. Megan Littlefield used to skipper a Grand Banks trawler, an' she's got arms like that." He made a circle with his hands indicating the circumference of Megan's biceps. "So she could clean the floor with most of the guys down at the wharf. Besides," he concluded, "she ain't the type to scare for no reason."

"But it was dark," said Bean, who didn't want to believe there was an entity as evil as the Black Moriah wandering about the island. "There's no streetlight by Littlefields. It coulda been anything."

Spooky shook his head emphatically. "Nope. It was almost a full moon last night. No fog. Besides, the porch light was on. She said that gave her all the light she needed."

"What about Pommy?" Ab asked, her curiosity rising.

"Like I said," said Spooky, absentmindedly turning the galamander's big iron steering wheel as if he were driving the machine, "he was on his way down to his float where he keeps his punt. It was 'bout five o'clock. He was goin' out to haul."

"I'm glad I'm not a lobsterman," said Ab. "Five o'clock's *way* too early for me."

"The ocean's calmer in the morning," said Spooky. "Anyway, he says he was just lookin' out the Reach to see what kinda weather he had comin' up outta the southwest when he saw something move over in the slag heaps. All he could tell from that distance was that it was black. At first he thought it looked like a bear. 'Course there ain't any bears on the island. So he runs back to the house an' gets his binoculars, then hoofs it back out to the field.

"Well, Pommy's prob'ly seventy, so he ain't exactly Rocketman," Spooky continued. "By the time he gets to where he's got a clear view, it was too late. It was gone."

"But *where* did it go?" Bean wanted to know.

Spooky shrugged. "He don't know. He says it was like it just disappeared right into the rocks." He snapped his fingers. "One second it was there, next it was gone."

No one was more interested in the sightings of the Black Moriah than Mrs. Prinderby, who had a soft place in her heart for misplaced spirits. "Something's clearly brought it back after all this time," she said as everyone sat around the dinner table at the Moses Webster House discussing the news of the day. "Some unfinished business."

"I vote for some lunatic in a Halloween costume," said Mr. Proverb. "He'll keep it up as long as he gets attention. If everybody just ignores him, he'll stop all this foolishness."

"There's a logical explanation," said Mrs. Proverb.

"Right you are, my dear," said Mr. Proverb. "There always is. Abigail, it wasn't long ago you thought there were ghosts in the walls of your bedroom, if I remember correctly. Turned out *that* had a logical explanation, didn't it?"

Ab had to confess that it did.

"Well, then, same is true in this case. Mark my words."

Ab cast a silent appeal toward her father. "Sorry, Abby," he said. "I think Mr. Proverb's right. I don't believe the Black Moriah is real; it's just somebody who's taken it in his head to scare people. If there's a mystery about it, it's *why*?"

"Just to get attention," Mr. Proverb insisted.

"I wouldn't be so sure," said Mrs. Prinderby, who had been listening patiently. "As Dickens said, 'There are more things in heaven and earth, Horatio, than are dreamt of in your philosophy.'"

"Shakespeare, my dear," said her husband, who had just returned from taking one of the long, hot baths that he had begun to enjoy of late.

He had been listening with only half an ear. Talk of spectral visitors didn't interest him, except that they kept his wife entertained.

"Shakespeare? Are you sure?"

The professor nodded. "Yes, dear. Shakespeare."

"He seems to have said everything worth saying, hasn't he?" Mrs. Prinderby brushed some salt from the table into her hand and tossed it absentmindedly over her shoulder. "Dust in the Devil's eye," she said automatically. "Anyway, whoever said it, it's true. We are surrounded by the realm of the unseen. Astral dimensions woven in and about and through our own that will not yield to discovery by our five senses.

"It takes someone with a special gift," she continued modestly, "a sixth sense, if you will, to comprehend events in the unseen dimension."

"Why don't we have a seance?" Ab suggested. "Maybe you can find some ghost we can talk to who knows what the Black Moriah's up to and what he's come back for."

"Abigail," said her mother sternly. "Did you hear what your father and Mr. Proverb said?"

Before she could protest further, Mrs. Prinderby spoke up. "I think a seance is a wonderful idea! I shall get my things together immediately and we shall convene this evening. Where shall we have it?" She looked around the dining room. "Not here, the vibrations are too weak; spirits avoid rooms with cinnamon. Ah! I know, the tower room! Perfect!"

With some effort, Mrs. Prinderby extricated herself from her chair, stood up, and embraced everyone with eyes magnified several times by her thick glasses. "I am no stranger to skeptics," she said. "Come one, come all, and let's see what there is to see."

Throughout the conversation, Mr. Lawson had been completely silent, and his mind seemed otherwise occupied. Now he spoke up for the first time. "Well, if it's skeptics you want, I'd be happy to participate," he said. "But unless you can find some location on the ground floor that vibrates to your satisfaction, I'm afraid I'll have to beg off. Two flights of stairs would be a bit much." He slapped his legs and pushed his wheelchair away from the table. "If my Uncle Fortescue shows up when you're rummaging among the dead, ask him where he hid his will, would you? The family's been looking for it for years."

"This is going to be fun," said Ab. "Wait 'til I tell Bean."

13
UNINVITED GUESTS

IN PREPARATION FOR THE SEANCE, Mrs. Prinderby spent half an hour "aligning objects to the spiritual plane," as she explained.

"That's so the spooks don't bump into the furniture," Bean whispered loud enough for everyone waiting in the living room to hear. They all laughed a little uncomfortably.

"I'm not sure what I think of all this," said Mrs. Proverb.

Her husband patted her hand. "Surely you don't think there's anything to it, my love. It's a parlor game, is all. No doubt there'll be thumps on the wall and that type of thing. I'm sure Mrs. Prinderby's arrangements will see to that, but it's all just a bit of fun."

Mrs. Proverb didn't seem so sure. She fidgeted nervously in her chair. "My sister and I had a seance once, when we were kids. About your age." She nodded at Bean and Ab. "We thought it was all a bit of fun, too." She hesitated. "But it didn't turn out at all as we'd planned."

"What happened, Mrs. P?" Ab asked.

"Well . . . Miranda, that's my sister, had been reading a book about ghosts and demons—she'd gotten it at the library—and had found this incantation—"

"Incantation?" said Spooky. "What's that?"

"It's like a phone call," Bean explained. "You dial a certain number and it rings on the other end of the line."

"Good analogy, Bean," said Ab's dad.

"The incantation is a formula, like the phone number," said Ab, taking up Bean's train of thought. "You say certain words, and it rings somewhere out there and wakes up the spirit that the incantation calls for."

"Cool," said Spooky. "So, what was the incantation, Mrs. P? Do you remember?"

"Oh, I remember, all right," said Mrs. Proverb with a visible shudder. "I'll never forget it. Nor will I ever repeat it."

"What happened?"

"Miranda and I were sitting at this little round table, holding hands,"

Mrs. Proverb began, collecting her memories, "when she recited the incantation. Almost immediately, a nauseating smell filled the room. Then the lights in the house flickered once or twice, then went out altogether, leaving us in the dark except for a little candle.

"We screamed, as you might imagine," she continued, speaking the words almost against her will, as if she'd rather let the memory lie. "Miranda jumped up from the table and ran toward the door. But just as she got to it, it slammed shut, and she couldn't open it. I went to help her, but it wouldn't budge.

"Suddenly, there was a series of soft thumps on the table. We were frightened, of course, but we were also curious. So we went back and sat down and tapped on the table."

The kids were doubtful. "I'd've jumped out the window," said Spooky.

"You were very brave," Ab told Mrs. Proverb. She wasn't sure what she would have done in the same situation.

"I thought so at the time," said Mrs. Proverb cryptically. "Not anymore. I think we were foolish. Like children playing with matches."

Bean was impatient. "What happened then? Did it tap back?"

"No. We waited, but there wasn't a sound. Finally, we heard the click of the door latch, and it swung open very slowly, squeaking the whole way. Then the lights came on."

Spooky was disappointed. "That's all?" he said.

"Not quite," Mrs. Proverb replied. "There was a full-length mirror in the hall outside the door. As the door swung open, we saw that it had been fogged over, like the mirror in a bathroom after you've taken a hot shower. Someone had written in the condensation. We could read it even from where we stood."

"What did it say?" Ab demanded.

"It was the name of the demon we'd summoned in the incantation."

Ab's mom gasped involuntarily. Mr. Peterson put his arm comfortingly around her shoulder.

"That's not the worst of it," Mrs. Proverb continued. "Miranda was much bolder than I. She went directly to the mirror and wiped it clean with the sleeve of her sweater. Then she looked into the mirror, screamed, and fainted. I'd never seen Miranda faint. She wasn't the type."

Spooky asked the obvious question. "What did she see?"

"I ran to get Mother. By the time we got back to the hallway, Miranda had come around and was propped up on her elbow, pointing at the mirror, staring at it.

"I looked, but I didn't see anything and told her so. So did Mother. Miranda got up slowly and looked for herself. Nothing. We asked her what she'd seen, but she wouldn't say.

"To this day," Mrs. Proverb concluded, "she won't speak of what happened that night. And she's a grandmother herself now. Needless to say, she'll have nothing to do with seances."

"All easily explained," said Mr. Proverb, whose own heart was racing a little more than he would admit. "My guess is Miranda arranged the whole affair."

"Oh, I don't think that's likely," his wife objected. "If you'd seen her face—"

Mr. Proverb held up a silencing hand. "Now, hear me out. The one thing every medium needs is an accomplice, someone to carry on in the background to do the thumping and the door slamming. I'd say Miranda had such an accomplice—probably your brother, Matthew. He'd have loved playing the ghost."

"That may be," said Mrs. Proverb, "but—"

"Let me finish," said Mr. Proverb mildly. "Taking the events in order . . ." He held up his fingers and began ticking them off one at a time. "The foul smell? That could have been anything—rotten eggs, for instance. The lights flickering off? Easy as flipping a breaker switch. The door was no doubt shut by the accomplice; probably there was a string involved in the process. He could have locked it from the outside, which explains why you couldn't open it." Mr. Proverb pushed down another finger. "Then the tapping. Probably nothing more complicated than someone under the table who managed to scamper back into the shadows before you returned. You said yourself there was no more tapping once you took your seats again."

"Then there would have to have been at least two accomplices," Ab observed doubtfully. "One holding the door, and the other under the table."

Mr. Proverb was willing to accept this. "Two accomplices then—"

"Three," Bean corrected. "If the breakers were in the basement."

Mrs. Proverb tried to recollect. "We had a cellar. They must have been there."

"Be that as it may," said Mr. Proverb with just a hint of impatience. "We may assume that while the door was closed, the accomplice in the hall brought in a teakettle or some such thing and steamed the mirror. Then he tucked it somewhere out of sight and unlocked the door. While it swung slowly open, he scampered off to hide, and the illusion was complete."

"Not quite complete," said Ab. "What about what Miranda saw in the mirror?"

"That's what proves my point most of all," said Mr. Proverb. "She was the only one to see anything, right? Yet she wouldn't tell you what it was. How likely is that?"

"But she fainted!" Mrs. Proverb objected.

"*Pretended* to faint," he countered.

Mrs. Proverb didn't seem to know what to think. "Well, it certainly seemed real at the time."

"Of course it did. That's what makes seances so convincing to the gullible."

"Still," said Mrs. Proverb with weakening conviction, "I can't believe she'd carry on the charade all these years. Certainly she'd simply tell me if she'd tricked me, and we'd have a good laugh."

"Ready!" came Mrs. Prinderby's singsongy voice from the top of the stairs, and everyone began to rise.

"Notice anyone missing from our little group?" said Mr. Proverb knowingly.

Everyone looked around and, almost as one, realized that one central character was absent: Professor Prinderby.

The little tower wasn't big enough to hold any accomplices. There was no table. No chairs. No incense or candles. In fact, the room was almost blindly bright, thanks to the naked lightbulb that hung from the ceiling in an elaborate little glass globe. Mrs. Prinderby had removed everything from the room, including the curtains, which now hung over the banister. The only concession to comfort was the old Persian rug that covered the floor from wall to wall.

This clearly wasn't what Mr. Proverb expected. "My word, Mrs. Prinderby, you don't seem to have read the psychics' handbook. Isn't it supposed to be dark and . . . ethereal?"

"The professor says it's the imagination that creates spirits in the dark. Eliminate the darkness, he says, and you eliminate tricks of the mind."

"It also makes it pretty hard to hide under the table," said Bean.

"Especially when there isn't one," Spooky observed. Once again his expectations were dashed. The tower looked more like an operating room than a likely place for a seance.

"Exactly," said Mrs. Prinderby. "If our little experiment is to be valid, I think it's important everyone be aware that I have nothing to hide."

Ab's dad was curious. "How many spirits have you spoken to with these seances, Mrs. Prinderby?"

Mrs. Prinderby creased her brow in thought. "You mean, *exactly* how many?"

"Roughly will do."

"Hmm." Mrs. Prinderby drummed her fingers on her chin. "None that I can recall."

"None?" said Mr. Proverb, as startled by her honesty as by the fact she professed to be a medium who had never communicated with a spirit.

"But I feel sure tonight's the night!" Mrs. Prinderby said with unbridled optimism. "The vibrations are very positive. Now, if we could all just form a little circle, boy girl boy girl, and join hands."

There was just room enough for the eight of them to carry out the instruction. When they had aligned themselves, Bean stood holding hands with Mrs. Prinderby on one side and Ab on the other.

"Now, I understand there are skeptics among us, but it is important that we all be at least receptive to the possibility of communicating with inhabitants of another spiritual dimension. Everyone try to clear your mind of intrusive thoughts. Think, 'I welcome the opportunity to learn from those who have gone before.'"

Spooky and Bean, who looked at each other from opposite sides of the circle, tried to keep from laughing, though Spooky widened his eyes and spun them wildly around in their sockets. "Good," said Mrs. Prinderby. "Now, if there are any restless spirits about who would like to communicate with the living, they will find us ready." So saying, she fell silent.

The rest of the people in the circle, waiting for Mrs. Prinderby to do something mysterious, began to be uncomfortable with the prolonged silence and flashed glances at one another, especially at Mrs. Prinderby. Her eyes were closed and she was smiling contentedly, humming almost inaudibly, and, to all appearances, having a wonderful time.

"I think we oughtta turn off the light," Spooky suggested after five minutes. "I don't think ghosts like lights."

"Guests," said Mrs. Prinderby patiently.

Once again, everyone fell silent. Soon, despite the ordinariness of their surroundings, an odd, tangible energy began to fill the room. "Ah, feel it!" said Mrs. Prinderby excitedly.

"I do feel something," said Mrs. Proverb, squeezing her husband's hand a little tighter.

Bean felt it, too, though he wasn't about to be the first male to admit it. It was as if someone else had entered the room, someone who took up space but couldn't be seen.

Mrs. Prinderby was tingling in every pore. "Oh, the vibrations are so intense! Anabel Twing, is that you, my dear, after all this time? Tap once for yes, twice for no."

All held their breath in anticipation, but for a moment nothing happened. Then, without warning, a distinct thump on the wall made everyone jump. All hands gripped a little tighter. Just as Mrs. Prinderby drew her breath to speak, the thud was repeated.

"You're not Anabel Twing?" said Mrs. Prinderby, alarmed.

The reply was two more thumps. Bean thought they sounded like a heavy book being dropped in another room, only the sound was definitely coming from the walls.

"Looks like we got a wrong number," said Spooky.

Mrs. Prinderby clearly hadn't been prepared for this eventuality. "Well, who are you?" she asked somewhat indignantly.

"Don't you have to ask 'yes' or 'no' questions?" Ab ventured timidly.

"Were you born on the island?" Bean asked the specter.

A slight delay, then a single thump.

"This isn't what we wanted at all," said Mrs. Prinderby. Her whole body seemed to deflate with disappointment. Bean could feel she wanted to let go of his hand, but he held it tightly.

"Are you Pitch Huggins?" said Ab, as if reading Bean's thoughts.

The responding thump this time was loud and emphatic.

"Who the heck is Pitch Huggins?" demanded Spooky. "I never heard've 'im."

Bean and Ab took turns telling the story. When they were done, everyone was holding hands a little tighter. Even Mrs. Prinderby seemed to have regained interest.

"Pitch Huggins is the Black Moriah?" Spooky deduced tentatively.

"Let's ask," said Ab. "Mr. Huggins, are you the Black Moriah?"

This time it was not a thump that responded, but a voice—a sinister voice dripping with evil. "Not *you,* girl," it said, choking out the words. "Not you."

The words, punctuated by a long hissing sound, were unexpected and frightening and were followed almost immediately by a whiff of the most nauseating stench imaginable. Everyone instinctively withdrew their hands and covered their mouths and noses.

"Not you, girl," the spirit repeated as the single lightbulb flickered on and off. "Or you, boy." There was no need to ask which boy the voice was talking about. It may have been his imagination, but Bean could feel a cold, foul breath on the back of his neck. "Evil is walking behind you. Come my way again and you'll wrestle with the dead, and I'll have your souls and your bones."

The ominous declaration was followed by another thud on the wall, as if someone had slammed it with the flat of the hand. Then all fell silent. It was several seconds before everyone dared to release a breath. Though the acrid smell still lingered in the air, it was much weaker than it had been initially. Mr. Proverb flew to the window and threw it open.

"What *was* that?" Mrs. Proverb asked shakily.

Ab's dad and Mr. Proverb ran out onto the landing and into the adjoining attic, where they found nothing but dusty boxes and bags, the contents of which probably had been long forgotten. Momentarily, they returned.

In response to the question in his wife's eyes, Mr. Peterson shook his head. "Nothing that we could see." He began inspecting the walls for signs of wires or other devices that could have been used to produce the sounds, smells, and voices.

Mrs. Prinderby was very agitated. "I'm so terribly sorry," she said. "Nothing like this has ever happened before. This is a very bad spirit." She began rummaging through her canvas bag and eventually produced a dog-eared old book.

"Where is your husband tonight, Mrs. Prinderby?" asked Mr. Proverb, studying the flustered medium closely.

"My husband?" said Mrs. Prinderby, oblivious to the suspicion in Mr. Proverb's voice and eyes as she flipped frantically through the book, running her finger up and down the pages as she read. "I'm not sure. He said he was going out."

Mr. Proverb looked at the others in the room. "Sound familiar?" he said. "Remember what I said about an accomplice?"

"Ah, here it is!" said Mrs. Prinderby, emerging triumphantly from her perusal. "The Rite of Sealing."

"What's that?" asked Spooky.

"It's a formula—an incantation, if you will—that imprisons spirits such as this until Judgment Day," Mrs. Prinderby explained. "So they can't do any mischief."

Spooky had an opinion on that. "Too late, if you ask me," he said.

"What do we have to do?" asked Ab a little anxiously. The specter's last words were still ringing in her ears.

"Read the words, I suppose," said Mrs. Prinderby. She read it out loud:

Penes Deum excelsum
Qui creavit caelum et terram
Te impero, spirite inquues
Habitare saecula in taciturnitate
Et exspectare Arbitrium Suum.
Te igitur signo in nomine
Patris, et Filii, et Spiriti Sancti.

Everyone listened until she was through, then waited to see if there would be any reaction. Nothing happened.

"What did that mean?" Bean asked.

"I'm afraid my Latin is very rusty. Can anyone translate?" Without waiting for a response, she said, "I wish the professor were here. He knows Latin well."

"I wish he were here, too," said Mr. Proverb, arching his eyebrow skeptically. "I'd like a word or two with him in plain English."

"Do you think it worked?" said Spooky. "Do you think he's . . . gone?"

Mrs. Prinderby looked up from her book. "Well, assuming the spirit knows Latin better than I do, I don't see why he shouldn't be."

"You know Latin," said Mrs. Peterson to her husband.

"Legal Latin," her husband clarified. "It's been a long time since I was in law school, but from what I gather, it's a sort of prayer that's meant to confine the spirit to a kind of purgatory or something."

"Like prison?" said Spooky.

"Sort of," said Mr. Peterson.

Mrs. Prinderby blew a long sigh of relief. "Well, I'm afraid our little interview wasn't very helpful," she said apologetically.

The small audience filed out of the room and down the stairs. "I don't like this, Michael," said Mrs. Peterson to her husband. "What did that mean about coming my way again and wrestling with the dead?"

Ab overheard her parents speaking, but she didn't intrude on their conversation.

"Much as I hate to say it," Mr. Peterson whispered as the little procession crossed the hallway on the second floor, Mrs. Prinderby at its head, "I have to agree with Larry. There had to be an accomplice involved."

"The professor?" Mrs. Peterson ventured.

"Who else?"

Ab wasn't so sure. She pulled Bean aside on the landing, and Spooky tagged along, naturally. "We'll be down in a minute," Ab told the others. She watched as the rest of the party disappeared into the living room at the bottom of the stairs.

"Well, what do you guys think about that?" Ab asked when they were alone.

"Spooky," said Spooky. "That wasn't like any seance I've ever seen on TV, but it sure made my skin crawl."

"Do you think Pitch is the Black Moriah and he's come back from the dead?" Bean asked.

Ab shook her head undecidedly. "My dad thinks it was the professor."

"Musta been," said Spooky, who would love to have had an explanation for the strange things he'd just witnessed. "But where was he?"

"Who knows?" said Ab. "Maybe they're con artists. Maybe they've been doing this kind of things for years. They could have all sorts of tricks."

Something about the notion rubbed Bean the wrong way. That kind of behavior didn't fit with the picture he'd developed of the Prinderbys. "Why would they?" he said. "What would they have to gain?"

Ab shrugged. "Who knows? People do things for lots of weird reasons."

Bean shook his head. "They don't seem like that kind of people to me. I mean, Mrs. Prinderby might be a little . . . ," he rotated his finger around his temple, "but I can't see her doing something mean."

Ab had to agree. "The professor either," she said. Bean nodded. "Unless it's all just an act."

"I guess it's possible," Bean conceded. "But I don't think so. The professor's so wrapped up in his research, he hardly knows what planet he's on."

The trio started slowly downstairs, with Spooky sliding down the banister, his fingers squeaking on the polished wood as he gripped tightly to slow his descent.

"So, what do we do now?" Ab asked.

Bean didn't know. Part of him wanted to challenge the dark oracle he'd heard, to go up to Pogus Point and dare the Black Moriah to show himself. A more sensible part of Bean wanted to go home and hide under the covers. Still another part was worried for Ab's safety and thought maybe it would be best if she and her family cut their summer short and headed back to New York. The thought carved a hollow ache in the pit of his stomach. What would he do for the rest of the summer without Ab around? Still, if she was in danger, he had to put his feelings aside.

As they approached the living room door, they heard voices in animated conversation. "That sounds like Constable Wruggles," said Spooky.

"Uh-oh, what's happened now?" said Ab.

The kids followed the voices through the living room and into the front hall, where Mr. Proverb and Mr. Peterson were talking with the constable and Professor Prinderby, who had evidently just arrived, clutching his briefcase as if it were a baby.

"Where have I been?" the professor was saying, apparently in response to a question.

"I found 'im sittin' up in the bandstand readin' and listenin' to his radio," Wruggles answered on the professor's behalf.

"CD," the professor corrected. "Edvard Grieg's *Peer Gynt Suite*."

Wruggles cocked his head and raised his eyebrows as if to say "whatever."

"Why?" the professor asked. "What's up?"

Mr. Peterson and Mr. Proverb looked at each other worriedly as all their neat explanations for the mystery of the seance came tumbling down.

14
"I'VE GOT A PLAN"

BEAN PUSHED INTO THE LITTLE CROWD and addressed Constable Wruggles. "Did you . . . find anything," he asked, "up around the Point?"

"Come out on the porch and we'll talk about it," said Wruggles.

Ab's dad and Mr. Proverb, preoccupied by the dissolution of their theory, went to the kitchen. The professor said something about wanting to sort his notes and tottered off toward his room, still cradling his briefcase. Shortly after, Daltry Lawson emerged from his room in his wheelchair, apparently in response to all the commotion. The kids didn't pay much attention as they went outside with Constable Wruggles.

"I found Link's skiff," the constable said. "It was floatin' around in Arey's Cove on the other side of the Point."

Bean felt an uneasy pang of guilt at the thought of having to face Link with the remains of his fine little boat. "What kind of shape was she in?" he asked hesitantly.

"Oh, she was fine," said Wruggles. "I took 'er back to Link's and hauled 'er up on shore with them other ones he's got there."

Bean would have heaved a sigh of relief, but he read the rest of the conversation in Wruggles's eyes. "But no sign of the guy who took it?"

Wruggles shook his head. "Neither in the boat or on land," he said. "Anybody who didn't know better would prob'ly figure you was just foolin' around, maybe got hit by a rogue wave, and fell overboard," he said. He was voicing his own thoughts but evidently didn't want to say so flat out.

"Well, they'd be wrong," said Bean. "I ain't foolish enough to fall out've a boat, 'specially not in five fathoms of rough water." A thought occurred to him. "Did you find the oars? There must be fingerprints!"

"Sorry," said Wruggles. "They got washed away. The locks were still in place, but no oars." He studied Bean carefully. He knew the boy had a tendency to exaggerate, but he wasn't a liar. "I'll keep pokin' around up that way, see what there is to see. I'll let you know."

Bean was relieved.

"What's been happenin' here?" Wruggles asked after a brief silence. He nodded toward the house.

"Parlor games," Ab said quickly. She felt that Wruggles's credulity had been stretched to the limit, and if they told him about having heard the voice of Pitch Huggins, he'd suspect they'd either gone completely crazy or were playing him for a fool.

"Parlor games?" said Wruggles. "Now, that's sensible." He tucked his thumbs behind his suspenders and peered out over the town, looking peaceful beneath a rising moon. "Moon low tide in about three days," he observed. "I bet the parkin' lot's gonna be flooded."

"How could it be flooded during a low tide?" Ab asked.

Bean explained. "A moon high tide comes with a moon low tide, which don't often happen in summer. It means the moon's in position to pull the tide higher than usual, and when it goes out, it goes out farther than usual. When the tide goes out that far, you see things folks don't often see."

"They call it a clamdiggers' tide, too," said Spooky, whose father dug clams from time to time. "They can go way out on the flats that are usually covered by water. Big ol' clams out there."

Wruggles studied the western sky. "Storm comin' up the coast, too. One of those tropical storms. We'll have to deal with that in a couple of days," he said.

"You can tell that by looking at the sky?" said Ab, impressed.

"Some can," said the constable with a chuckle. "But I watch the weather on the six o'clock news. Should blow through pretty quick. Hope it hits at low tide, is all I can say. If she hits at high tide, she could do some real damage." He walked down the steps. "See you kids later. Behave yourselves," he said over his shoulder. Then, as if struck by another thought, he turned around and came back up the steps partway. "I mean that. You three stay out of trouble. There's something goin' on around here that I don't like the look of. I want you to promise me you won't go up to Pogus Point, or anywhere around there, 'til I've had time to dig around a little more. Got that?"

Bean began to protest, but Constable Wruggles held up his hand. "Promise me," he said firmly. "Three days, is all. Just promise me you won't go up there for the next three days."

"We promise," said Ab. Bean shot her a sharp glance, but he finally relented.

"Okay, three days."

"Spooky?"

"You don't have to worry 'bout me," said Spooky emphatically.

"Good," said Wruggles, patting his substantial belly. "Well, good night."

The kids said good night, then watched as he walked down the steps, got in his SUV, and drove away.

"Well, I guess that means the professor wasn't behind what happened at the seance after all," said Ab. In a way, it would have been much easier if he had been. At least that would have explained things. Now, all they had was another mystery.

Bean had been thinking. Ab tapped him on the head. "What's going on up there?" she asked.

"You should know better than to ask 'im that," said Spooky with a quick laugh.

"I was thinkin'," Bean replied, "I bet the Widowmaker's bone dry durin' a moon low tide."

"You're not thinking of going up there, are you?" said Ab, alarmed. "You can't. You just promised."

"I promised I wouldn't go up there for three days." He looked at his watch. "Three days from now is the moon low tide." He smiled.

"I wouldn't go up that way anymore *anytime*, if I was you," said Spooky. "Not 'til someone's figured all this stuff out."

Bean felt like saying "and that someone should be me," but he didn't.

"I think Spook's right," said Ab. "This is getting way too serious, Bean. Somebody's going to get hurt."

"What's the big deal?" Bean wanted to know. "We go up to the Widowmaker and poke around, is all. See if there's anything there. No harm in that, is there?"

"But what about Pitch Huggins?" Spooky reminded them. "Don't forget what he said at the seance."

"I ain't afraid of Pitch Huggins," said Bean. To Ab it sounded as if he were trying to convince himself.

They turned their eyes in the direction of Double-Dead Road and thought of the raspy, threatening voice they'd heard, and the foul stench that accompanied it. "Or the Black Moriah," said Bean, as if challenging the fear that swelled within him.

That night Bean didn't sleep well. He tossed and turned, drifting in and out of nightmares that woke him in a cold sweat and seemed to lurk in the darkened corners of his room long after his eyes were open.

He and Ab had had lots of adventures over the years, and they'd all been exciting—some even a little dangerous. But this business of the Black Moriah, or Pitch Huggins, or whatever it was, was different. It was evil, and it seemed to hang over Pogus Point like a black cloud. The fear that came with it wasn't the tingly kind of fear kids feel when they tell ghost stories around a campfire; it was real fear.

"Fear is not a bad thing," his father had said once. "It's what makes us cautious and careful. It gives us respect for things like fire, electricity, heights, sharp objects, poison—anything that might hurt us. But when you fear something that your mind has made up, like when you imagine there's a monster under the bed, then you have to face that fear and overcome it. Take a peek under the bed, and the monster will vanish."

Was the Black Moriah like that, just a monster under the bed? What about the voice of Pitch Huggins? Clearly it wasn't Mrs. Prinderby, and it couldn't have been Mr. Prinderby; Wruggles had seen him at the bandstand.

A litany of questions chased themselves in circles through his mind most of the night, and Bean wound his covers into knots before eventually falling into a fitful sleep.

For the next two days, Bean, Ab, and Spooky kept their word to Constable Wruggles. During that time, the boys helped Captain Kittredge work on his submarine, which he called *Jellybean,* and Ab spent a lot of time sailing with her parents.

Of course, now and then the kids would overhear gossip at the post office or in the hardware store when the boys went to fetch things for the captain. Apparently a group of men had staked out Pogus Point near the hollow where Betty Lou had seen the apparition, in hope of laying their hands on whoever was terrifying the womenfolk. After two long, foggy nights with no sign of the Black Moriah, or of anyone pretending to be the Black Moriah, they began to lose interest. On the third night, only two men went on the stakeout. When nothing had happened by midnight, they went home, knowing that the storm would hit by morning.

Earlier that same night, under the glare of the spotlights on the sub's barge, the kids had been sitting on the submarine eating ice cream cones and passing tools to the captain while he put the finishing touches on the repairs. The kids had been discussing the fact that no one had seen the Black Moriah since the night of the seance.

"The seance must've worked," said Spooky, licking a blob of blueberry ice cream from the front of his shirt. "Mrs. Prinderby sent 'im away."

Ab shivered at the memory.

"Mom's freaked," she said. "I bet she's told me fifty times not to go up to Pogus Point. Every time I leave the house, she wants to know where I'm going and when I'll be back. I mean, it's always been like that in New York, but not on the island. Makes me feel like a little kid."

"She's just worried," said Spooky. "I don't blame her, after what Pitch Huggins said."

"Oh, for pity sakes, it wasn't Pitch Huggins," Bean complained. "He's dead and gone."

"But they never found his body," Spooky reminded them.

"Maybe not," said Bean, "but it was, like, seventy or eighty years ago. If he was still skulkin' around in the woods after all this time, he'd be a hundred. Get real."

"Then what was the voice we heard?" said Ab. Deep down she, too, doubted that Mrs. Prinderby had really been in touch with a spirit from "the other side." Ab wanted to know that there was a logical explanation, but what else *could* explain the strange things that had happened during the seance?

"We're missin' something," said Bean. He pitched his napkin into a nearby trash barrel and tossed the remainder of his ice cream cone to a seagull that had been waiting patiently nearby.

Captain Kittredge emerged from the submarine. With a tool in each hand and his stubbly white hair encircled by a blue and white kerchief, he made an impression on Ab. "You look like a pirate, Captain," she said.

Kittredge laughed. "I'd have made a good one, don't you think?" he said, brandishing a wrench as if it were a sword. "Avast, me hearties!" he snarled in his best Bluebeard impersonation.

Ab thought he'd have made a great pirate.

"All fixed?" Bean asked.

The captain sat on the edge of the hatch. "She'll get me to Rockland, all right. I'll make repairs to the body once I get her back in the shop." He looked at the sky. "No stars tonight," he said. "Looks like that storm's not going to miss us, so we'd best tie the old girl down." He patted *Jellybean* affectionately. "Give me a hand?"

They spent the next five to ten minutes helping Captain Kittredge lash the submarine to the deck of the barge with ropes. "There!" said the captain when the last knot was tied. "She shouldn't go anywhere, as long as this storm is anything short of a hurricane. Thank you, gentlemen," he said, shaking the boys' hands. "And lady," he added, bowing courteously to Ab and squeezing her hand lightly. "Now, I'm going to get these old bones to bed. I've got a five-hour ride across the bay once the storm blows through."

The captain noisily gathered his tools and dropped them in his toolbox, which he put in the sub before closing the hatch for the night. Reaching into the barge's deckhouse, he flipped a switch. At once, everything was plunged into relative darkness. Already the wind had begun to pick up, and though it was only 9:30, Main Street was deserted. Even the Harbor Gawker, the Pizza Pit, and Boongie's video store, which were usually open until eleven, were closed. The captain thanked the kids again, bid them good night, and strode across the parking lot to the motel.

The kids watched him go.

"You'd never think that guy was over eighty years old, would ya?" said Bean.

The old man had certainly made an impression on them, and the stories he told as he had worked on his beloved little submarine—about his career as a submarine captain in the navy and, later, as an attaché at various American embassies around the world—made even the fancies of Bean's colorful imagination seem a little dull.

"You really think he did all them things he said?" Spooky wondered.

Bean shrugged. "I'll ask my dad," he said. "Someday." Meantime, it was more fun believing that the captain's incredible stories were true.

Ab was gazing out over the harbor. "Look how low the tide is," she said. "Some of the lobster boats have grounded out."

"Told ya," said Spooky, referring to nothing in particular. "Tomorrow it'll be even lower. You'll almost be able to walk out to Powder Island, 'cept you'd get stuck in the mud."

"And at high tide, all this will be underwater," said Bean, gesturing across the parking lot. "My dad says he remembers a moon high tide that covered Main Street and poured over into the pond, so it looked like the stores were built on water."

For a while the trio entertained their thoughts, until Ab broke the silence. "I'm tired," she said. "Let's go home."

When they reached the fountain at the end of the sidewalk to the Moses Webster House, Spooky continued up the hill to his house, while Bean and Ab lingered by the fountain. "What are you thinking?" said Ab.

"Nothin'," Bean replied.

"Yes, you are. I can tell, because you haven't said anything in almost two minutes. That's a record."

She knew him too well. There was a thought in the back of his mind that had been trying to bubble to the surface, but until Ab had spoken, he hadn't been able to get a handle on it. Suddenly it dawned on him. "It's something Spook said."

"About what?"

"He said nobody's goin' up to Pogus Point anymore."

"Because of the Black Moriah," said Ab. "Who can blame them?"

That was it. Nobody was going up to Pogus Point anymore.

"What if that was the whole point?" he said, becoming animated by his thoughts. "What would you do if you was lookin' for something up there—a pirate treasure, or whatever—an' you didn't want anyone else snoopin' around?"

Even though she was tired, Ab could see where he was headed. "Scare them away!" she said, as if a light were coming on. "You think someone's pretending to be the Black Moriah so people will be too afraid to go up to Pogus Point?"

It made sense. "That's just what's happened, ain't it?" said Bean.

It was indeed. "So, whoever's behind it can take their time to dig around, because nobody's going to bother them," reasoned Ab.

"If that's what's happened," said Bean, "it's a heck of a good plan."

"But who?"

"The guy who tried to drown me out at the Widowmaker. He must be Steerforth. With *Jellybean,* he could cruise up an' down the shore underwater without anyone knowin' what he was up to. But it got away from 'im somehow."

"And we found it," said Ab. "And messed up his plans."

"So," Bean reasoned, "he had to use the inflatable."

"And you found him."

The thoughts were flowing freely between them now, with one voice picking up as soon as the other left off. It was Bean's turn to pick up the train of thought. "So he thinks if some kid can find out what he's up to, he'd better come up with a different plan. One that'll keep people off his back while he looks for the treasure."

"The Black Moriah," they both said at once.

Bean was impressed. The Black Moriah was a good idea, and it had worked. By throwing a scare into the townsfolk, the stranger had already bought himself three whole days and nights to poke around to his heart's content. "And the only one he's had to worry about is Constable Wruggles," said Ab.

Bean had a sudden, outrageous stroke of inspiration. "What do you s'pose would happen if the *real* Black Moriah turned up all of a sudden?"

"What are you talking about?"

Bean smiled. "I bet everyone's playin' cards with the Proverbs, don't you?"

The Proverbs were avid cribbage players, and nightly games around the card table in the parlor had become a tradition since they had taken over the Moses Webster House. Ab glanced at her watch. It was almost ten o'clock. "Sure. So?"

"So, they're about to find out that we've just seen the Black Moriah."

15
TOO MANY BLACK MORIAHS

"*THERE YOU ARE!*" said Mrs. Peterson as the kids came in the front door. "We were just about to send the dogs out." That's what she always said when the kids were a little late. "Where have you been?"

"Just down helping Captain Kittredge with the sub," replied Ab.

"Fifteen for two," said Ab's dad, playing an eight. "How's it coming?"

"He says it's seaworthy again," said Bean. He took a seat on the sofa near the bookcase where he could see the Prinderbys' reaction to the news he was about to relate. Mr. and Mrs. Prinderby were seated across from each other, playing partners against the Petersons. The Proverbs, who loved cribbage but weren't very good at it, had evidently been knocked out of contention in the previous round and were now pouring coffee and arranging dessert within easy reach of their guests. Daltry Lawson was sitting in an easy chair under the lamp in the corner behind the Prinderbys, reading a newspaper. "The captain says he's gonna take the sub back across the bay tomorrow," said Bean.

Daltry Lawson looked up. "Is that a good idea? What about the storm?"

"That's s'posed to blow through by dawn, accordin' to the weather radio," said Bean.

"Oh, it'll be fine," said Mr. Proverb, placing a buttered cranberry scone in front of Mrs. Peterson. "The bay will be calm by midmorning."

"Me an' my dad are followin' him over in the launch, just to make sure," said Bean.

Lawson's eyes fell back to the newspaper. "That'll make a long day," he said. "That thing only goes four or five knots."

Bean shrugged. "I s'pose. If we get there by three or four, we'll be back in time for supper."

116

Ab was on pins and needles waiting for Bean to drop his bombshell. She caught his eye and prodded him with a nod. He nodded back. "I s'pose you heard he's been seen again."

"Who's been seen, dear?" said Mrs. Proverb. She was standing behind Mrs. Peterson to see what card she was going to play next.

Bean fixed his gaze on Professor Prinderby, who seemed to be having difficulty counting his points. "The Black Moriah," Bean said. "Mandy Philbrook saw 'im about two hours ago, up by the schoolhouse turn."

Whatever response he'd expected from the Prinderbys, he was disappointed. The professor continued looking at the cribbage board and scratching his head, and his wife rearranged her cards for the umpteenth time.

Mr. Lawson dropped his newspaper, and Ab picked it up and handed it to him.

Mrs. Proverb's reaction was more emphatic. "Oh, no. Not again! I'd hoped that business was over with." She cast a worried look at her husband.

"It's all right," said Mr. Proverb, patting his wife's shoulder comfortingly. "Just someone out playing pranks. Some people just have too much time on their hands."

"Well, whoever it is, and whatever they're up to—" Mr. Peterson looked at Ab over the top of his cards—"you two stay away from that end of the island."

"But—" Ab began to protest.

"No buts," said her father, sensing that the words of the seance were still ringing in his wife's ears. "As long as that nutcase is around, you stay away. You hear?"

Things weren't going at all the way Bean had planned. "We were just kiddin'!" he said spontaneously.

Suddenly all eyes were on him. "You were what?" said Mr. Peterson, turning to fix Bean with a severe stare.

Bean felt about four inches tall, but it was too late to back out now. "We just made that up about Mandy Philbrook. Nobody's seen the Black Moriah."

There was no misinterpreting the anger in Mr. Peterson's eyes. He turned to Ab, who practically melted beneath his gaze. "Why on earth would you do such a foolish and irresponsible thing? Do you think it's funny that half the town is terrified that there's some maniac on the loose?"

117

Ab hung her head. "No, sir," she said. She wanted to clobber Bean for putting her in that situation. "We're sorry."

"You've heard of the boy who cried wolf when no wolf was there," said Mrs. Proverb sternly. "Nobody believed him when a real wolf showed up."

Bean got the point. "We're sorry. We were just kiddin' around."

Mr. Peterson gave each of the kids a long look that left no doubt as to how he felt about their idea of kidding around, then he returned to his cards. "I thought you had more sense between you than to pull something as idiotic as that," he said. "You haven't told that story to anyone else, have you?"

"No, sir," said Bean, who was feeling as low as a snail's trail. "It was stupid."

"It was indeed," said Mrs. Peterson. She looked at her daughter. "I'm surprised you'd be a part of such nonsense, Abigail. I expect better of you."

Ab said nothing. All she could think about was getting Bean alone and giving him a good piece of her mind.

Mrs. Peterson turned to Bean. "I think you'd better go home, Arthur," she said. "It's getting late, and I'm sure your mother will be wondering where you are."

The message was clear. At the moment, Bean was about as welcome as a burp in church. He got up and slunk toward the door. "I'm really sorry," he said. "It won't happen again. We just thought—"

"I'd say you didn't think at all," Mr. Peterson cut in.

Mrs. Peterson was becoming more agitated. "All I can think about is that dreadful voice we heard at the seance the other night."

"That's what I was thinking, too," said Mrs. Proverb.

The women's husbands exchanged skeptical glances.

"Now, I'm sure there's a rational explanation," said Mr. Proverb. He looked at Mrs. Prinderby, who, as if feeling his eyes on her, looked up from her cards.

"I had so hoped to speak to Anabel," she said distractedly. She played a card. "That's a three, for . . . what is it now, twenty-two?"

"What do you think about the seance, Professor?" asked Mrs. Peterson. She'd been wanting to get his opinion, and this seemed like the perfect time.

The professor looked up. "I don't believe in them," he said flatly. "It can be explained scientifically."

Although someone may have expected Mrs. Prinderby to take exception to her husband's disbelief, she didn't. "Harold is not a believer," she said good-naturedly. "But he lets me have my hobby, and I let him have his. Still," she said, "I wish he'd been there. Perhaps he'd feel differently."

The professor looked at his wife and smiled, then went back to wrestling with the complex mathematics of the game. "If I play a three on her three, that's two points, correct?" he said.

The conversation drifted off in other directions as the adults resumed their game. Ab got up and walked to the door with Bean.

"Where are you going?" Mrs. Peterson asked.

"Just out on the porch with Bean," said Ab. "I'll be right back."

"See that you are," said her mother. "Nowhere else."

"No, ma'am."

Bean wasn't looking forward to being alone with Ab. He knew what was coming, and as soon as the door closed behind them, it did.

"Are you crazy?" she said, hitting him sharply on the shoulder with her fist. The blow nearly knocked him down the steps. "Ow!" said Bean, regaining his balance. "That hurt!"

"You're still alive," Ab snapped. "You made me feel like a fool in there."

Bean knew the feeling. "I know. Sorry. I guess it wasn't such a great idea. I just thought we'd get some kind of reaction outta the Prinderbys. I was sure of it."

"Well, we didn't. The only reaction was that I came *that* close to getting grounded," said Ab, holding her thumb and forefinger half an inch apart.

Bean sat down on the step. "Well, at least we can write off the professor as a suspect."

Ab conceded that much was true. "I was expecting this big bombshell. And the only thing that happened was that Mr. Lawson dropped his newspaper. Big deal."

Bean replayed the scene in his mind. "Why do you think he dropped it?"

"How should I know? It just slipped off his lap," said Ab. "You're not going to try to make something of that, are you?"

"But he was holdin' it with both hands," Bean recalled out loud. "Maybe he was startled."

"'Oh, please," said Ab. Even she was losing patience with him. "I suppose you're going to say that he's the Black Moriah. Are you forgetting he's in a wheelchair? Now, as I recall," she continued sarcastically, "nobody mentioned that the Black Moriah was chasing them in a wheelchair. You think they just overlooked that little detail?"

Bean hung his head again. All the facts were stacking up against him. Then he remembered something Lawson had said. "How do you think Lawson knew that *Jellybean* only goes four or five knots?" Bean asked.

"Common sense," said Ab.

Bean wasn't so sure. "I don't think it's common knowledge how fast a minisub can go."

"Oh, so he's the one who stole the sub, too? *His* name was Steerforth, remember? And Captain Kittredge said he was slim—which Mr. Lawson definitely is not—and that he had grayish hair and blue eyes. Lawson's hair is brown, and his eyes are green. Besides, don't you think it would be a little difficult to get a wheelchair through the hatch?"

Bean overlooked Ab's scorn. "All them's things that can be changed," he said, though the notion was pretty far-fetched, even to him. "Except he showed up the day after I followed the guy in the boat out to the Widowmaker, didn't he?"

Ab didn't reply.

"What if he doesn't really need that wheelchair?"

"What do you mean?"

"What if he's fakin' it?"

"Oh, come on, Bean. Get real. Why would he do that?"

"So no one will suspect he's Steerforth, of course," said Bean. This new thought began to open up a whole new realm of possibilities. "It would explain why Wruggles hasn't been able to find the guy who dunked me, wouldn't it? 'Cause he don't exist. It would also explain why Lawson's shoes are scuffed, an' why there's blisters on his hands—from rowin' the dinghy. An' how 'bout them scratches? What if he got 'em while we was out in the Widowmaker?"

In spite of herself, Ab was beginning to wonder if Bean had a point.

"Well, you're right about him not showing up until the next day," she said, her curiosity piqued. "If he doesn't really need the wheelchair, he could easily have snuck out those nights and pretended to be the Black Moriah."

"It'd be risky," said Bean. "I mean, if anyone here saw 'im out of his wheelchair."

"Then it would have to be a risk he figured was worth taking," said Ab, who was quickly coming over to Bean's side of the argument. "But he's not from around here. How would he have known about pretending to be the Black Moriah to scare people away while he looked for the treasure?"

"He could've found that out up at the historical society," Bean guessed. "My mom says the whole story's in one've them books 'bout island history."

The conversation trailed off for a few minutes as they entertained their own thoughts, then Bean spoke up. "What can we do to get 'im out of that wheelchair?"

"Oh, no!" Ab replied, frightened at what she was afraid Bean was planning. "You're not going to run in the house yelling 'fire' or anything stupid like that, are you?"

She watched with horror as a smile spread across Bean's face, as if he didn't think that was such a bad idea. "No," he said, much to her relief. "I got a better idea."

This last statement didn't exactly fill Ab with confidence. "I don't like the sound of that."

"All you have to do is—"

"*Me!* What do you mean, all *I* have to do? If I get in any more trouble, they'll ground me and my children and my grandchildren. No way."

"Just listen a minute, will ya?" said Bean. "You won't get in any trouble."

"Famous last words," said Ab.

"Listen, the room next to his is empty, ain't it?"

"It's the library," said Ab. "People go in and out."

"But after eleven or twelve tonight, nobody'd be in there, would they?"

"So?"

"So, you go down there after everyone's in bed, and listen for his footsteps."

"What makes you think he's going to be up after everyone's in bed?"

"Don't you worry," said Bean. "I'll take care of that."

"I don't like the sound of that either," said Ab.

"What's the big deal? You go down and listen. What kinda trouble can you get in for that?"

"The question is, what will you be doing? I don't want any more surprises. Besides, what are you going to do, sneak out of the house?"

"Won't have to," said Bean confidently. "I'm gonna stay in the tree house tonight."

Bean's dad had built the tree house in the backyard several summers ago. Since then, Bean had spent many summer nights there. With two bunk beds, electricity, and a little kitchen—where he cooked his specialty, chicken noodle soup—it was the envy of the neighborhood.

"What are you going to do?" said Ab, raising her voice as a gust of wind shook the old lilac bush beside the porch.

At that moment, the door opened and Ab's dad appeared against the dim light from the front hall. "Ab? Time to come in." He gave Bean a look that meant it was time for him to go home. Bean got up and headed down the walk.

"Good night, Ab," he said. "Good night, Mr. Peterson. Sorry 'bout the—"

"Just don't let it happen again," said Ab's dad. He liked Bean a lot, but it worried him that whenever the two kids got together they managed to get in trouble. "Good night."

Ab went in with her father, then, when the door closed, stood with her nose pressed against the window watching Bean jog down the walkway and across the street. What was he up to now?

"I don't know," said Bean's mom when he told his folks he wanted to spend the night in the tree house. "That storm's coming. What if the tree gets blown down?"

"That won't happen, will it, Dad?" Bean appealed to his father.

Captain Carver placed an arm on his wife's shoulder. "It's been through worse," he said reassuringly, sensing the concern in her eyes. "I don't think there's any problem, but take the walkie-talkie out with you. If the storm gets too bad, I'll call you in and you come right away. Capiche?"

"Capiche," said Bean. He gave his mother a quick kiss on the cheek, took the walkie-talkie from its holder by the kitchen sink, and grabbed a waterproof flashlight from the hall closet. "See you in the morning!" he yelled as he ran out to the backyard.

Thirty seconds later, the trapdoor of the tree house slammed shut behind him. He turned on the light, spread out the sleeping bag on the bottom bunk, and got out his dog-eared copy of *The Last Battle,* from *The Chronicles of Narnia.* Knowing he had about two hours to wait, he began to read.

Two hours and ten minutes later, a tremendous clap of thunder slapped him awake. He hadn't even realized he was asleep. The tree house was swaying like a ship in a gale. Rain rapped angrily at the window. A quick glance at his watch told him he had missed his appointment.

In a flash, he leapt from the bed, smacking his head sharply on the top bunk. Reeling from the blow, he clicked off the light—so anyone who happened to check would think he was asleep—and crawled down the ladder. He jumped the last few feet to the ground and landed with a thud.

Immediately he wished he'd had the foresight to bring his storm gear, although the rain wasn't cold. It was a good thing, because he was soaked to the skin in a matter of seconds.

The stout old tree that held the tree house wasn't in any danger of blowing over, but a row of feathery maples across the street was whipping about like people doing the wave at a baseball game. The rain, which was falling almost horizontally, pelted his face and neck as he ran across darkened yards to the rear of the Moses Webster House.

"Be there, Ab!" he said to himself.

The backyard of the Moses Webster House was enclosed by a granite wall five feet high, most of which was covered with a hundred years' growth of beach rosebushes. In the middle of the yard was a huge forsythia, not fifteen feet from Daltry Lawson's bedroom window. Bean scurried under the forsythia, where the thick canopy of leaves created a little hut-shaped shelter from the rain.

A quick flip of the switch assured him the flashlight was working. He parted some of the branches immediately in front of him and directed the beam at Lawson's window. From this angle, he figured, the light would shine on the ceiling of the room. Bean shut it off, waited for a count of three, and turned it on again. A moment later he repeated the sequence.

If Lawson was awake, surely he would get out of bed to see what was happening. If so, Ab would hear his footsteps. Such a simple plan.

Bean decided to do it one more time, but just as he was about to flick the switch, there was a blinding flash of lightning. This time, instead of the blank, darkened window, the brief flash revealed a face—looking straight at him!

"What're you doin'?" came a voice from behind.

16
MISSING

BEAN DROPPED THE FLASHLIGHT and nearly choked on his heart before he recognized the voice. "Spooky?" he said into the darkness of the forsythia cavern. "Is that you?"

"Who'd you expect? Santa Claus?"

"What're you doin' out here?" Bean demanded. He groped through the tall grass and picked up the flashlight.

"Ab called a while ago an' told me you were up to something," Spooky explained. "I saw the light on in the tree house, but I figured you had more sense than to stay out there in a storm like this. Then I saw the light go off, so I come to see what you were gettin' yourself into."

There was another flash of lightning, and Bean was reminded of the face in the window. "We'd better get outta here," he said. "I saw something."

"Saw what?"

"A face in the window."

"What window?"

"Daltry Lawson's," said Bean, pointing.

"The guy in the wheelchair? What would he be doin' lookin' out the window?"

"Good question." Bean watched with eagle eyes and waited for the lightning. He didn't have to wait long, but all the next flash revealed was an empty window.

"Quick!" said Bean, scampering through the branches in the opposite direction. "Let's get outta here."

"Why?" said Spooky, following close behind. "What're we runnin' from?"

They were just clear of the forsythia when, in a brief interval of silence while the wind drew its breath for another blow, they heard the distinctive sound of rattling glass.

"Shh! Somebody's openin' a window!" Bean hunkered down and crawled around the forsythia for a better look. At the moment there was nothing to see, and he had a mighty urge to turn on the flashlight, but a subtle aftershock of lightning pulsed at that moment, revealing a darkly clad figure climbing out of Daltry Lawson's window. "Did you see that?"

"See what?" said Spooky, who was trying to tie the hood of his raincoat in place so no more rain would run down his neck.

"He's comin' after us!" Bean whispered sharply. "Quick, this way!" With that, Bean was halfway down the yard and Spooky was right on his heels. They dropped to their knees behind a huge old oak tree and peeked around the trunk.

"What're we lookin' for?" said Spooky. "Who's after us?"

"Daltry Lawson," Bean explained, squinting toward the house through the darkness and the sharp raindrops that pelted his eyelids. "He just came out the window."

Spooky sat back against the trunk and looked quizzically at his companion. "In a wheelchair?" There was a loud clap of thunder in the distance.

Bean hurriedly explained his theory, and had just finished when another flash of lightning lit up the night. This time they saw nothing out of the ordinary. No figure in black rushing at them across the lawn, as he'd half expected. Nothing.

"Where'd he go?" Bean asked aloud.

"I think you're seein' things," Spooky suggested. "Even if what you say is true, why would he be goin' out on a night like this? There's nobody around to scare."

Good question, Bean thought. For the next five minutes they stayed put, waiting to see what would happen. Nothing did.

"My butt's soakin' wet," said Spooky at last. "And you look half drowned. Let's go back to the tree house."

Bean continued staring at the Moses Webster House during intermittent flashes of lightning. Nothing changed. After a few more minutes, he began to wonder whether he had seen something or his mind had just been playing tricks on him. Reluctantly, he agreed to Spooky's suggestion.

Back in the tree house, Bean and Spooky stripped, hung their clothes over the little electric heater, and crawled into their sleeping bags. Spooky had taken the top bunk and before long was contentedly sucking his thumb and snoring.

Spooky was fourteen and had always sucked his thumb when he was tired, and he didn't care who knew it. He sucked it in school, at basketball games, at church. Everywhere and anywhere. When anyone teased him about it, he simply said, "Better than cigarettes," and that was the end of the argument.

For a long time Bean lay awake, staring at the underside of Spooky's bunk as the storm rose and fell outside. Had he really seen someone coming out Daltry Lawson's window, or had it just been a shadow cast by the lightning? And even if Lawson wasn't really confined to a wheelchair, Spooky had made a good point: What on earth would he be doing out on a night like this? Certainly there was no reason to play the Black Moriah when no one would be around to see it. And just as certainly, he wouldn't be going anywhere near the Widowmaker in such wild weather. So, what would he be up to?

At that moment, a limb cracked outside and Bean imagined the Black Moriah making his way up the ladder to the tree house. He looked at the trapdoor in the floor, half expecting it to slam open at any time. He leaned over and, nearly tumbling out of bed, reached down to close the hook-and-eye latch to lock the door.

Afterward, he lay still staring holes into the darkness until, unable to sleep, he turned on the flashlight and took out the rough copy of the poem Ab had made in the submarine.

Three score and four, nor scarcely more
One gets there by degrees
Then nought and twice times six and seven
Count minutes o'er the seas

126

Three score and eight the bosun's mate
Shouts fathoms to the shore
Then eight and half of eight and four
And one completes the lore
A cave, a stone, my mark alone
And none remain to save
For hoard, and men and secrets keep
Forever in their grave
A cave, a stone, my mark alone
And none remain to tell
But follow these and you shall find
Thy treasure, Anabel.

What did it mean? Several times he read and reread the words, but the more he read, the foggier his brain got. He was sure it was a riddle. He was also sure the riddle was a clue to the whereabouts of the treasure that Daltry Lawson—if he had been the man in the submarine—was seeking.

All of a sudden he had an idea that made him sit bolt upright. Numbers! The poem was full of numbers. What could they mean? Hungrily he scanned the text again, and two words stood out: minutes and degrees. "Latitude and longitude!" he yelled out loud.

"What?" said Spooky sleepily.

"The poem!" said Bean, switching on the light.

"No poems," said Spooky. "Go to sleep."

Bean punched the bottom of Spooky's bunk. "Get up!"

Spooky, startled awake, smacked his head on the ceiling. "Ow! What'd you do that for?"

Bean swung his feet to the floor. "Get down here. I figured out the riddle."

"What riddle?" Spooky asked crankily as he climbed out of his nice warm sleeping bag and dropped to the floor. "What time is it?"

"Never mind that," said Bean. "This poem we found in the submarine is a code."

Spooky was suddenly interested. "A code? For what?"

"Latitude and longitude."

Coming from a long line of seamen, Spooky knew that latitude and longitude were the measurements by which seafarers determine locations. He sat down beside Bean and looked at the paper Bean had spread out on his bunk.

"Look at this," said Bean, tracing the words with his hand. "'Three score and four, nor scarcely more, one gets there by degrees.' A score is twenty. We learned that in school, remember?"

"Sure," said Spooky drowsily. He didn't really remember much of anything at the moment. "So?"

"Then three score is sixty, plus four is sixty-four. 'Nor scarcely more' prob'ly means an' a little bit. Then right afterward it says 'one gets there by degrees.' That means sixty-four degrees."

Spooky glanced ahead and read the next line aloud. "'Then nought and twice times six and seven, count minutes o'er the seas.' Nought is zero. Twice times six is twelve and seven would be . . . ," he counted quickly on his fingers, "nineteen. Zero one nine minutes." Now he was fully awake. "Sixty-four degrees an' nineteen minutes," he said, completing the formula. "That must be the latitude. What's the longitude? What's next?"

Bean read aloud. "Three score and eight the bosun's mate."

Spooky did the math. "Three score and eight is sixty-eight."

"'Then eight and half of eight and four,'" Bean continued. "That means eight plus four plus four—sixteen!"

"Sixty-eight degrees, sixteen minutes longitude!" Spooky concluded triumphantly. "We're on to something, Beanbag!"

A worn old nautical map of Penobscot Bay hung on the wall beside the window. Bean jumped up, ignoring the cold, and studied it closely. He placed the index finger of his right hand at the top of the map where longitude was measured, and the index finger of his left hand at the left edge of the map, which indicated latitude. Slowly, following the degrees and minutes that were marked in light blue ink across the surface of the map, his fingers met at sixty-four degrees and nineteen minutes latitude and sixty-eight degrees, sixteen minutes longitude. Bean removed his fingers and stared at the place they had joined. "The Widowmaker!"

Spooky, poem in hand, was now at his side. "'A cave, a stone, my mark alone,'" he read. "The Widowmaker's a cave. What do you think the rest means?"

Bean studied the words. "A stone . . . it's all stone. Granite. I don't know . . . . 'My mark alone.' Maybe he made a mark on a stone."

"Makes sense," said Spooky. "If you're right about Lawson, he figured it out just like we did. That's why he was snoopin' around the Widowmaker."

"But why the submarine?" Bean wondered.

Spooky shrugged his shoulders. "Dunno. The Widowmaker's not deep enough for a sub."

"I wonder what his mark is?"

Spooky eyes drifted to the initials he and Bean and Ab had carved in the walls of the tree house. "Initials," he said. "I bet he carved his initials in the rock."

"Abnezar Twing," said Bean. "A.T."

"All we need to do is find those initials, and we got the treasure!" said Spooky. "If we can get there before the Black Moriah!"

Bean looked out through the rain lashing at the window. "Nothin' we can do tonight," he said. "The moon low tide's tomorrow night, 'bout eleven o'clock. I bet that's when he's gonna make his move."

"So, what do we do?" asked Spooky.

"Simple," said Bean. "We get there first and catch 'im in the act."

"Oh, is that all?" said Spooky skeptically.

Bean had begun to shiver. He jumped back into the sleeping bag and pulled it up around his neck. "Get some sleep," he ordered. "We're gonna need it."

The boys were awakened by a loud rapping on the trapdoor. Bean forced himself awake and cast a bleary glance at his wristwatch. "Six-fifty," he groaned.

"Bean? Are you up there?"

It was Ab. The hook rattled in the lock as she pushed against the trap-door. Suddenly Bean remembered he and Spooky didn't have any clothes on. "Wait a minute!" he said, jumping out of bed. He grabbed his skivvies and pants from the hook above the heater and slipped them on. They smelled mildewy and were still miserably damp and cold. Goosebumps popped up on his skin as he slipped them on. Taking his shirt from the hook, he kicked the latch with his toe. "Okay, come on in," he said. The words weren't out of his mouth before the door banged open.

"I heard him!" said Ab excitedly as she pulled herself up through the opening. "You were right. He's faking it!" Spooky, peeking out of his sleeping bag, peered over the edge of his bunk. "Spooky!" said Ab. "So, you came over."

"Had to," said Spooky. "Somebody's got to keep an eye on 'im."

"What happened?" Ab demanded.

Taking turns, the boys recounted the events of the previous night, including the code they had broken.

"Bean! Are you awake!" his father was calling.

Bean pressed the button on his walkie-talkie. "Yeah, Dad?"

"Come on in the house. I need you to help me right away."

There was an unsettling edge of urgency in his father's voice. Bean pulled on his shoes and, without tying them, squeezed by Ab and started down the ladder. "I'll be right back. Wait here."

Minutes later, Ab and Spooky were warming themselves with a cup of tea when Bean scrambled back up the ladder and burst through the hatch with a wild look in his eyes. "The sub's gone!" he said, grabbing his soggy socks from the floor and stuffing them in his pocket. "And so's Captain Kittredge!"

17
In the Grip of a Fleshless Hand

"What happened?" said Ab with alarm. "Has the captain taken it back to the mainland?"

"He wouldn't have tried that without a boat to follow," said Bean. "My dad was goin' to go with him 'bout noon. They had it all planned out. Besides, the sea's still too rough after the storm. Won't settle down for a couple of hours yet."

"Did they check his room at the Tidewater?" Spooky asked.

"'Course they did, first thing. He didn't check out, and he ain't there."

Ab was perplexed. "He didn't leave a note or anything?"

Bean shook his head. "Nope."

"Prob'ly just went out for breakfast," Spooky guessed.

Again Bean shook his head. "Nobody's seen 'im. They've been lookin' all over town since they found the submarine missin'."

"Is the barge gone, too?" Ab wanted to know.

"Nope. It's there," said Bean. He was about to add something else when Spooky interrupted.

"Maybe the sub blew overboard somehow."

"Nope. The derrick's swung out over the side," Bean explained, referring to the metallic arms that had lifted the submarine from the water and held it in place. "And the cables were lowered. She was put over on purpose sometime durin' the night."

"Who'd be fool enough to do something like that in a storm?" Spooky wanted to know.

"Someone who's desperate," said Ab.

"You don't think the captain's gone lookin' for the treasure, do you?" Spooky asked.

"He's got too much sense to try something like that," said Bean. "Besides, he may be in pretty good shape, but he's gotta be pushin' a hundred."

"Then where is he?" Spooky demanded.

"I don't know," Bean replied.

"We've got to find him," Ab volunteered.

"Can't," said Bean, taking his coat from the hanger over the trapdoor. "Not now. Dad needs help resettin' the channel marker out in the Sound. The storm dragged it too close to the ledges. I've gotta go with 'im. Spook, he wants you to come, too, if you can."

"Sure!" Spooky said. It was a chore he and Bean had helped with several times in the past, and usually he got to take the helm of the powerful little Coast Guard launch while Bean and his dad did the heavy work. He liked that.

"Wruggles's got the fire department out lookin' for the captain," said Bean reassuringly. "He's bound to turn up sooner or later."

"But what about the Widowmaker?" worried Ab. "Tonight's the moon low tide."

"Don't worry," said Bean. "We'll be back by suppertime."

The first thing Ab did was go back home to see if Daltry Lawson had shown up. She had a hard time concealing her dismay when he rolled out of his room in his wheelchair to take his place at the breakfast table. He looked tired, but so did everyone first thing in the morning. Other than that, he seemed in high spirits and had a healthy appetite. Bean must have been wrong about him, which meant there had to be another explanation for the footsteps she had heard in his room, and for the dark figure Bean had seen sneaking out the window.

For the rest of the day, Ab joined in the search for Captain Kittredge, but neither hide nor hair of him was found. It was as if he'd vanished from the face of the earth.

Seven o'clock that evening had come and gone while Ab waited at the public landing, watching anxiously for a sign of the launch bearing Spooky, Bean, and his dad back from their long day's work on the water. Every time she saw a boat enter the harbor, her hopes rose, only to fall again when she realized it was just another lobster boat returning to port for the night.

Finally, unable to bear it any longer, she went to Bean's house. "Mrs. Carver," she said as she entered the kitchen, careful not to let the screen door slam behind her, "have you heard anything from Bean?"

"Oh, hi, Ab," said Mrs. Carver kindly. She was standing at the sink doing dishes. "Yes, his dad called on the ship-to-shore radio about an hour ago." She pulled the plug in the sink and dried her hands on the dish towel. "They were just on their way in when they got a call from the Coast Guard that a ledge marker up at the Thoroughfare had blown over during the storm, so they had to go up there and reset it."

"Oh," said Ab. On one hand she was relieved; on the other, she was afraid they'd miss their chance of solving the riddle of the Widowmaker and the Black Moriah. "When do you expect them back?"

"Not tonight," said Mrs. Carver, who was used to her husband being called out on emergencies. "They're meeting a Coast Guard cutter up there. I expect they'll stay overnight." She saw the worry in Ab's face. "They'll be okay, hon," she said, patting Ab on the shoulder. "I'm sure they'll be back by midmorning."

"That's too late," said Ab, thinking out loud.

"Too late for what?"

"Oh, nothing special," said Ab, backtracking quickly. "We just . . . we had plans."

"Well, I'm afraid you'll have to make other plans tonight," said Mrs. Carver.

Ab nodded. "I guess I will," she said. "Thank you." She was about to leave, but turned and said, "Mrs. Carver? If you hear from Bean, tell him . . . I'll take care of things."

"What things?" Mrs. Carver asked out of curiosity.

"Oh, just . . . things," Ab demurred. "Tell him I'll see him tomorrow. 'Bye."

The screen door slammed behind her as she left the house. "Sorry!" she called over her shoulder.

Ab walked slowly up the sidewalk toward the Moses Webster House. Nothing was making sense, but somehow, she was sure, all questions would be answered at the Widowmaker that night. But someone would have to be there. Of course, her first thought was to get help—probably from Constable Wruggles—but she could easily imagine the skepticism with which he or any other adult would greet the news of Bean's theory. If only Daltry Lawson had disappeared instead of Captain Kittredge, there would be something to offer as proof. But it hadn't worked out that way.

Proof. That's what was needed.

"The three days are over," she said to herself. "That means it's all right to go up to Pogus Point."

She knew that argument wouldn't hold much water with her parents, but she was trying to rationalize the plan that was taking shape in her mind. "All I need to do is go up and watch from the cliffs above the Widow-maker to see if anyone shows up. There's no danger in that."

By the time she got home, she'd convinced herself that this was a reasonable course of action. Furthermore, she had resolved to get permission to stay in the tree house, so she would be free to come and go long after everyone had turned in for the night.

"It's all right with me if it's all right with Mrs. Carver," said Ab's mother. "Though I can't imagine why you'd want to spend the night up there alone. It's a boys' place, you know. I'm sure it's a mess."

"But they always get to stay up there," Ab argued, though inside she cringed at the thought of crawling into Bean's sleeping bag, which she was sure was damp. Who knew what kinds of things lived in there? "And they're always saying how great it is. I just want to try it, is all."

Ab looked to her dad for support. He caught the eagerness in her eyes. "Well, I don't see any harm in it. It's a nice, safe place, and she's not twenty feet from the Carvers' window if she needs help."

Ab thought this would be a good time to explain about the walkie-talkies that Bean's folks used to keep in touch with him when he was in the tree house.

"Okay, Mom?" she asked for final approval.

"All right," said her mother, somewhat assured by Ab's explanation. "But take the alarm clock with you so you'll be back in time for breakfast, hear?"

"Yes, ma'am," said Ab meekly. "And I'm going to take my own pillow and sleeping bag."

Late that night she watched from the darkened tree house until the lights in the Carvers' house and the Moses Webster House were turned off. About ten o'clock, Mrs. Carver had called on the walkie-talkie to check that everything was all right, which Ab had assured her it was. "Sleep tight," said Mrs. Carver.

"You, too," said Ab.

Real tight, she added to herself.

She waited a while longer, just to be sure. While she waited, she worked up the courage she would need for the task at hand.

Fortunately, Bean had left his flashlight on the little shelf beside his bunk. Ab checked it with a flick of the switch, tucked it in the pocket of her black pea coat, and quietly opened the trapdoor.

Outside, the moon was full and bright. This was both good and bad. Good in that she'd be able to see where she was going, especially up the steep path through the bracken to the cliff top overlooking the Widow-maker. Once there, she'd be able to clearly see anyone going in or out. The moonlight was bad in that she would have to be careful to stay out of sight herself.

For a while she stood at the edge of the Carvers' back lawn, looking down Double-Dead Road. All at once she wondered if this was such a good idea. "Sounds like something Bean would do," she said softly. Nevertheless, she couldn't see any other way. Gathering her courage, she started down the road, keeping to the shadows as much as possible. She held the flashlight in front of her with her finger on the switch, ready to turn it on at the first sign of anything.

"There is no Black Moriah," she told herself as she passed the old ball ground and approached the hollow where Betty Lou had seen the apparition. "There is no Black Moriah." She thought she sounded like the cowardly lion in *The Wizard of Oz* when he said, "I do believe in ghosts. I do believe in ghosts!"

"It's only someone trying to scare people," Ab said into the darkness. Her voice sounded small and unconvincing in the heavy silence that surrounded her.

Until this point she'd felt that the danger, if any, lay in front of her. Once she passed the hollow, though, she sensed it behind her as well. As she walked, she turned in slow circles, her senses tingling with apprehension. Bean had always said she didn't have any imagination. Well, he'd sure be impressed with it now. Try as she might, she couldn't keep from imagining that any second the Black Moriah, in all his evil fury, would leap out at her from the surrounding shadows and seize her with his fleshless fingers. She kept sniffing the air for the slightest evidence of the foul smell that seemed to precede his appearance.

Despite the heavy pea coat and her blue jeans, Ab felt cold through and through and shivered uncontrollably. The farther she went, the more strongly she felt the urge to turn and run home as fast as her trembling legs could carry her. "Why am I doing this?" she scolded herself. "I could be in my nice, warm bed."

Her footsteps slowed as she approached the turnoff to the cemetery. If anything terrible is going to happen, she thought, it will be now. She quickened her footsteps until, without being aware of it, she was running toward the small comfort of the solitary streetlight that marked the fork in the road. To the left the road branched off toward Roberts Cemetery; to the right was Pogus Point.

From here on there were no signs of civilization except for Billy Pringle's shack, which marked the spot where Pitch Huggins's place had burned to the ground that night so many years ago. No other houses. No streetlights. Nowhere to run.

Billy Pringle was a legend on the island. Over the years, she'd heard all kinds of strange stories about him, most of which suggested that he didn't have all his marbles. Still, she'd never heard anything bad about him, just that he was odd. Often, when she and Bean passed on their way to the quarry, she'd seen Billy sitting on the rickety apple crate that served as his front step. He'd smile and wave, and instead of saying hello or nice day, he'd ask questions that seemed to have no point—"Two and a half teaspoons of stardust in a clamshell?"—things like that, and he'd go on smiling and asking questions long after the passersby passed by.

Ab's footsteps slowed as she drew abreast of the shack. She was surprised to see the door wide open. There was no sign of Billy, and no lights inside, which wasn't so odd because, according to Bean, Billy didn't have any electricity.

It occurred to her, of course, that Billy could be the Black Moriah, but that made no sense. Billy had no interest in treasure. He was a collector, but as far as she knew, all he did was wander the shoreline picking up things nobody wanted and bringing them home to fill his dooryard, which looked like a flea market somebody had dropped a bomb on. Besides, whatever anyone said of him, everyone agreed he was harmless.

Slowly, in the silence, she became aware of a sound coming rhythmically through the open door. Snoring. Billy was asleep.

In a minute or two, Ab had put the shack behind her and was beginning to feel she might actually reach the Widowmaker after all, in spite of her fear.

"What's a princess doin' out?"

The voice froze Ab in her tracks. She spun around reflexively and clicked on the flashlight, shining it in the speaker's face.

"Like sunshine!" said Billy Pringle happily, pressing his forefinger against the lens. "Howdy-do. Good mornin'. Fine day. What's a princess doin' out?"

Ab stuttered and stammered and tried to swallow. "Billy," she finally managed to choke out. "I thought you were asleep." She looked back at his cabin, the door of which still stood wide open. "I heard snoring."

"My dog," said Billy flatly. "Gets monkeys up his nose."

"Monkeys?"

"Monkeys," said Billy without further explanation. "What's a princess doin' out?"

Ab took that to mean that he wanted to know what she was doing out so late at night.

"I was just . . . I have to . . ." She was talking and trying to think of something to say at the same time. The knot of fear that was crammed in her throat didn't help.

Billy nodded. "Me, too. I was just . . . I have to . . . Me, too." He held up a plastic milk jug he'd filled with blackberries. "Matty turns these into pies," he said.

Now that the initial scare was over, Ab wanted to get on with the business that had brought her to the lightless road in the middle of the night, but she couldn't bring herself to be rude to Billy Pringle. "Who's Matty?" she asked.

"Aunt Matty," said Billy. Offering no further explanation, he headed back toward his house. Ab watched after him. She was surprised that he didn't go into his cabin, as she'd expected, but instead struck off up a little path through the woods that, she knew, came out on the road to Roberts Cemetery. "Where do you suppose he's going with those blackberries?" she asked aloud.

When he was out of sight, she turned her attention to the road ahead. Oddly enough, something about the brief, startling interview with Billy Pringle had dispelled the unreasonable specters of her imagination. The moon lit up the road like a deep blue river threading its way through a dark canyon of firs and spruce trees. She clicked off the flashlight and continued her secret mission.

The narrow path that wound up to the cliff top overlooking Hurricane Reach, though overgrown, was bright with the reflection of moonlight on bits of quartz and mica in the ledge. She easily threaded her way through scratchy, fragrant juniper bushes and scrub pines to the ledge where Bean had witnessed the curious actions of the man with the map. She lay down on the outcropping and peered over the edge.

The moonlit ripples on the Reach, far below, scintillated as if they were tossing fistfuls of diamonds back and forth. The view was bright and breathtaking. From this high up, she could see all the way to the southern and western horizon, and the ocean was like a shimmering carpet of blue and silver, studded with islands whose shores were trimmed with white granite.

The moon hung in the southern sky like a huge night-light, so anyone moving about on the shore below would be easy to see.

To the north, Indian Creek was drained almost dry by the low tide, with just a thin silver trickle, like mercury, oozing under the bridge. The effect of the tide wasn't as dramatic in the Reach, which was much deeper than the creek, but still Ab could see that the waterline was much lower than normal.

For what seemed like forever, nothing happened. She began to feel drowsy and wasn't as cold as she had been. She rested her chin on her crossed arms and was just about to close her eyes for a minute or two when she noticed something not ten feet away that startled her awake: a rope, tied by one end to an ancient iron ring, the kind that stonecutters wedged into granite in times long gone. The other end of the rope dropped over the face of the cliff and out of sight.

Ab crawled over to investigate. The rope was new and only slightly worn at the place where it went over the side. Clearly it had been used to lift something—or someone—heavy over the edge.

Her heart began to race. What if the man with the map was using the rope to lower himself to the cave? What if he was already down there? Or, even more horrifying, what if he was nearby, watching her?

She had two choices. She could hide in the bushes, which were sparse and too low to provide cover, or she could go down the rope herself. Was it her imagination, or did she hear a noise somewhere in the darkness behind her? Too frightened to think clearly, she stuck the flashlight in the deep pocket of her pea coat, then she took off the coat and tied it around her waist, grabbed the rope tightly in her fingers, and lowered herself over the side.

Just below the lip of the outcropping, the rope dangled free of the cliff face for about thirty feet, and Ab found herself flailing in midair. She wrapped her legs around the rope, threaded it tightly around her hands and feet, and slowly shinnied down to the next ledge. Once her feet were on solid rock, she looked up. There was no way she was strong enough to pull herself back up. She'd failed the rope climb in gym class, and that had been a thick rope with knots to rest your feet on.

The ledge she was standing on was only about eighteen inches deep and two to three feet wide, and there was nowhere to go but down. Looking up again, she half expected to see the face of the Black Moriah peering at her over the ledge. Perhaps he'd have a sharp knife in his hand. She could envision it flashing in the moonlight as, with an evil laugh, he cut the rope, leaving her to die miserable and alone on the granite shelf. "I've been hanging around Bean too long," she said to comfort herself. "This imagination stuff isn't all it's cracked up to be."

Though no face appeared, Ab still felt anxious to find a safe place to hide. A quick look over the edge showed that the rope went straight down against the cliff side, so at least she'd be able to rappel off the granite wall. The thought gave her a little comfort. But not much.

Summoning all her strength, she wrapped the rope around her forearms and lowered herself carefully over the ledge. By the time she ran out of rope, about six feet above the shore, her arms had been scraped raw and sore. But with a short jump to a large, flat rock on the beach, she was safe—at least until the tide started coming in again. She looked across the Reach to Lane's Island. That would be a long swim, even for her.

First things first, she thought. She was no more than twenty feet from the Widowmaker. The Orphans, looking sinister in the surreal light, stood with their bases revealed. Carefully she made her way from rock to rock along the shore, trying to keep out of the mud.

Finally, she was at the cave, a pitch-black cavity in the rock about eight feet high. She untied the pea coat from her waist, put it on, and dug the flashlight from the pocket. She clicked the switch and shined the beam into the cavern. The floor of the cave, which was below the beach outside, was still covered with water, but she could see the bottom only four to five inches beneath the surface. She'd have to wade.

She took off her shoes and tied them to her belt, then rolled up the cuffs of her blue jeans and stepped into the water. The cold went through her like an electric shock, and she splashed across the algae-covered bottom toward the ledge on the opposite side, where she could climb out of the water.

As she crossed the cavern, seaweed grabbed at her feet and legs. She remembered Bean telling her that many sailors—washed overboard—had been caught in long branches of kelp and dragged under. "And that's the way they were found," he had said with a maniacal grin, "wrapped up in the branches of the underwater forest." He'd made a ghastly face. At the time, she had told him to not be so immature. At the moment, though, she was having difficulty shaking the image from her mind.

The seaweed at the cave's entrance wasn't deeply rooted, and there was no way it was going to keep her from getting to the other side. She was just a step away from the ledge when she slipped on a slimy stone that stood at a slight angle from the cave floor. She was about to go down when, in an effort to grab hold of the rock, she dropped the flashlight into the water. As she bent to pick it up, her attention was drawn to an object it illuminated: a square metal plate set vertically in the cave wall just below the normal low-tide line.

Still bending, she lifted the flashlight and scanned the metal surface. It was rough, hand-beaten iron, like that she had seen on sculptures at the Metropolitan Museum in New York. Around the edges, other strips of iron were fixed in place with heavy bolts or rivets. On the right-hand side was a thick ring of cast iron, much of which had been eaten away by the sea over a long period of time. It's a door! she thought. She ran the fingers of her free hand around its edges and detected a set of corroded hinges on the left side.

Wondering if there might be a hasp of some kind holding it in place, she felt under the curtain of seaweed that covered the top part of the door. There was no hasp, but she did discern a series of unnatural grooves in the smooth surface of the stone just above the door.

Lifting the seaweed, she bent lower still—until her forehead was nearly in the water and her dangling hair was soaking wet—and shined the light on the indentations. The marks were coated with algae, and time had worn the edges smooth, but there was no mistaking the letters that had been carved there: A.T.

A sudden splash outside the cave was followed by the gut-wrenching sound of someone sloshing through the mud along the shore. She shut off the light, but it was too late.

"Who's in there?" snarled a low, wicked-sounding voice, followed by a steady hissing noise.

A wandering breath of air oozed into the cave, and that's when she smelled it—the unmistakable stench that had filled the tower room the night of the seance.

18
IN THE DEVIL'S LAIR

WHEN THE LAUNCH motored into the harbor the next day, Spooky, who was in the bow with Bean, was the first to notice the little knot of people waiting on the float at the public landing. Because of the moon high tide, the float was nearly level with the town parking lot. "Looks like something's goin' on," Spooky said, nudging Bean in the ribs and directing his attention to the landing.

As they drew closer, they were able to identify the faces: Bean's mom, Ab's parents, Constable Wruggles, Tiny Martin—the fire chief—and several others.

"What's up?" Bean asked, jumping from the boat with the painter in his hand.

"Bean," said his mother, "do you know where Ab is?"

Bean was filled with a sudden foreboding, and his heart sank. "No. Ain't she home?"

"She stayed in the tree house last night," said Mr. Peterson, pushing to the front of the little crowd. "And she isn't there this morning."

"She stayed in the tree house?" The thought struck Bean as odd. Ab didn't like the tree house. She said it always smelled of mildew and was full of spiders. Immediately he had a suspicion of what she'd been up to.

"Last night," said Mrs. Carver, "she asked me to give you a message. She said if you called I was to tell you she'd take care of everything. But she didn't say what that was. Do you know what she meant?"

"Why the welcoming party?" said Captain Carver, jumping from the boat. "What's going on?"

Several of the adults began to speak at once. "Hold on," he said, raising his hand. "One at a time. Missy, you tell me."

When she had finished, everyone looked at Bean. "What was Ab talking about when she said she'd take care of everything, Arthur?" his father asked.

Reluctantly, Bean explained his theory about the Black Moriah, the Widowmaker, and the moon low tide, careful to omit his suspicions about Daltry Lawson for the time being.

"You mean to tell me, you think she went up to the Widowmaker to see if she could find the Black Moriah?" Wruggles asked in disbelief.

"To see if she could find out who's *pretendin'* to be the Black Moriah," Bean corrected. "And to find out what he was up to."

Wruggles shook his head. "You kids. Sometimes I wonder if you've got a brain between you. How could you let her go up there after what happened to you?"

"What do you mean?" said Bean's dad. "What happened?"

Wruggles leveled a severe gaze at Bean. "This one's my fault," he said. Pulling Bean's folks aside, he related what had happened at the Widowmaker three days earlier.

"And you didn't tell us?" said Captain Carver angrily.

Wruggles looked sheepish. "Well, no, I didn't. To tell the truth, I half expected that Bean was just lettin' his imagination get away with him, and I figured you folks had been through enough this summer without . . . Well, at the time it just seemed best to keep that little story to myself. Hindsight's twenty-twenty, they say. I'd do it different if I had to do it over again. I'm sorry." He gave a little bow in Mrs. Carver's direction. "Sorry, Missy."

"What is it?" said Mr. Peterson, pushing his way forward. "What are you talking about?"

Captain Carver explained.

"You mean, there actually is someone up at this cave, someone who tried to drown Bean?" He turned hotly on Constable Wruggles. "And you didn't do anything?"

Wruggles sensed it would do more harm than good if he protested his innocence at this particular moment. "What's done is done," he said. "You can have my badge later. But for now, I'm still the constable. Everyone in the boat. Cap'n, take us up to the Widowmaker."

"That's under fourteen feet of water by now," said Tiny Martin. He took the painter from Bean and clambered into the bow, where he helped the women aboard. "What do you expect to find?"

"I don't know," said Wruggles, "but we've got to start somewhere. Come on, you boys. Hop in."

They wove a crooked wake through the anchored boats as they crossed the harbor. By the time they passed in front of the crab factory, where a cloud of seagulls was squawking loudly, Bean had sidled up beside Constable Wruggles in the bow. "What about Captain Kittredge?" he asked.

Wruggles shook his head. "No sign of him yet, either," he said with a sigh. "Or the submarine. It's like the earth just opened up and swallowed 'em." Bean noticed how weary he looked as he voiced his frustration. "I tell you, Bean, I'm afraid we've opened a can of worms here that's just beyond us." He bent close so only Bean could hear. "To tell you the truth, if the Petersons want my badge after this business is over, well . . . I'd almost be relieved not to be constable any longer."

Bean felt there was nothing he could say. They passed under the Lane's Island bridge and headed across the inlet toward Pogus Point.

The water in Hurricane Reach was perfectly calm. With the tide as high as it was, Bean's dad had no trouble maneuvering between the Orphans and the cliff.

"I don't see any cave," said Mrs. Peterson anxiously. "Where is it? Are we in the wrong place?"

"It's down there," said Tiny, pointing to the depths below.

Mrs. Peterson cast a frantic glance at her husband.

"It's all right," he said, though it was obvious he was worried. He put his arm around his wife's shoulder. "She'll be okay."

"She can't have gotten into the cave," Constable Wruggles said reassuringly. "The only way in's by boat, and she didn't have one, did she?"

Mr. Peterson shook his head.

"Well, then," said the constable, "I guess we'd best start lookin' up there." He nodded toward the top of the cliffs. "I expect we'll find her curled up under a tree somewhere, fast asleep."

Captain Carver took them back across the Reach and tied up at Link Dyer's dock.

Nobody said much of anything as they walked across the bridge. Wruggles plodded on ahead. "We were warned," said Mrs. Peterson at last.

"Now, now," said her husband patronizingly. "Don't start that."

"Well, we were, weren't we? Plain as day."

"What do you mean?" asked Captain Carver. "Who warned you?"

Mr. Peterson told him about the seance—the voice they had heard and what it said.

"Mighty strange," said Captain Carver, casting a skeptical glance at Mr. Peterson, who simply shrugged and raised his eyebrows helplessly. "Why didn't you tell us about that, Bean?"

"'Cause I knew what you'd say," Bean replied. "'It's all in your head, Bean,' or 'there's a logical explanation for everything, Bean.'"

There was no denying that's just what would have happened. "Still," said his dad, "you should have told us."

Bean's mom wasn't a superstitious person, but neither was she one to tempt fate in regard to Bean's safety. The threat rang in her ears. "Maybe Bean should go on home," she suggested.

"No way!" Bean protested immediately. "If Ab's in trouble, I want to help find her."

Captain Carver gave his wife a look that said he agreed with his son. There was no way Bean could be expected to stay home and wait while Ab's fate hung in the balance. "Nothing's going to happen to him with all of us around," he said, and the subject was closed.

The little group searched from one end of Pogus Point to the other for the rest of the morning. As Ab's disappearance became general knowledge, people from all over the island joined the search, and by late afternoon more than half the town was involved.

"Seems we've spent most of the summer lookin' for them kids," griped Buster Greenlaw to anyone who would listen. "If they don't know how to stay out of trouble, they ought to be kept to home."

Most of the searchers ignored Buster's comments, but more than a few felt he had a good point.

Bean and his dad spent most of their time combing the tumble of rocks leading up to the overlook above the Orphans. There, in the powdery gravel of a little hollow, Bean made an important discovery. "Dad, look!" he called. His father, who had been calling Ab's name down cavelike gaps in the slag, ran to his side.

"What is it?"

"Footprints," said Bean. "They're Ab's."

Captain Carver dropped to his knees and looked at the clear marks in the dirt. "What makes you think so?"

"This," said Bean. He pointed at a distinctive mark in the tread. "She stepped on a broken bottle a few days ago. That's the mark it made when I took out the glass."

"You're sure?"

Bean nodded earnestly.

"We'd better tell the others," said his dad.

"You go," said Bean. "I'm gonna look around up here some more."

"Okay," his dad replied doubtfully. "But stay here. Don't go anywhere or do anything without telling me first. And don't get too close to the edge."

"Okay," Bean replied. He watched until his father was out of sight, then he turned and began to walk slowly along the face of the cliff. There was simply nowhere Ab could have climbed down to the Widowmaker. And Wruggles was right; the only other way in was by boat. So where was she? For the first time, he was beginning to feel genuinely fearful. The possibility that something had happened to Ab had seemed unreal until now. Something had told him she'd turn up at any minute. But she hadn't.

He looked out over the western bay where the setting sun spread a dazzling golden carpet on the sea. In another hour it would be dark. What if Ab hadn't been found by then? What could he do? Where could he look that no one else had thought to look?

Unconsciously, his eyes had drifted back to the ledge just as he was about to trip over a rusted iron ring wedged in the granite. The island was littered with these decaying reminders of the quarrying industry, so he'd have thought nothing of it until something caught his attention—a tangle of rope fibers that had been pinched between the ring and the spike securing it to the ledge.

Good detective that he was, he didn't touch the evidence, but lay down on the rock to get as close as possible to study it. "New rope," he said. He glanced across the speckled granite to the outcropping. Crawling on his hands and knees, he examined the edge closely and found another knot of fibers flattened against the stone at the point where the earth dropped away. He poked his head out and saw the thirty-foot drop to a small ledge.

"Dad!" he screamed, jumping to his feet. "Dad!" He practically flew down the path, nearly colliding with his father and Constable Wruggles, who were running up the hill in response to his call. "Dad, I know how she got down to the Widowmaker. Come on!"

"So, you figure she lowered herself down there with a rope?" said Wruggles after Bean had outlined the evidence. Wruggles leaned forward for a tentative glance over the edge. "Take a pretty brave girl to do that, 'specially at night."

"Or desperate," said Captain Carver. He dropped to one knee at the cliff's edge. "I think we can say Bean's right. The question is," he looked around to make sure no one else was in earshot, "did she make it safely to the bottom?"

"Dad!" said Bean, shocked by the suggestion that Ab could have fallen.

Captain Carver stood up and put his hand on Bean's shoulder and squeezed it forcefully. "It's one of the things you have to consider in rescue work, son. You can't pretend things are always going to work out right. It's not going to do Ab any good to ignore the evidence."

Wruggles took up the unpleasant train of thought. "She couldn't have survived a fall like that." He looked out on the water. "If that's what happened, the tide would have taken her."

Bean began trembling, and tears suddenly pooled in his eyes. "No!" he cried. "You're wrong! You're wrong!" He picked the rope fibers out of the crack at the cliff's edge and waved them in front of his father's face. "Somebody must have untied the rope!" he said in desperation.

Captain Carver appealed to Constable Wruggles with his eyes. "Could've been poorly tied," said Wruggles, taking upon himself the unhappy task of explaining the worst-case scenario. "Prob'ly the knot come loose, and . . ."

Bean's head was spinning, and he felt as if the whole world were spinning with it. Nothing seemed real. Nothing made sense. He had to get away. He had to be anywhere but here. Blindly, he hurled himself back down the path.

"Here!" Constable Wruggles called. "Where are you goin'?" He started to follow, but Captain Carver caught him by the elbow.

"Let him go," he said. "He's got to deal with this."

The two men stood for several minutes, staring down at the Orphans.

"What're we gonna tell the Petersons?" said Wruggles at last.

"Nothing, for the moment," said Captain Carver. "Not 'til we're sure. That wouldn't be fair to anyone."

"You think that's what happened?"

Captain Carver lowered his eyes with a sigh. "The only alternative is no better," he said.

"You think she got in the cave . . . ," said Wruggles, who had been thinking the same thing, "and couldn't get out before the tide come in?"

"We have to check it out."

Wruggles took out his cell phone and punched in some numbers. "Mosey? Wruggles here. I need you to do some divin' out at the Widow-maker." He explained the situation. "How soon can you get here?" He listened. "Okay. We'll be watchin' from the cliff over the Orphans." He flipped the phone shut. "He'll be here as soon as he can get his stuff together. Twenty minutes, prob'ly."

Captain Carver nodded. "I can't help thinking this is all tied together somehow, the submarine and Captain Kittredge missing. Now Ab. It just can't all be coincidence."

"I tell you, Captain," Wruggles confessed. "I'm right over my head."

"Maybe you should call for help from the state police," Captain Carver suggested. "I don't know what they can do—search dogs, I guess. Helicopters . . ." His voice trailed off as he thought about Bean.

"I may do that," said Wruggles. "Why don't you go see if you can find your boy. This hit him pretty hard."

"Yeah. I think I will."

Several people reported seeing Bean running toward the quarry. Captain Carver soon found himself ducking the overhanging branches on the gravelly path through the woods to the ancient swimming hole. As he neared it, he heard the sound of crying echoing from the cliff sides. A few steps farther, he emerged from the trees onto a grassy knob of rock. He saw Bean on the other side of the quarry, sitting cross-legged on a big granite boulder, his head buried in his arms and his shoulders heaving under the convulsions of his sorrow.

Short of finding Ab alive and well, there was nothing the captain could do. He sat and waited. Tears formed in his own eyes and fell silently down his face as he watched his son wrestle with the desolate realization that he probably would never see Ab again.

19
LIFE WITHOUT ABIGAIL

WRUGGLES AND TINY MARTIN watched anxiously from the cliff top as Mosey Brown broke the surface and climbed into his flat-bottomed skiff. It seemed to take forever for him to take off his mask, regulator, and tanks. When he had, he sat down and looked up at them and shook his head. "No one in there!" he yelled. "I found a rubber boat, deflated. You think she coulda been in that?"

"No!" Wruggles called. "I already know about that." He decided that the discovery of the inflatable confirmed Bean's story of the other day. "Anything else?"

" 'fraid so," said Mosey. Reluctantly, he untangled a knot of soggy material from among his equipment on the floor of the boat. He shook the folds out and held it up.

Even from that distance, Wruggles could identify Abby's pea coat. "Where was it?" he asked.

148

"In the cave," Mosey said. "Just washed up there, I'd say. Sorry."

"Okay," said Wruggles. "Thanks. You gonna be home if I need you again?"

"Yup."

The sun had gone down, and Bean and his dad had rejoined the search by the time Wruggles and Tiny Martin came down from the hill. Wruggles shook his head in response to the query in Captain Carver's eyes.

"Can I see you for a minute, Cap'n?" said Wruggles. He took Captain Carver by the elbow and drew him aside. He explained about Abby's pea coat. "Don't look good, I'm afraid." He looked at Bean. "I thought maybe he'd best hear it from you."

The captain nodded sadly. "I appreciate that." He hesitated. "You're sure it's her coat?"

"No doubt," said Wruggles. "Had her name tag in it. I've had Hutch Swenson contact everyone who lobsters in the area to keep a lookout. Nobody's seen anything."

"I don't believe it, Dad," said Bean, as he absorbed the disheartening news of Mosey's discovery. "I don't. Ab's not . . ."

It was all he could say. He buried himself in his father's arms and, for a long time, they just stood there, and everyone left them alone.

The search continued through the night, with women from the church providing coffee and sandwiches. At first light, the searchers were joined by state troopers and investigators from the mainland.

Bloodhounds followed Ab's scent to the edge of the cliff, confirming Bean's suspicions, but there the trail went cold and the dogs just wandered around in confusion, like everyone else.

For four days the townspeople searched, but there was no sign of Ab. The professionals from the mainland were the first to give up. "My guess," said the lead investigator, "is she went over the cliff, the rope broke—like Wruggles said—and she fell. I expect in the next few days some fisherman will . . ." He left the rest unsaid.

One by one the searchers, all exhausted from lack of sleep, went home to resume the normal routine of their lives. In the end, even the Petersons and the Proverbs surrendered to the cold facts that Ab was gone. After a few days, the pastor gently suggested a memorial service, knowing that such a ceremony would help the Petersons put the terrible ordeal behind them so they could come to grips with life without Ab.

As for Captain Kittredge, it was generally assumed that—for whatever reason—he had launched the sub himself, perhaps to test the repairs before attempting to cross the bay. The consensus was that the repairs hadn't held and the sub had sunk, probably somewhere in or around the harbor.

On the morning of the fifth day, Captain Carver was called away on Coast Guard business. His wife was worried about Bean, who hadn't slept much since Ab had disappeared. "He spends all his time up on those cliffs," she said, handing a lunch cooler to her husband as he climbed into the launch at the public landing. "I think we should keep him home for a few days."

"I don't think that would be a good idea," said her husband. "He's got to work this out for himself. I don't see how keeping him home would help."

"But it's not healthy. He doesn't eat or sleep. This is just tearing him up."

Captain Carver proposed a compromise. "Let's see how he's doing when I get back tomorrow afternoon. If he isn't any better, we'll have Pastor Arey talk to him. I just don't know what else to do right now."

They exchanged a quick kiss. "He's got to grieve, my love. It'll take time, but he'll pull through. Don't underestimate him."

The launch eased away and Mrs. Carver stood for a long time watching from the float. Then she climbed the ramp and went home.

Bean's mother wasn't the only one worried about him. Spooky stayed with him in the tree house and tagged along on his frequent walks to the cliff on Pogus Point. Neither of them said much, but Bean's mom was comforted by the fact they were together.

On the night of the fifth day, about nine o'clock, they were sitting on the cliff, mindlessly tossing rocks into the water far below, when Bean finally began to open up. "I miss her," he said.

"Me, too," said Spooky.

"It's all my fault," said Bean, talking as much to himself as to his companion.

"No, it ain't."

"Yes, it is. I put the idea of goin' up to the Widowmaker in her head. If we'd just done like everyone said and minded our own business, she'd be—"

"Then it's my fault, too," said Spooky. "I found the submarine in the first place."

"That's stupid," Bean snapped. "What were you s'posed to do, just leave it there and not tell anyone?"

"I coulda told Wruggles and let him worry about it."

If only they had, thought Bean. Why did they ever get caught up in this whole mess? Who cared about submarines? Who cared about stupid old pirates and their treasure? Without Ab, none of it mattered. Even in his sadness, though, a nagging thought kept coming back to him. "Somebody came out of Lawson's room that night. I saw him."

"Well, it wasn't Daltry Lawson," said Spooky. "I've had my eye on him for days, and he ain't got out of that wheelchair. He just hangs around the Moses Webster House, readin' and writin'. He's harmless."

"Then who was it?" Bean demanded, angry with himself for not being able to put the pieces together.

"You're sure there was someone there?" said Spooky. "I mean, you just had that much time." He snapped his fingers. "Coulda been a shadow or something. Who knows?"

Even Bean was beginning to doubt what he had seen. Had there been a face in Lawson's window? Had it been just a trick of the light? "But Ab heard footsteps," he protested. "She heard the window go up. You did, too."

"I ain't sure what I heard," said Spooky, "in all that thunder and rain. Maybe the wind just rattled the window. I don't know."

They sat for a while in silence, until Spooky's stomach growled. "I'm hungry," he said. He was also cold and tired, but he kept that to himself. "Let's go back to the tree house and get something to eat."

"I ain't hungry," said Bean. It was strange not having Ab around to correct his English. "I'm not hungry," he amended. "You go."

"It's gettin' late. Your mother will want to know where you are."

"Then tell her," said Bean. "I'll be there in a while."

Spooky rose to leave. He felt he should say something, but he didn't have the words. "I'll heat up some chicken noodle soup," he said. "When you're ready."

Bean nodded and listened as Spooky made his way down the hill in the dark.

Not two minutes had passed when Bean heard a frantic scrambling in the bushes and Spooky reappeared. "What'd you come back for?"

"Shh!" Spooky whispered sharply, clapping his hand over Bean's mouth. "Listen!"

For a moment, Bean heard nothing but the beating of his own heart. Then, somewhere nearby came the sound of scuffing gravel and crunching leaves. Something was out there.

Spooky leaned close and whispered in Bean's ear. "I was almost out on the road when I saw someone comin'."

"Who?"

"Couldn't tell," said Spooky. "All I saw was a flashlight. But he's headed this way. We gotta hide."

"Probably just Wruggles," Bean guessed.

Spooky doubted it. "Could be the Black Moriah."

In all the excitement, Bean had nearly forgotten about the fearsome apparition that had haunted Pogus Point but hadn't been seen since Ab disappeared, despite all the people who had been trampling the area night and day during the search. "I don't think the Black Moriah uses a flashlight," Bean said. Still, there was no harm in being cautious. "We can get under that spruce tree over there."

Seconds later, careful not to make a sound, the boys had crawled into the fragrant hollow beneath the gnarled old tree and held their breath as the footsteps drew closer.

Low-lying clouds obscured the moon, so it was too dark to make out more than a shadowy figure behind the glare of the flashlight. Slowly and methodically the intruder made his way up to the clearing. He stood there for a minute, surveying the area with his flashlight. Once or twice the boys had to duck as the light's beam swept in their direction.

Apparently satisfied that he wasn't being followed, the furtive figure scrambled down a little ravine leading to the massive heap of slag that blocked the view to the southeast.

"You recognize him?" said Spooky when the figure was out of earshot.

"No," Bean replied. He knew that it was as easy to recognize someone by the way they walked and carried himself as by his voice or face, but there was nothing familiar about this individual.

At the bottom of the ravine, just after he dropped out of sight, the flashlight beam stopped waving wildly about and became still. "He's put down the light," Bean deduced.

A moment later, there was the unmistakable sound of a large rock being dragged.

"What's he up to?" said Spooky.

The movement of the light indicated that the stranger had picked it up again. A moment later, the light vanished from sight.

"Quick!" said Bean, scrambling from their cover. "We gotta see where he went."

The boys ran across the cliff top and began feeling their way down the dangerous jumble of stones toward the juniper-covered ravine.

"Where'd he go?" Bean whispered, but there was no reply. He spun around. "Spook?" he said. But Spooky had disappeared. "Spooky!" Bean cried in alarm, no longer caring if anyone heard him.

There was a muffled reply that seemed to come from the ground itself. Then Bean made out the words. "Down here!"

"Keep talkin'!" said Bean as he crawled across the jagged stones. "I'll find you!"

Fortunately, Spooky was in a talkative mood. He'd fallen into a crevice that had been hidden by thick tangles of juniper. Seconds later, Bean was peering into the pitch-black hole.

"You down there?"

"Yeah."

"You okay?"

"Yeah. I banged my crazy bone something wicked."

"Can you climb out?"

There were some scuffling sounds as Spooky tried to find a way out. "I don't think so." For the first time he became aware of the echo of his own voice. "Hey, this must be a pretty big place. I can hear my voice echo."

"Don't move around," said Bean. "There could be another drop-off."

Too late. Spooky had taken an exploratory step in the darkness and the earth had fallen away beneath him. Bean heard his scream, then a loud splash.

"Spook!" Bean yelled. "Spook! What happened?"

The violent thrashing sounds issuing from the cavern answered the question. Somehow, Spooky had fallen into deep water.

"Spook!" Bean repeated helplessly. "Spook!"

A series of spits and sputters indicated that at least he was alive.

"Saltwater!" Spooky exclaimed at last.

Bean, holding himself by a juniper branch, leaned into the hole as far as he dared. "How deep?"

"Not very," said Spooky, still choking from time to time to force the water from his lungs. "I can touch bottom. It's slimy."

"I'm going for help," said Bean. "You gonna be all right?"

There was a brief pause. Clearly the idea of standing up to his neck in stagnant water at the bottom of a black hole didn't appeal to Spooky. "I guess," he said. "Can't you find a rope anywhere?"

"Sure, I've got a pocket full of it," said Bean, hoping a feeble attempt at humor would ease the desperation in his friend's voice. "Don't worry. I'll be back before you know it."

"Yeah, sure," said Spooky meekly. "I'll just wait here, okay?"

Bean laughed, but it wasn't sincere. He had no idea what Spooky had gotten himself into, or what other dangers might lurk in the darkness at the bottom of the hole. "There's bound to be some rope in Billy Pringle's yard," Bean said. "I'll be right back."

With that he stood, then ran blindly down the slope. More than once he missed the narrow path and found himself knee-deep in blackberry bushes. By the time he felt the road under his feet, he was scratched from head to foot. But none of that made any difference. He had to get Spooky out of the hole.

The door to Billy Pringle's house stood open. In the pale light of the distant street lamp, Bean could make out the figure of someone sitting on the front step. "Billy?" he said tentatively. "Is that you?"

"Should be," said Billy. His voice was distinctive, as was the odd little raspberry he made at the end of his sentences. "Hard to tell in the dark."

"I'm Bean," said Bean.

"You're a frog," said Billy.

"If you say so," Bean replied. He'd spent many hours talking to Billy over the years, so nothing he said was surprising. "I need some rope, Billy. You got any?"

"Sure," said Billy. "Help yourself."

Bean looked around the junk-filled yard. All he could make out were some of the larger items: a washing machine, some chairs, lots of tires, some pot buoys, a rusted car chassis or two. None of it was any good, he knew. That would have made it useless to Billy. He collected only the things nobody else wanted. "Any idea where I could find some rope?"

"In the refrigerator," said Billy, as if it was the first place anyone would look.

The doorless refrigerator leaned against a nearby tree at a perilous angle. Bean picked his way through the refuse and reached inside. He pulled out a fistful of odds and ends of rope, none more than three feet long, in keeping with Billy's philosophy of uselessness. "I shoulda known," he said to himself.

"Find what you need?" Billy asked. "Men's and boys' apparel is on the second floor."

There was no second floor.

"Yeah," said Bean. "I think so. You don't have any longer pieces?"

"Sure," Billy replied. He got up and walked effortlessly through the debris to the refrigerator. "I got some longer than a dog. Some longer than a cat. Some longer than an alarm clock. Some—"

"No," said Bean, thinking of Spooky waiting in the darkness. "I mean, longer than these."

"Those are my ropes," said Billy, a little confused. "How can I have rope longer than my ropes?"

"Never mind," said Bean, grabbing a handful. "I'll tie 'em together."

"I'm good at that!" Billy volunteered, grabbing a handful himself. "You know what we can do? Tie 'em all together and make one great big long one!"

To Billy it had been an original idea. He was a little disappointed when Bean didn't show suitable enthusiasm, but he began tying the ends together anyway.

"All I need is twenty or thirty feet," said Bean.

Billy had already begun expertly threading the ends of two pieces of rope together, but Bean's comment made him stop. "You do?"

"Do what?" said Bean, tying furiously.

"Need twenty or thirty feet," Billy clarified.

"That's right."

Billy thought this over. "You'd trip on 'em," he said at last.

Bean laughed in spite of himself. He remembered that one had to be very specific when talking with Billy Pringle or the conversation could end up miles off track. "No," said Bean. "I need a piece of rope twenty or thirty feet long. If we tie a bunch of these together, we should be able to make what I need."

"Oh!" said Billy. "I see."

Apparently that was all the information he required. He set to his task as if it were the most important thing he'd ever done. "There!" he said at last. He handed Bean the rope he'd made, a good fifteen feet long. The knots were perfect.

Bean took the multicolored rope and tied it to his own, which had been made up of four pieces and was about ten feet in length. He coiled it around his arm. "That should do," he said. "Thanks, Billy."

"You're welcome," said Billy proudly. He returned to the apple crate and sat down.

Bean wondered how long he would sit there. Perhaps he sat there every night. The thought brought inspiration. "Billy?" he said after gingerly making his way through the junk to the road. "You ain't seen anything strange up here, have you?"

"Up where?" asked Billy. He wanted to make sure he understood.

"Up here. On the roads around Pogus Point."

"I seen you," said Billy.

Bean rephrased the question. "Have you seen anyone around here late at night that you didn't recognize?"

Billy thought about this. "Yup. I did."

"Who was it?" Bean asked excitedly. This might be the first real clue to the identity of the Black Moriah.

"I don't know," said Billy. "I didn't recognize him." Once again Bean had asked the right question in the wrong way. "I mean, what can you tell me about 'im? Can you describe 'im?"

"Sure," said Billy, and that was all.

"Would you, please," said Bean with more patience than he felt.

"Now?"

"Yes."

"To you?"

"Yes."

"Well," said Billy thoughtfully, "he was pretty tall. He wore a hood up over his head, but it wasn't a hood really, it was a dark green wool blanket he tucked down his coat and pulled up over his head like a hood. It looked black in the dark. The coat was black, too. An' he smelled bad."

No doubt Billy Pringle had seen the Black Moriah.

"And black pants and black socks," Billy added for good measure.

"A regular Goth," Bean said to himself. He looked at Billy. "Has anyone asked you if you've seen the Black Moriah?"

"Nope."

"Do you know what the Black Moriah is?"

"Not even if you hit me over the head with it."

People didn't give Billy Pringle much credit. None of the investigators had taken the time to ask him if he'd seen anything out of the ordinary. Mind, you had to ask very carefully or you might end up with a description of the weather patterns in Outer Mongolia. "I don't s'pose you have a flashlight," Bean asked.

"Sure, lots of 'em."

"I mean, one that works."

"You mean one that makes light?"

"Yeah."

"Nope."

"Or a phone?"

"One that works?" Billy asked again.

"Yeah."

"Nope."

"Well, thanks for the rope," said Bean. He turned to start back down the road.

"I got a stick of margarine!" Billy offered helpfully.

"No, thanks, Billy. I need something that'll let me see in the dark."

"A seeing-eye dog?"

"No."

"I guess you're right," said Billy. "Cats see better in the dark. So do owls. I don't have either of them."

Bean decided to try one last approach. "How do you see in the dark, Billy?"

"Not very well," Billy replied. "Unless I've got a candle goin'. But then it ain't dark anymore, is it?"

"Do you have a candle an' some matches that work?" said Bean anxiously.

"Sure."

"May I borrow them?"

"Sure. They're inside. I'll go in an' get 'em."

"Great."

Billy went inside and, after a little banging around, reemerged with a lighted candle. "I couldn't find it at first," he said. "It was too dark." He strode easily across the debris, like Jesus walking on the water, and brought the candle and a pack of matches to Bean. "Here."

"I'll bring it back in a few minutes," said Bean. With that, he blew out the candle and ran back down the road.

As he neared the crevice where Spooky had fallen, Bean couldn't help but wonder if he would run into the man with the flashlight. Where had he gone? What was he up to? If only Spooky hadn't fallen down the hole, all the questions might be answered by now.

"Spook? You still there?" Bean called into the hole.

"Yeah," said Spook weakly. "An' I'm freezin'. Did you get some rope?"

"Yeah," said Bean, cinching one end of the rope around the trunk of a nearby birch tree. He tossed the other end into the hole and was relieved to hear it splash.

"Hey!" said Spooky, grabbing the rope. "Warn me when you're gonna start throwin' things on my head, will ya?"

Despite the complaint, Bean could tell Spooky was relieved. "Can you pull yourself up?"

Spooky didn't reply. Instead, he applied all his strength to the task of dragging himself up the rope and, within a minute, was clear of the hole.

"You okay?" asked Bean.

"I will be," said Spooky, shaking the water from his hair like a dog. "That place is huge down there."

"We'll have to check it out sometime," said Bean disinterestedly. At the moment he was more concerned with getting Spooky back to the tree house, where it was warm and dry. "Here, take my coat."

Spooky didn't argue. "Did you see the guy with the flashlight?"

"Nope," said Bean as they made their way down the path.

"Too bad," said Spooky. "I'll bet there's another hole up there, just like the one I fell in. That's where he went."

"Maybe so," said Bean sleepily. Exhaustion had finally caught up with him. He was too tired to think straight, and it was taking all his concentration to navigate the path in the pitch dark. Then he remembered the candle. "Hold on a second." He wrestled the candle and matches from his pocket. "Here, hold this." He searched for Spooky's hand in the dark and slipped the candle between his fingers.

"Hey!" said Spooky. "You had this all the time?"

Bean struck a match, but it just smoldered and died. "'Course not. Billy gave it to me."

He struck another match, with the same result.

"He give you them matches, too?" Spooky asked.

"Yeah."

"Then you might as well forget it. They're prob'ly older'n dirt."

"Third time never fails," said Bean. He struck a third match and it burst to life. He applied it to the candlewick. "Hold still, will ya? You're shakin'."

Spooky didn't reply. He just kept shaking, but not because he was wet and cold.

Bean looked up and, in the golden glow of the match, saw a look of raw terror in Spooky's eyes. He was looking over Bean's shoulder.

"What is it?" he said, not wanting to know.

Spooky made some gurgling sounds in his throat. Then, all at once, Bean heard a slight hissing sound and was overwhelmed by the suffocating stink of rotting flesh.

They'd found the Black Moriah.

20
No Flesh on His Bones

A LOW, GUTTURAL MOAN sent chills down Bean's back. Suddenly he forgot his exhaustion. There was no time to think. No time to react logically. He had one thought: run! And that's what he did, with no doubt that Spooky would be on his tail. Right behind them, they could hear the footsteps of the foul-smelling demon in black.

As they hurtled blindly down the hill, holding their hands in front of their faces to fend off the branches that seemed to grab and tear at them like countless fleshless hands, they slipped and fell. Frantically, they scrambled to their feet and resumed their flight. But they couldn't out-distance the ghastly specter that pursued them. It didn't slip or fall, but plodded after them as if it could see in the dark.

Halfway down the hill Bean made a wrong turn. A split-second later he found himself surrounded on all sides by a dense circle of trees. They were trapped.

"Go!" Spooky cried as he careened into Bean in the darkness. "Go!"

"I can't!" said Bean. "It's a dead-end."

Directly behind them, they could hear the heavy footsteps and the labored, raspy breathing of the Black Moriah.

"What do we do now?" said Spooky, shaking in his sneakers.

All at once Bean's emotions got the best of him. His terror, fear, anger, and frustration, combined with bone-deep fatigue, made him lash out at the unseen enemy. He turned to confront the Black Moriah. "I've had it with you!" he screamed. "What did you do with Ab?"

The demon stopped suddenly in its tracks. Then, without warning, Bean charged.

"What're you doin'?" cried Spooky, trying to grab his friend as he flew by in the darkness, but he missed. He watched in helpless disbelief as the shadow that was Bean flung himself upon the shadow that was the Black Moriah. Half expecting the hideous creature to devour his assailant in a single bite, Spooky was stunned when, with a mighty lurch to free himself from Bean's grasp, the inhuman beast turned and fled, with Bean in hot pursuit.

"I don't believe he's doin' this," gasped Spooky, scurrying up the gravel-covered slope. "I don't believe *I'm* doin' this!"

Hampered by the darkness in which he repeatedly tripped and slid, Bean was no match for the Black Moriah, who seemed to have a supernatural ability to see in the dark. In a matter of seconds, he was no more than a wildly fleeing shadow in the distance, threading his way through the sharp-edged boulders of the slag heap. As Bean watched breathlessly, the figure disappeared. Bean pulled to a stop. "Where's Ab?" he yelled at the top of his voice. "If she's hurt, I'm gonna haunt you the rest of your life!"

Spooky came panting up beside him. "What're you, nuts? Where'd he go?"

"Into the rocks," said Bean. He bent over and put his hands on his knees, trying to catch his breath.

"He ran," Spooky puffed.

"He sure did," Bean agreed.

"Why, I thought he was gonna pull your head off an' stuff it down your neck. What made you run at 'im like that?"

"I don't know," Bean confessed. He was having a hard time believing it himself.

Spooky was impressed. "I wouldn't've done it."

Neither would Bean, if he'd been thinking clearly.

"You had 'im," said Spooky, his voice full of admiration. "You actually had 'im."

Bean took a deep lungfull of air. "He ain't no more the Black Moriah than I am."

"But how'd he run so fast in the dark?" Spooky wanted to know. He tossed a sharp glance among the rocks where the apparition had disappeared.

Bean didn't know, but he had a strong suspicion that, as his father would have said, there was a logical explanation.

There was no point in trying to follow the Black Moriah to his lair in the dark, where he clearly had an advantage. There was also the danger that one of them, or both, could fall down another hole. Reluctantly, Bean decided to go back to the tree house. Suddenly, he was hungry.

"You look like you been rollin' around in the briars," Spooky observed as he slurped the last drops of chicken noodle soup from his plastic bowl. Bean was covered with scratches and they itched like crazy, but he was too excited to notice. "What do we do now?" said Spooky. "Tell Wruggles what we found?"

Bean had gone through two bowls of soup and a peanut butter and jelly sandwich, and it seemed like the best food he'd ever tasted. "We got no evidence."

"We got our story," said Spooky.

"Yeah, as if people don't already think we're crazy. All we got to do is tell 'em we grabbed the Black Moriah, but he got away."

Spooky could see Bean's point. "So, what do we do? You think he's got Ab?"

The thought that the Black Moriah might have kidnapped Ab and hidden her away somewhere was oddly comforting, but it was almost more than Bean dared hope. "I don't know," he said. "I gotta get some sleep."

He collapsed on his bunk and didn't move a muscle until his watch alarm went off at five o'clock in the morning.

"What'd you set that thing so early for?" Spooky complained groggily.

"I forgot," said Bean. Then, with a sickening feeling in his heart, he remembered that Ab's memorial service was planned for that afternoon.

"Go back to sleep."

Vivid memories of the events of the previous night came flooding back into Bean's mind. "I can't sleep," he said. "Ab might be out there some-where. We gotta find 'er." Somehow he felt that he had to find Ab before the memorial service—that if she were officially pronounced dead, it would be too late. It didn't make sense, but that's how he felt.

He bounced out of bed, fully dressed, and splashed his face with cold, soapy water from the dishpan where Spooky had washed the soup bowls.

Spooky pulled on his sweater and sneakers. "You wanna go back up there?"

"Where else? Maybe there's a trail we can follow an' find out where he went."

162

Spooky wasn't too optimistic about finding any kind of trail across bare granite, but he didn't say so. Bean was more like his old self again, and he wasn't going to do anything to discourage him.

"That Black Moriah don't know what he's in for. Let's go," said Bean. He was already halfway down the tree. Spooky grabbed a couple of peanut butter Power Bars from the shelf and stuffed them in his pocket, then scrambled down behind Bean.

"Wait there," said Bean from the back step of his house. "I gotta get something."

He opened the screen door quietly, went into the house, and came out two minutes later carrying the bag containing his father's video camera by the strap. "If we see anything this time, we're gonna get *real* proof," he said.

"Bean!" Bean's mother called sleepily from her bedroom window. "I thought I heard the trapdoor slam. Where are you off to so early?"

"Oh, just out an' around," said Bean, slinging the bag over his shoulder.

"Don't you want some breakfast?"

"Nope. We ate late last night."

Mrs. Carver was encouraged by the upbeat tone of her son's voice. "You're sure?"

"Yup."

"Is that Dad's video camera?"

"Yeah. We're gonna take some pictures. See ya!"

"Be careful with it," Mrs. Carver cautioned, "or he'll have your hide." She went back to bed. Her husband had been right. Bean was back.

As the boys climbed the familiar hill to the ledges overlooking Hurricane Reach, Bean felt he knew the path by heart. About halfway to the top, he saw something in the grass and bent to pick it up. "Here's the candle," he said.

"An' here're the matches," said Spooky, retrieving them from a nest of blueberry bushes.

"Remind me to get 'em back to Billy," said Bean, tucking the objects into his pocket.

Spooky nodded at a box canyon of trees off to their left. "That must be where we ran off the path."

Bean searched the cliff side for footprints, but there was no dusty gravel or dirt that would have captured them. Slowly, the boys made their way across the cliff top to the ravine where the Black Moriah had disappeared.

"Last I saw of 'im was over there," said Bean.

Spooky's eyes followed to where his companion was pointing. "I don't see anywhere he could've gone."

Neither did Bean, but common sense told him the Black Moriah hadn't simply evaporated into thin air.

Spooky scanned the area. "Where's the hole I fell in?"

"Over there somewhere." Bean nodded toward a broad tangle of juniper and blackberry bushes, and Spooky went to investigate.

"We shoulda brought a flashlight," said Spooky.

"It's daylight," Bean said offhandedly. Remembering he had heard the man with the flashlight move a stone, and convinced that that man and the Black Moriah were one and the same, Bean began pushing and kicking at some of the larger rocks in the area where he'd last seen the specter. Nothing happened.

"It ain't daylight down there," said Spooky, who knelt to look under a thick juniper bush.

"You find it?"

Spooky dropped a stone into the blackness, and half a second later there was a responding splash. "I'd say so," he said, holding up the rope they'd used the night before. "Give me the candle. I wanna look."

Bean, not getting any satisfaction from his attempts to move the rocks, lit the candle and handed it to Spooky, who was already halfway down the hole.

Spooky held it below him. "This thing don't give much light," he complained. "I see the ledge I was standin' on."

"Go on down," said Bean. "I'm right behind you."

A moment later, the boys were standing on a flat shelf about a foot wide. "Hold the candle down here," said Bean, bending down.

Spooky did as he was told. "What'd you see?"

"This is strange," said Bean, running his hand over the ledge. "It's smooth."

"Just a piece of cut granite that landed that way," said Spooky.

"I don't think so." Bean took the candle from Spooky and edged carefully along the shelf. "The wall's the same," he said. "This place is manmade."

"Can't be," said Spooky in disbelief.

Bean bent down and ran his hand over the lip. "Check it out," he said. "This is all cut and dressed stone."

Spooky conducted his own investigation and arrived at the same conclusion. He stood up. "Let me have that." He took the candle from Bean and held it overhead. "Look at that."

In the dim halo of candlelight, Bean could make out heavy iron girders overlaid with thick wooden beams that formed a roof over the cavern.

"What do you s'pose it is?" Spooky asked.

"Something to do with the quarry days," said Bean. "Otherwise it'd be made of concrete."

"Get out the camera and take some pictures," said Spooky.

Bean dug out the camera and turned it on. "Dang! No tape! I can't believe . . . Hey, wait a minute." He pushed a little button on the side of the camera, and the built-in spotlight made a bright circle on the opposite wall, a good thirty feet away.

Spooky blew out the candle. "Look at the size of this place."

Bean scanned the wall with the spotlight. "Look there. Stairs."

Sure enough, a set of perfectly symmetrical steps was carved into the sheer granite face of the far wall. "There must be another way in at the top of them stairs."

Bean examined the end wall to the left in the same way. The light revealed nothing but a flat surface of cut stones about thirty feet wide and forty feet high. The wall on the other end, though, held a surprise. "Doors!" they cried in unison.

Judging from the location of the hinges, the massive oak doors, which took up more than half the wall and were framed with wrought iron, had at one time opened inward. It was obvious from the rust and overgrowth of slime covering them that they hadn't been opened in a very long time.

Bean lowered the light to the dark abyss at their feet, revealing a black rectangle of stagnant, murky water skirted by another shelf two to three feet wide just above the surface.

"I musta just missed that when I fell in last night," said Spooky, alarmed at how close he'd come to hitting the ledge.

Bean dragged the beam of light slowly along the surface of the water, searching for anything that might give a clue as to the former use of the underground room. But nothing prepared them for what appeared in the pale halo of light.

"The *Jellybean*!" Spooky cried.

The discovery nearly took Bean's breath away. "We found it!"

This exultation was followed immediately by the obvious question. "But how did it get here?"

Bean directed the light at the doors to the cavern, concentrating the beam on the hinges. There was no way they had been used, not in a hundred years. He handed the camera to Spooky. "I'm goin' down."

"What? Why?" Spooky sputtered. "All we wanted was evidence. That's evidence, ain't it? Let's go tell Wruggles."

Bean grabbed the rope and descended into the darkness. "We will," he said, breathing heavily as he descended to the lower ledge. His sneakers slapped loudly as he dropped the last five feet. Spooky kept him in the spotlight as he crawled up on the sub, which had been secured to rings in the shelf by ropes at the bow and stern.

"It's padlocked!" said Bean.

Spooky was feeling more and more uneasy. "Let's go, Bean. This place is givin' me the creeps. We oughtta get help."

Ignoring his companion, Bean grabbed the padlock and, in frustration, slammed it sharply against the turret. Nothing could have prepared him for the shock when, as the initial concussion echoed and died, it was answered by a series of sharp thuds on the hatch—from the inside.

"Somebody's in there!" said Bean with alarm. All he could think was that Ab was imprisoned in the submarine. Had she been there the whole time? How much air did she have? "Quick! Get me a rock."

Without argument, Spooky scrambled up the rope and out of the hole.

"Ab!" Bean yelled in the darkness, pounding on the hatch. "You in there?"

Two more thuds replied, these much weaker than the first.

"Hold on! Hold on! Spooky? You comin'?"

"Got one," said Spooky, lowering himself down the rope with one hand while cradling a rock in the other. The camera strap was slung over his shoulder. "Here." He handed Bean the stone.

"Good," said Bean. "Stand back." He leaned close to the turret. "Cover your ears," he yelled.

A second later both boys were nearly deafened as Bean repeatedly smashed the rock against the padlock. Fortunately, the lock hadn't been built to withstand much abuse, and after five or six blows, it flew to pieces. Spooky trained the light on the hatch as Bean flung it open. "Ab!" he cried desperately into the darkness.

It wasn't Ab's voice that replied. "Sorry to disappoint you."

"Captain Kittredge!" said Spooky. He shined the camera light into the sub and on the captain's upturned face, which was deathly pale, his blood-shot eyes rimmed with dark circles.

"Captain," said Bean, struggling to conceal his disappointment, "are you alone in there?"

"The loneliest I've ever been," said the captain. He reached up and gripped the lip of the hatch with his frail hands. "I'm afraid I can't . . . I need some help."

Bean reached down, seized the captain under the armpits, and helped him out of the sub.

"Thank you," said the captain, clearly exhausted. He slid down the side of the sub, planted shaky feet on the mooring ledge, and massaged his ringing ears. "I thought I was going to end my days in there," he said, closing his eyes and sighing deeply. "Speaking of which, what day is it?"

Bean told him.

"Only six days," he said. "It seemed like forever."

"How'd you get in there?" Spooky asked.

"I was kidnapped. I went to check the sub the morning after the storm, and he came up behind me."

"Who did?"

"Turns out it was Steerforth, the fellow I'd rented it to. He said he had a gun, which I had no reason to doubt, and made me help him winch the sub over the side. Then he made me get in and he got in, too."

"Musta been wicked cramped," said Spooky.

"That's putting it mildly," the captain replied. He stretched his arms and legs, inhaling slowly and deeply. "Fortunately, I had enough of my wits about me, once we got here, to incapacitate *Jellybean,* so it wouldn't be of any use to him."

"What'd you do?" Bean asked.

"A simple matter of dropping the lead ballast. She can't go under now."

"And a submarine that can't dive is just a funny-lookin' boat," Spooky deduced. "Good idea!"

The captain massaged his elbows. "Seemed so at the time. Of course, it didn't make him too happy. Next thing I knew, I was alone in the sub, bound and gagged. I finally managed to free myself not three or four hours ago. But, as you know, the hatch was locked. What time is it?"

"About six o'clock," said Bean with a quick glance at his watch.

"How can it be dark already?" the captain wanted to know.

"Six in the morning," Bean clarified. "We're in some kinda cave."

Spooky ran the spotlight around the cave.

"A flood shed." The captain nodded knowingly. "I've seen similar places."

"Flood shed?" said Bean.

"Yes," the captain replied, looking at the ceiling as Spooky ran the light over the rafters. "The quarrymen dug it out, down below the low-water line, then knocked out the wall between the pit and the sea. I can smell this is saltwater. Those doors were in two parts, like a huge Dutch door," he explained. "The top part would be open at high tide to let shallow barges in. For boats with a deeper draft, the bottom doors would be open. With the bottom doors shut, the barges would stay afloat even at low tide so they could be loaded with granite blocks and equipment."

"Like the locks in the Panama Canal," said Spooky, recalling a show he'd seen on the History Channel.

"Very much like that, young man," said the captain. "No doubt that's how Steerforth got the sub in here, through those bottom doors. Rotted away by now, I should imagine. How did you know where to find me?"

Bean would have loved to take credit for good detective work, but he couldn't. "Dumb luck," he said. He related the string of events that had brought them here.

"Dark business," said the captain when Bean had finished the story. He patted Bean on the shoulder. "I'm sure Abby is all right."

"You think he kidnapped her, too?" Bean asked hopefully.

"I expect so," the captain replied thoughtfully. "Otherwise, she'd have turned up by now, one way or the other."

"Then we gotta find her, before it's too late."

"I wouldn't worry about him hurting her," said the captain. "He fed me once a day, and let me out to . . . take care of business. He won't do any worse by a little girl, I shouldn't think. He's not interested in us; we just happened to be in the wrong place at the wrong time."

Bean didn't share the Captain's optimism. It was all too likely that Steerforth had been the one who tried to drown him. He tried not to think about it.

"What's he up to?" asked Bean. "Did you talk to 'im?"

"Not too easy when you're gagged," said the captain.

Still, piece by piece, Bean thought, things were falling into place.

"So, now do we tell Wruggles?" asked Spooky.

"You bet," said Bean enthusiastically. "We're gonna get the whole town back up here to find Ab."

Captain Kittredge put a hand on Bean's shoulder. "Wait a second," he said slyly. "I think I may have a better idea."

The plan was simple: Enlisting only Constable Wruggles and Tiny Martin, the strongest man in town, they would hide near the quarry and wait until the kidnapper returned to feed his prisoners, then catch him in the act. What could be easier? Bean and Spooky volunteered to wait for the rest of the day. Meantime, for the plan to work, Captain Kittredge would have to stay out of sight, so Bean told him how he could get to his house without being seen by taking a little-used trail over Armbrust Hill. Once there, he would inform Bean's mother of their plans, have her contact Constable Wruggles, and then get some much-needed sleep.

Spooky was appointed to find a perfect hiding place while Bean kept a lookout. From his vantage point high atop the cliff, Bean could see in all directions. It was unlikely that anyone would approach through the thick forest and dense undergrowth to make the treacherous climb up the north or south side of the slag heaps. Nor was anyone likely to scale the cliff.

So Bean concentrated his efforts on the path sloping sharply down to the east.

After a while he grew bored, so he started scanning the horizon in all directions through the viewfinder of the video camera. With its powerful 600x zoom lens, he could pull even Matinicus Island—fifteen miles away— so close it seemed he could reach out and touch it. A seagull floated effortlessly into the circles of his sight, and Bean followed it to the old lobster pound on Lane's Island. Once upon a time, the pound—a little cove that had been dammed off to form a holding pen for lobsters—would have been a hive of activity by this time of the morning, but it was no longer in use, and everything was eerily still.

Bean's eyes were drawn to a slight motion near the trees at the edge of the cove. At first, it seemed like a bundle of laundry or a sail bag, probably fallen from some passing yacht, that had washed up on the shore. It pulsed rhythmically at the prodding of the gentle, curious waves. He zoomed in for a closer look and instantly saw that it wasn't a bundle at all.

21
BACK FROM THE DEAD

BEAN LOWERED THE CAMERA as if to verify with his naked eyes what he'd seen. "Ab!" he cried. He looked through the camera again, and this time zoomed in as tightly as it would go. She was curled up in a ball and didn't move. The question was, was she just lying there, or had she been washed up by the tide?

His heart trembling with fear, he focused the camera on her face. Her eyes were lightly closed and she seemed to be sleeping. Positioned the way she was, there was no way to tell if she was breathing. Whatever the truth was, he had to know. He stuck the camera in the crotch of a tree and raced across the cliff top toward the path.

"Spooky!" he yelled. "Where are you?"

"Can't you see me?"

Bean scanned the area frantically. "No! Where are you?"

"I'm hidin'," said Spooky. "If you can't see me, neither can he."

"Never mind that," said Bean, running toward the path. "I've found Ab!"

"You what?" said Spooky, bursting from a little cavern beneath a clump of trees on the far side of the clearing. "Where?"

"On Lane's Island. Come on, we gotta get to her!"

With that, Bean was gone, and it was all Spooky could do to keep him in sight as they ran across the bridge at Indian Creek, along the road skirting Armbrust Hill, over the bridge to Lane's Island, and down the dirt road toward the old lobster pound.

A narrow path, nearly invisible beneath several years' worth of undergrowth, branched off through the woods to the right. Spooky knew that it ended on the shore at the head of the cove. Here, Bean suddenly pulled up.

"What's the matter?" said Spooky, stopping beside him. "Where is she?"

Bean nodded toward the cove. "There."

Spooky, puffing loudly, brushed his sweaty hair from his eyes and peered through the trees. "Where? On the shore?"

"Yeah," said Bean, gulping his breath nervously.

"So, what're we waitin' for?" Spooky demanded. "Let's go." He started to run but quickly realized that Bean wasn't following him. "What's your problem, Beans? Come on!"

Bean began to walk slowly forward, but his heart clearly wasn't in it. "What if she's dead?" he said flatly.

It was Spooky's turn to stop. "Oh," he said. He thought a minute, then said with a good deal more resolution than he felt, "Well, if she is, there's nothin' we can do about it. But if she ain't, what if she needs us?"

It took no more than that to shake Bean to his senses. Within ten seconds, he and Spooky had worked their way through the undergrowth onto the shore. There, still curled up in a ball in a nest of decaying eelgrass, was Ab.

"Ab?" said Bean tentatively as they approached, half afraid he'd wake her, half afraid he couldn't.

Ab didn't stir.

Both boys were filled with apprehension as they made their way slowly along the shore.

"Ab?" said Bean a little louder.

This time she responded. Her eyelids flickered briefly and, like someone being troubled from a sound sleep, she grumbled and turned over.

Bean's heart ballooned with joy and nearly floated from his chest. Laughter burst uncontrollably from his lips as he raced to close the distance between them. "Ab!" he yelled. "Wake up!"

Spooky watched from a little distance. He felt relief, too—more than he ever had before—but he knew that Bean and Ab had something special and this moment was just for the two of them. "It's like a perfume commercial," he said with a sigh. It was the only romantic thing he could think of.

"Who do you think you are?" said Bean, dropping to his knees. "Sleeping Beauty?" He wanted to pick her up and hold her, but he didn't know how she'd take that, so he poked her in the ribs instead.

"Hey!" said Ab groggily. "Knock it off."

Bean tickled her and, laughing in spite of herself, she turned over, propped herself up on her elbows, and forced her eyes open. "Bean?"

"You can just call me Prince Charming," said Bean with a grand sweep of his hand.

"And a few other names," said Ab sarcastically. She looked around, yawning and rubbing her eyes. "What are we doing here?"

"You tell me," said Bean. "This is where we found you."

"We, who?"

"We, me," said Spooky, who figured this was as good a time as any to make his presence known.

"Who else?" said Ab. "Anyone want to tell me what's going on?" She sat up and modestly adjusted her clothing.

"You've been gone for six days, Ab," said Bean slowly. He'd seen television shows where people had received a smack on the head and forgotten everything they knew, and even who they were. Maybe that's what had happened to her, except she seemed to remember who he and Spooky were, and herself, too, come to think of it. Maybe something else was wrong. Maybe she'd been drugged the whole time. He'd seen that on TV, too. "Nobody knew where you were." He explained about the memorial service. Suddenly, Ab realized the horror that her parents must be going through.

"We've got to stop that," she said. She tried to stand, but was too wobbly on her feet. She sat down again.

"Take your time," said Bean. "No rush."

Ab rubbed her head. "I'm remembering now," she said, as if waking from a dream. "I was in a little stone room."

"A stone room?"

"Yes. Sixteen steps long and eight steps wide." It was all coming back now. She trembled suddenly. "With a thick iron door, and no windows. No one could hear me from there." She began to cry as the memory overtook her. "When I screamed, it nearly made me deaf."

Bean sat beside her and put his arm around her shoulder. "It's okay now, Abs," he said softly. "You're okay."

Without a word, she flung her arms around him and buried her face in his neck. Bean sensed she needed to cry, and he didn't tell her not to, he just let the tears come. Spooky waited patiently, skipping rocks across the placid waters of the lobster pound. Finally, after a few choking sobs, Ab began to talk.

"I was in the Widowmaker when he caught me," she said, sniffing.

"Do you know who it was?" Bean asked.

"The Black Moriah," said Ab. "Or whoever's pretending to be him. The smell was just awful, but it was fish bait."

"So, he smelled like you?" said Spooky approvingly.

Ab was suddenly aware of how smelly and grimy she was. She was embarrassed and pulled self-consciously away from Bean. If she smelled bad, he didn't notice, or at least he was far too happy to notice.

"Don't worry about it," said Bean, wishing she'd lean against him again. She didn't. "What happened then?"

"He grabbed me. There was no way out. He put this cloth over my mouth—."

Ab was still operating in a fog, under the effects of chloroform. It took a great deal of effort for her to concentrate. "Well, next thing I knew I was in the little stone room."

"You don't know how he got you there?" Bean asked.

Ab shook her head. "There were some candles and a blanket, and that was all. No matches. I kept a candle going the whole time, and he'd come to bring me my food and let me out—blindfolded—for a few minutes to go to the bathroom in a bucket. I wasn't outside, though. I peeked. I was in a big room. Then he'd lead me back to the little room and take my blind-fold off, and there'd be a fresh candle going."

"He never said anything?" Spooky asked.

"Not a word."

"So, you don't know who it is?"

Again, Ab shook her head.

"Did you escape?"

Ab considered the question carefully. "I don't think so. If I did, I must have been walking in my sleep, because I don't remember getting out, or how I got here."

"He musta knocked you out with chloroform and then rowed you over here some time before dawn, no more'n two hours ago."

"How do you know that?" she asked.

"If you'd been here longer, you'd be covered with dew," Bean explained.

"Pretty good thinking for a Beanbag," said Ab.

The sound of her teasing was like music to Bean's ears.

Spooky had been thinking. "The question is, why did he bring her here?"

Bean shrugged. "We can worry 'bout all that later. I think now we'd better get her home. Her folks are gonna freak big-time."

"It might not be a good idea just to walk in on 'em," Spooky suggested. "You'd prob'ly give 'em heart failure."

Bean and Ab nodded. "Good point," they said in unison. "You run ahead and break it to them, Bean. I'll be right behind you," said Ab. She squeezed his elbow. "No theatrics, okay? No 'Hey! You'll never guess what I found. Come on, guess!'" she said.

"Don't be so immature," said Bean, mimicking Ab and dragging out the last syllable for what seemed like a minute and a half. She stuck her tongue out at him, and he responded in kind. Then, without warning, tears began to form in her eyes. "Let's go."

In order to avoid prying eyes, they took the same path over Armbrust Hill that Captain Kittredge had taken. Then they crossed Fog Hollow to the backyard of the Moses Webster House. There, Bean opened the back porch door and told Ab and Spooky to wait until he called them. Ab, still a little groggy, sat down on a big plastic bag of pine bark mulch and leaned her head against the wall. Spooky paced back and forth. "They're gonna freak," he said. "The whole town's gonna freak. They're all ready for that memorial service."

"Mrs. Proverb?" Bean said quietly, rapping on the trim of the kitchen door, which stood open. He could see the proprietress at the counter, peeling apples.

Mrs. Proverb turned halfway. "Bean? Come on in. Take a seat." She nodded at the table. "Have you had your breakfast?"

"No," said Bean. "I was—"

"You haven't?" She looked at the clock on the wall. "Why, it's nearly eight. I have some blueberry muffins in the warmer. Help yourself."

"Thanks," said Bean. "Maybe later. Are Mr. and Mrs. Peterson around?"

"They're upstairs," said Mrs. Proverb, returning to her chore with a heavy sigh, "getting ready for the memorial service, and packing."

"Packing?"

"Yes. I'm afraid Mrs. Peterson isn't bearing up very well after . . . well . . ." She didn't conclude the thought. "You know. And Mr. Peterson decided it's best if they go back home to New York. They have to get away from the island. Too many memories."

"I have something to tell them," said Bean, trying to conceal his excitement. It was important not to shock Mrs. Peterson, especially in her emotional state. "Do you think it's okay if I go on up?"

"I don't suppose they'd mind," Mrs. Proverb replied, though there was no enthusiasm in her voice. "You have to say good-bye, of course, so . . . Just be sure you knock first."

At the top of the stairs, Bean could hear Mrs. Peterson crying, as she had been for the last six days. From where he stood, he could see her sitting in the seat by the bay window. She had a tissue in her hand and was pressing it under her nose. Even from that distance, he could see that her eyes were filled with tears. Mr. Peterson was carefully folding clothes and putting them in suitcases. Neither of them was saying anything.

"Mr. and Mrs. Peterson?" said Bean, climbing the last step to the upstairs foyer.

Mr. Peterson came to the door, a pair of Ab's jeans draped over his arm. "Oh, hello, Arthur," he said. He cast a sidelong glance at his wife. "I'm afraid this isn't a very good time for a visit."

Bean wanted to shout that it was the best possible time, but he restrained himself. "I've got something to tell you, Mr. Peterson."

"What is it?"

"Well, would you mind?" He gestured for Mr. Peterson to meet him in the hall. "What?" Mr. Peterson responded, his patience clearly tried. "I have a lot to do."

Bean stole a look at Mrs. Peterson, to be sure she couldn't overhear. He took Mr. Peterson by the elbow and pulled him into a book-lined alcove. "Mr. Peterson," he said slowly, trying to form the words in the gentlest way he could. "Ab's all right. We found her."

For a second, Mr. Peterson just stood there. Then, as if someone had struck him behind the knees, he sank to the floor, his mouth open, trying to form words that wouldn't come.

"She was kidnapped," said Bean, putting a reassuring hand on Mr. Peterson's shoulder. "Whoever done it kept 'er in some kinda cellar or something. . . ."

Mr. Peterson looked up at Bean in shock.

"Oh, he didn't do . . . nothin' happened to 'er or anything," Bean added hastily. "He fed 'er an' took care of 'er all right. She's downstairs now. I figured you might wanna come see 'er before you tell . . ." He nodded toward the Petersons' bedroom.

Mr. Peterson followed Bean's eyes. Then, looking back at Bean, he nodded, but he was still too overcome by emotion to say anything.

"C'mon," said Bean, helping Mr. Peterson to his feet.

"I've . . . I've got to go downstairs for a minute," Mr. Peterson called to his wife. She didn't seem to notice how his voice was shaking. She kept staring out the window. "I'll be right back."

By the time they reached the bottom of the stairs, Mr. Peterson had mastered himself, and it was all Bean could do to keep up. Together, they burst into the living room. "Where is she?" he snapped, turning in circles as if he expected to find her on the couch or in one of the chairs. "Where is she?" he demanded, seizing Bean by the shoulders and shaking him.

"Out on the back porch," said Bean, his teeth rattling in his head.

Suddenly, Mr. Peterson stopped shaking him and squeezed him so hard it hurt. "Bean, you're not lying, are you? You've got more sense than—"

"No, really!" said Bean with alarm. "We didn't know what would happen if she just walked in on everybody, so she's waitin' out there 'til I could tell you."

Mr. Peterson let him go.

Bean thought it best to avoid Mrs. Proverb's natural curiosity at the moment, so he led Mr. Peterson to the back porch. When he opened the door, Spooky appeared. "Alvin," said Mr. Peterson. "Where is she?"

Spooky pointed to Ab, who had curled up and fallen asleep again on a bag of pine bark.

The sight of Mr. Peterson bursting into silent tears was one neither Bean nor Spooky would ever forget, and in those tears they saw how much he loved his daughter, and how much he had suffered thinking she was gone. He walked across the stone floor without making a sound, as if Ab was an apparition and the slightest noise would make her disappear. Slowly he sank beside her and ran his hand across her cheek, wiping aside a stringy clump of her hair. "Ab?" he whispered.

Responding to the sound of her father's voice, Ab opened her eyes. "Dad?" she said.

All at once, Mr. Peterson picked her up in his arms as if she were no heavier than a rag doll and gripped her to his chest, burying his face in her neck. He burst into uncontrollable tears. So did Ab.

Bean and Spooky quietly left the porch and waited outside.

There were a lot of tears that morning as the town embraced the news that Ab had been found alive and well. The doctor at the medical center pronounced her physically fit, though he cautioned the Petersons that there was no way of telling how the experience might affect her mentally or emotionally.

After allowing an appropriate amount of time for the reunion, Constable Wruggles came to the Moses Webster House to interview Ab and get a firsthand account of what had happened to her. She told him what she had told Bean and Spooky.

"Well," said Wruggles when she had finished, "I don't know what to say. We've never had a kidnappin' out here."

"What are you going to do?" asked Mr. Proverb.

Wruggles shrugged his shoulders. "I'm not sure. Sounds to me like this room she was kept in must be left over from the granite days, but there was never any quarryin' on Lane's Island, where she was found."

"She must've been moved there, then," Spooky suggested logically.

"Musta been," Wruggles agreed, "but from where?"

Bean had been thinking. "Is there anyone left on the island who worked in the quarries?"

Wruggles considered this. "Hmm, I see what you're gettin' at. Yeah, two men that I can think of—Stump Budrow and Connie Young. Connie's at the convalescent center over in Rockland, and he ain't doin' too well from what I hear." Wruggles tapped his temple meaningfully. "Stump's the best bet." Wruggles glanced at his watch. "Most likely he's down to the hardware store this time've day. I'll go have a talk with 'im—see if he remembers anything like that."

"Can I go with you?" Bean asked.

"Me, too," said Spooky.

"Don't see why not," Wruggles replied. "How 'bout you, young lady?" he added, looking at Ab.

Mr. Peterson spoke up. "I don't think that would be a good idea. Ab's been through enough already. She needs her sleep."

"I've been sleeping all morning, Dad," Ab protested mildly. After a long, hot shower, a couple of Mrs. Proverb's excellent blueberry muffins, and a few hours' nap, she felt refreshed and was just as eager as anyone to get to the bottom of what had happened to her. "I'll be okay."

"Oh, Ab," said her mother, distressed, "I'd really rather you stayed here with us. Let the boys and Constable Wruggles take care of this."

Wruggles interrupted. "I can imagine how you feel, Mrs. Peterson. But it might be good if she was there. Maybe she an' Stumpy between 'em can come up with a clue for us."

In the end, Mrs. Peterson reluctantly gave her permission, provided her husband went along as well.

The walk downtown normally took about two and a half minutes, but Main Street was crowded with people who all wanted to greet Ab and tell her how glad they were that she was okay and how they'd been thinking of her and praying for her. By the time Wruggles and his four followers stepped from the sidewalk into the cool, welcoming gloom of the hardware store, a good fifteen minutes had passed.

Stumpy Budrow sat in his customary chair near the potbellied stove and, as usual, had been talking island politics with a couple of his cronies. Wruggles pulled up a chair and stated his business. It took two or three tellings to get the whole story out, because Stump was hard of hearing, but finally he got the message.

"I see," he said. He cast his mind back nearly seventy years to when he was a boy, doing odd jobs around the quarry. "Sounds like a powder bunker," he said after a while.

Bean had never heard the term. "What's that?"

Drew Meescham, who owned the hardware store, was the town historian. He had been sorting nails at a nearby counter and listening with interest. "That's where they kept the explosives," he explained. "It had to be someplace pretty well away from the quarry. Usually a little room cut in stone, the way Ab described."

Wruggles turned to Stump. "Where was this powder bunker, Stumpy?"

"Oh, there was lots of 'em," said Stump. "Every quarry had two or three."

"What about up by the Widowmaker?" Bean asked. "Was there any up there?"

Stump struggled with his memory. "Musta been," he said at last. "Sure. But I didn't work up there, so I can't tell you where it mighta been. When they closed the quarries, they heaped up slag on them old sheds. Pretty well buried by now, I imagine. Prob'ly collapsed under all that weight."

"Sheds?" said Bean. "Is that what you call the powder bunker?"

"No, no. The flood sheds were big rooms cut in the rock," Stump explained. "The bunkers were usually cut into the side walls of those sheds."

Drew Meescham, whose special interest was the island's quarrying days, spoke up. "They were cut into the cliffs and opening onto the ocean, so barges could be brought right in and loaded with cut granite between tides, then floated out again."

"The locks," Spooky interjected, then he explained Captain Kittredge's theory about the use of the room.

"Makes sense," said Stump after Spooky had repeated himself a couple of times. "The captain was right. There woulda been two doors—one above high water, and the other below. They'd open 'em both to bring in the barge, then close the bottom one, so when the tide went out, she'd still be afloat."

"When they heaped up slag, like you said," Bean theorized, "wouldn't it have covered both doors?"

Stump considered this. "Not necessarily. More 'n likely they pushed the big rocks in first—boulders. They prob'ly heaped up in such a way that they left an openin'. Same as the caves that are all through them slag piles."

"The fella in the submarine must've found out about that somehow," said Wruggles.

"That's what Captain Kittredge said," said Bean.

All at once things fell together in Bean's overheated brain. "Oh, my gosh! Captain Kittredge! I forgot all about 'im."

So had Spooky. In all the excitement and relief of finding Ab and returning her to her parents, the captain had clean slipped their minds. Between them, in animated fits and starts, the boys told how they had found the sub, with Captain Kittredge trapped inside. When they finished, you could hear a pin drop.

"Where is he now?" said Wruggles.

"Up in the tree house. We had this plan." He outlined the captain's scheme.

"Mighta worked," Wruggles said, wagging his head appreciatively. "'Course, it's too late now. The Black Moriah let Ab go."

Bean protested. "But he doesn't know we found Captain Kittredge."

"Bet he does by now," said Wruggles. "Whoever this is, he's a pretty savvy fella. I don't think we can count on 'im slippin' up like that."

Everyone nodded in agreement.

Drew had been thinking. "With that setup, this fella could drive the sub in and out without anyone bein' the wiser."

"But why?" said Mr. Peterson. "What's the point?"

"I know the point," said Bean. "He's lookin' for pirate treasure." Slowly and carefully, repeating himself often for Stumpy's sake, Bean laid out the evidence, from Professor Prinderby's scholarly investigation right up to their theories about the Black Moriah. "But that plan fell apart the day Spook found the sub down to Indian Creek. It must've got away from 'im somehow."

"That's when the Black Moriah showed up," Ab observed. "We figure that without the minisub, he thought he lost his secrecy, so he decided to try scaring people off so he could be free to look for the treasure."

"Sounds like he didn't count on a coupla kids who don't scare so easy," said Drew when the story was finished. "I've heard tales of buried treasure—you hear 'em all the time up an' down the coast of Maine. I take 'em with a grain of salt. But that business of the poem and everything you've told us sounds like the professor might just be onto the real McCoy."

"I'm gonna have to shut down the ferry, so no one can get off the island," Wruggles decided. "Folks're gonna be madder'n wet hens, but there's nothin' else I can do. Meanwhile," he added, turning to Bean, Ab, and Spooky, "you kids go to the tree house an' get the captain. We got us a spook to catch."

The kids told Captain Kittredge what had happened. "Too bad," he said as they steadied him on the tree house ladder. "The simplest plans are always best." He jumped the last three steps to the ground. "Oh, well, can't be helped." He tousled Ab's hair. "The important thing is you're okay. Must've been horrible for you."

"I'd rather have been where I was than locked in the sub," said Ab.

Kittredge smiled and looked at the boys. "This is an exceptional young lady," he said, patting her on the back. He sat down on the bottom wrung of the ladder. The kids thought he was resting from the climb down from the tree house, but he was studying Ab carefully. "What do you remember?" he said after a while.

Ab felt a little uncomfortable under the intensity of the captain's gaze. "What do you mean?"

"You were kidnapped for a reason," said Kittredge. "You must have

181

been getting close to something. What were you doing just before you were captured?"

In all the panic and confusion, and the struggle to survive, Ab had nearly forgotten what she had found tucked away in the seaweed at the Widowmaker. Her eyes lit up. "I did find something!"

22
"A Cross, a Stone, My Mark Alone"

WHATEVER AB HAD IN MIND, she kept it to herself as everyone waited on pins and needles for the next low tide, which was at eight o'clock that night. Even Bean couldn't get more than an inscrutable smile from her when he begged to be let in on the secret. Meanwhile, over a steaming bowl of Mrs. Carver's homemade haddock chowder, Captain Kittredge told his story to Constable Wruggles.

"Two kidnappin's," said Wruggles when the story was ended. "Looks like I'm gonna hafta call the sheriff's office again."

"I'm going to take a nap," Ab said with a twinkle in her eye. "Wake me up for supper. It could be a long night. Constable Wruggles, I think we're going to need Hutch Swenson's boat. And Bean? Make sure you've got good batteries in your flashlight. And you'd better bring your hip boots."

The search party consisted of the kids together with Bean's and Ab's dads, Constable Wruggles, Tiny Martin, and Hutch Swenson. As directed, Hutch had his boat waiting at Link Dyer's wharf by 7:55 that evening.

"Ab, you have to tell us what this is all about," said Mr. Peterson, who had been as exasperated as Bean with his failure to get any firm information from his daughter.

"You'll see, Dad," she responded with a smile. "Mr. Swenson, take us to the Widowmaker."

Hutch glanced at Mr. Peterson for approval. With the doctor's warning of the possibility of mental and emotional repercussions from her kidnapping ringing in his ears, Mr. Peterson decided to play along, at least for a while. He nodded.

"Whatever you say," replied Hutch. Once everyone was in the boat, he throttled the engines forward, and the launch surged across the placid waters toward the jagged spires of the Orphans, reddish gold in the light of the waning sun.

Ab didn't say anything for the remainder of the brief trip. She stood in the bow like the figurehead on an old Spanish galleon, and stared straight ahead as the gaping mouth of the Widowmaker came into view. "Pull up between the cliff and the Orphans," she said at last, turning to the harbormaster. "Get us as close as you can so we can get into the cave."

Hutch looked doubtfully at Constable Wruggles.

"This is her show," said Wruggles with a shrug. "Best do as she says."

Hutch expertly nudged the boat to within a foot of the ledge at the lip of the cave and, wedging a boat hook into a crevice in the cliff face, held them in place. "Go to it," he said.

Ab pulled up the hip boots she'd borrowed from Mr. Proverb and stepped over the side onto the ledge.

"Ab, you be careful," said her dad, holding her hand.

"I will," she said. "You be careful, too. It's slippery in there, and there's kind of a little pool that drops off. It shouldn't be too deep, but everyone roll up your boots."

"There's nothin' in there, Ab," Bean whispered worriedly in her ear as he climbed over beside her. He was wondering if maybe Ab's ordeal over the past few days had left her a little light in the head. "I been inside."

"So have I," said Ab confidently. "You just didn't look in the right place. Neither did the Black Moriah."

She didn't sound insane, Bean thought. They ducked as they entered the cave, and the rest of the party followed suit.

Holding tightly to both Bean's hand and her dad's, Ab lowered herself into the pool, which, as she suspected, was only a little deeper than the last time she was here.

"Are you sure you know what you're doing?" said her father. "You can't see much in this light. The bottom might drop away at any minute."

"It's flat," said Ab. "Come on in, the water's fine!"

A little dismayed by her breezy confidence, Bean, Spooky, and the rest of the men followed her example, and soon all were up to their knees in the brine. They could feel the frigid water even through their thick rubber boots.

"This way," said Ab, crossing to the far side of the cavern.

"This is a lot bigger'n it looks outside," Wruggles observed.

Each of the searchers had a flashlight, and the conflicting beams zigzagged across one another in the darkness like light sabers, providing random glimpses of the craggy wall.

The men waited impatiently while Ab, bent so low that her ponytail dragged in the water, began sifting through the thick growth of kelp that clung to everything below the low-water line.

"Ab," said her father at last, "what are you looking for? Did you lose something?"

For a second Ab didn't reply, then she almost giggled. "No, I found something. Bring your lights over here."

Once again, feeling it best to placate her, the men and boys complied with Ab's wishes. "Shine them down here," she said, pointing at the curtain of seaweed.

"I don't see nothin'," said Spooky.

"At least tell us what we're s'posed to be lookin' for, Ab," said Bean with mounting frustration.

Ab plunged her hands into the frigid water, seized two fistfuls of seaweed, and—perhaps a little more dramatically than was absolutely necessary—lifted them clear of the tide, revealing the door she had found just before the Black Moriah captured her.

"It's a door!" exclaimed several voices at once.

Mr. Peterson and Constable Wruggles bent to examine the weathered iron hatch.

"Well, I'll be," said Wruggles. "So it is."

"This has been here a very long time," added Mr. Peterson, examining the door closely in the beam of his light. "A very long time."

"That's not all," said Ab with a good deal of self-satisfaction. "Look at this." With all her strength, she ripped the cloak of seaweed from the wall and threw it aside. Then she took the flashlight from her pocket and trained the beacon on the area just above the door.

At first it was hard to make out the deep, algae-covered scratches in the surface of the rock, but playing their lights back and forth to highlight the indentations, they were finally able to make out the writing.

"An X," said Mr. Peterson in disbelief.

"An' look below it," said Bean, pushing to the front of the little throng. "A.T. . . . Abnezar Twing."

"*A cross, a stone, my mark alone*," said Ab almost breathlessly. "I knew it! Whatever's behind there is Abnezar Twing's treasure."

"So, open it, already!" Spooky cried, unable to contain himself any longer.

"That's not going to be as easy as it sounds," said Mr. Peterson, standing up. "It's probably corroded shut after all these years."

"Stand aside," Tiny Martin commanded as he plodded noisily through the water. With his mighty legs braced on the cave floor, he gripped the sides of the door with his weathered fingers and pulled with all his might.

The group held its collective breath expectantly, but nothing happened.

"She's in there pretty good," said Tiny at last, his face red and beaded with sweat. "What we need's a lever."

"Wait a second," said Wruggles. "I got just the ticket." So saying, he fairly ran back to the mouth of the cave and called out, "Hutch, you got that wreckin' bar you was usin' to jack them moorin's?"

The answer was a loud clang. A moment later, Wruggles returned to the group and handed the six-foot-long steel bar to Tiny. "Give 'er a go with that, Tiny."

Tiny slammed the wedge-shaped end of the bar between the door and the rock a couple of times until he got a good hold, then, positioning himself to maximize his leverage, began rocking the bar backward and forward, in and out.

"It still ain't budgin'," Spooky observed unnecessarily.

For several more minutes Tiny grunted and strained and groaned, refusing to give up. The veins on his forehead popped out until Bean thought his head would explode. Tiny's powerful muscles bulged and throbbed with the strain of his effort until, just as the mighty man's strength seemed about to give out, a deafening screech of metal ricocheted through the cavern.

At once many hands seized the edges of the door and pulled as it began to yield. Bean, Ab, and Spooky watched, wide-eyed and speechless, as at last the ancient hinges gave up the fight with a haunting squeal and the door scraped slowly open, revealing a dark black opening.

Tiny stood aside. "Have at 'er," he said, wiping the sweat from his brow. "She's all yours."

"You sayin' someone should go in there?" said Wruggles, clearly uncomfortable with the thought.

Mr. Peterson got down on his knees. Icy water poured into his boots, but he didn't seem to notice. He shined his light into the darkness. "Steps!"

"Steps?" said Wruggles. "Where do they go?"

"Can't tell," said Mr. Peterson. "Up and out of sight."

"Up?" said Bean.

"Up."

"Well," said Tiny, "*I* sure can't fit through there."

Wruggles patted his prodigious belly. "Me neither."

"Nor I," said Mr. Peterson. "I think it best if we notify the authorities on the mainland."

"No way!" Ab and Spooky chorused at once.

"We can't!" said Bean, casting a pleading glance at his father. "Not after all we been through!"

Captain Carver dropped to his knees beside Mr. Peterson and shined his light into the opening. "Looks solid enough, as far as I can tell." He stood up. "It'll take someone small."

Ab cringed. "Not me! I've had enough of places like that."

"Me neither," said Spooky. He didn't offer any reasons, but the look of sheer terror in his eyes said enough.

"I'll go," said Bean.

Surprisingly enough, his father didn't object. "I'll let you go in, Bean. But only a step or two at a time. If there's any kind of cave-in, or any fallen rocks, you get out of there, you understand?"

Bean understood. The men moved aside as Bean positioned himself in the little doorway.

"Get me a rope," said Captain Carver. Tiny Martin trudged across the cave and had Hutch Swenson toss him a stout nylon line, which he brought back and gave to Captain Carver.

"Tie this through your belt," said the captain. "If I tug on it, you get out. No questions asked. You got that?"

"Yes, sir," said Bean, cinching the rope through his belt loop. Though his hands shook and his heart felt as if it were trying to beat him up from the inside out, he was eager to get on with the job.

"And take this," said his dad, switching off his flashlight and tucking it into Bean's rear pocket. "Just in case."

Taking a deep breath to steady his nerves, Bean shined his flashlight up the rough-hewn steps and crawled through the opening.

"I don't think this is such a hot idea," said Wruggles as Bean's nether regions disappeared through the doorway.

"I agree with Wruggles," said Mr. Peterson. "We've got no idea what's in there."

"The way I see it," said Captain Carver, again lowering himself to his knees and shining the light up the steps after Bean, "if he doesn't run into any kind of landfall in the first few feet, he finds an open tunnel. This old cave isn't likely to collapse all of a sudden after all these years. I trust Bean to have enough sense to get out if it gets dicey."

Ab and Spooky shined their lights into each other's eyes and exchanged doubtful glances.

"Can you still see him?" said Ab apprehensively.

Captain Carver had squeezed through the door as far as he could go, and his voice, muffled by his body, sounded miles away. "He's okay," he called. "Bean?" he said as he watched his son stand up and begin to climb the steps, "what do you see?"

"More steps," said Bean. "It goes up about fifteen feet, I'd say, then I can't see where it goes."

"Okay," said Captain Carver, gripping his fingers tightly around the rope. "Remember, if you suspect anything's wrong, you get your fanny back down here."

"I will," said Bean. "Man, it's dark in here." He didn't like the feel of the place. The walls seemed to close in on all sides, and he felt as if the musty smell would suffocate him. But something stronger was calling him, something deep inside—the need to discover an answer to the mystery of the Widowmaker. Screwing up his courage, he continued his climb. Within seconds he had put twenty shallow steps behind him and reached a small platform, where the tunnel disappeared in thick darkness.

For two or three seconds nothing happened, and all was quiet on Bean's end of the rope.

"Bean?" said Captain Carver.

There was no response.

"I told you this wasn't a good idea," said Wruggles nervously.

"Bean!" Captain Carver repeated, his voice edgy with tension.

Suddenly, at the top of the tunnel, Bean gasped. Half a second later, his flashlight came crashing down the steps, casting wild shadows as it tumbled. Smashing into the iron frame of the door, it went out.

"Bean!" Captain Carver called again, reflexively trying to force himself through the door. But even Bean, skinny as he was, had had difficulty fitting through the tiny opening, so there was no way a full-grown man could make it.

"I'm okay, Dad," said Bean, his voice little more than a raspy whisper.

Captain Carver let out a sigh of relief as he saw his son's auxiliary light flick on. He backed briefly out of the doorway. "He's okay."

"What happened?" Spooky demanded.

"I don't know yet," said Captain Carver. He stuck himself into the opening again. "Bean? What happened? Are you all right?"

"Yeah," said Bean, his voice choked with an emotion his father couldn't interpret. "But you're never gonna believe what we just found. No one'd *ever* believe this."

"What is it?"

"Just a minute," said Bean. He'd finally run up against something even his imagination wasn't big enough to take in.

The cavern in which he found himself was twice the size of the flood shed where he and Spooky had found the minisub, but its rough sides— sloping upward and inward at odd angles to a point where the walls nearly joined at the top—made it clear this wasn't a man-made shelter. All of this he noticed at a subconscious level, but the bulk of his attention was focused on the huge object that filled the cavern. From the moment the beam of his flashlight fell on a distinctive arrangement of ropes and rigging, there was no doubt what he'd found—an ancient wooden frigate, demasted but otherwise fully intact.

So astonished he couldn't speak, Bean slowly swept the light from stem to stern. The ship's poop deck loomed high in the gloomy shadows at the far end of the cave, its single door wide open. The deck was well ordered, with ropes carefully looped in tight coils and everything else at the ready. The foredeck, which Bean knew was called the forecastle, was also slightly elevated above the main deck, though not as high as the stern.

"Bean?" His father's voice drifted up from below like a call from another world. "What have you found?"

"Just a minute," said Bean, trying to catch his breath. How could he describe this to anyone? They'd think he was crazy. He needed witnesses. "Tell Ab and Spooky to come up here."

Captain Carver relayed the message.

"No way," Spooky said flatly. "Not for all the warts on a witch."

"I can't let her do it," said Mr. Peterson, folding his daughter in his arm. "Not after all she's been through."

Ab looked up at her father. "Please, Dad," she said. "If you don't let me go, it's like I've been through it all for nothing. Please?" She wasn't whining or begging; she was simply asking his permission. He knew that she would abide by his decision.

Mr. Peterson agonized for long seconds. "Is it safe?" he asked finally.

"Bean? Is it safe?" Captain Carver asked.

"Yeah. It's safe. It's a huge cave. Tell 'em they gotta see this."

"Dad?" said Ab. She wouldn't ask again.

"All right," said Mr. Peterson, though his heart clearly wasn't in it. "But you get out of there at the least sign of trouble. You hear me, young lady?"

"Yes, sir," said Ab, although part of her had been hoping he would forbid her to go. It would have been a good excuse. Overcoming her fear of what lay beyond the little door, she got on her hands and knees and crawled through the opening.

"You be careful," said Mr. Peterson.

"I will," Ab assured him. Lighting the way with her flashlight, she began to climb the stairs. "Bean? Where are you?"

Bean had shut off his light and was standing in the dark. "Up here. Come on."

"Where's your light?"

"In my hand," said Bean. He wanted her to discover the ship the same way he had. "Don't worry, come on up."

When she got to the top of the steps, she shined the light in Bean's face. "What are you doing?"

Bean reached out and, taking her hand that held the flashlight, gently directed it to the ancient ship. "Look what we found."

"Ab?" said her father from below, where he had wedged himself beside Captain Carver in the narrow opening. "Are you okay? Is everything all right?"

Ab didn't reply. For once in her life, she was speechless.

"She's okay," Bean said on her behalf, watching with profound satisfaction as Ab's eyes widened. He could see the veins in her neck pulsing with excitement. "What do you think of that?"

Ab was transfixed by the name etched among the ornate carvings that rimmed the ship's forecastle. "*Destiny*," she said, once she found her tongue. "It's Abnezar Twing's pirate ship." Her voice was reverent with awe.

"That'd be my guess," Bean replied.

For the next minute or so, they studied the ship in the wide beams of their flashlights. Huge drops of water fell from the darkness high above and splattered to the deck. In places, the wood had been nearly worn through by countless thousands of drops over hundreds of years. Now and then the ship creaked and groaned under the burden of its age and weight.

"This is what the guy in the submarine was lookin' for," said Bean. "That's why he disguised himself as the Black Moriah and tried to scare everyone away."

"But I never imagined anything like this," Ab replied, her voice weak with amazement. "How did it get here?"

Bean couldn't even imagine an explanation to that riddle. He shrugged. "Do you think—"

Bean completed her thought. "Do I think there's a treasure some-where in the hold? You bet I do."

"Do we go aboard?"

"I don't think that'd be safe," said Bean with uncustomary caution. "There's no way of tellin' if the wood's rotted out. We could go right through 'er."

"So, what do we do?"

"We gotta get everyone in here somehow and figure it out. Let's go back down."

Ab didn't move.

"Ab? Come on. Let's go tell everybody."

Still Ab didn't move. Her light was fixed on something in the bow of the ship. Bean swept his light in that direction and saw what it was that had riveted Ab's attention. His heart jumped to his throat. "A skeleton!"

"And look," said Ab, pointing the halo of her light a little farther up the bow, "another one!"

"Don't look now," said Bean as his light trapped a heap of skeletons in the shadow of the forecastle.

Tattered rags of clothing clung to some of the bones. Some wore boots. All had a sword fastened to a belt around the waist.

A shiver tripped up Ab's spine as she counted the dead crew. "Six men," she said. "Somehow Twing killed them and sealed them in here. I'm sure it has something to do with the explosion Mrs. Prinderby talked about."

"What explosion?"

Ab reminded Bean of the story Mrs. Prinderby had told about the *Dauntless* and its pursuit of the *Privilege* and the *Destiny*. "When the two ships left Portland," she concluded, they had twelve men between them. Six hands per ship. This," she scanned the bones with her flashlight, "was the crew of the *Destiny*."

"Makes sense," said Bean, recalling the details of the story. "Twing didn't just bury his treasure, he buried the ship—crew an' all."

Ab thought of the poem. "'And none remain to save/For hoard and men and secrets keep/Forever in their grave.' No witnesses," she said.

"Until now," Bean added. "He musta figured he'd come back for the treasure one day. But he went down with the *Privilege*."

"Bean, let's get out of here. I'm not having fun anymore."

Somehow, though, their feet were rooted to the spot as images spun through their minds of what it must have been like for the sailors in the last days of their lives, on a ship trapped in a grave of stone, locked behind the little door at the bottom of the stone steps.

"Kids?" came a call from below. "What's going on up there?"

The sound of Captain Carver's voice brought them back to their senses. "Just a minute," Bean called. He turned to Ab. "Well, I guess we know what the guy passin' himself off as the Black Moriah was lookin' for all along."

Bean deliberated with himself a minute longer. "They'll never believe this."

"You're right," said Ab. "We've got to have proof, or they're just going to think we're crazy. We should have brought a camera."

With a sickening feeling in the pit of his stomach, Bean remembered his father's video camera, which he and Spooky had left wedged in the crotch of a tree on the cliffs above. "Oh, man, I'm gonna be toast," he said, more to himself than to Ab.

"Why?"

Bean explained.

"Well, there's nothing we can do about that now," said Ab. "You'll just have to go get it once we're out of here. But for now, if we could just get something . . . a sword or one of those cannonballs, even a piece of rope."

Bean shook his head slightly. Deep inside, he wanted Ab to talk him into going aboard the ship, but something told him it was a dangerous idea. "I don't know . . ."

"Oh, come on, Bean," Ab goaded. "Look, there's a board over there. We can make one of those bridge thingies."

"A gangplank," said Bean. It felt nice to correct her for a change.

"Whatever," said Ab. She sidled along the ledge to where the plank lay and picked up one end. "It seems sturdy enough."

Bean relented. "Okay, but we just go up to the gunnel and grab whatever we can reach, all right? That's all we need to do."

"Whatever you say," said Ab, but something in the tone of her voice left Bean unconvinced.

They picked up the plank and lifted one end over the chasm between the ledge and the ship, then dropped it onto the gunwale.

"Bean? Ab?" called Captain Carver from the Widowmaker. "The tide's coming in. You'd best get down here right away."

"Okay," Bean called. "Just a minute or two. Don't worry. We're okay."

"What's going on up there?" Ab's father wanted to know. "Ab, don't you do anything foolish."

Too late. Ab, on her hands and knees, was already halfway across the gangplank. A moment later, she jumped over the gunwale and landed with a resounding thud on the deck. "It holds me!" she cried triumphantly.

"Are you nuts?" Bean whispered sharply, not wanting their fathers to overhear. "I told you not to—"

"Look," Ab interrupted, jumping up and down on the deck. "It's solid as anything."

Bean allowed that it sounded pretty solid. Holding his arms out to his sides like a tightrope walker, he spanned the chasm and dropped gently to the deck. It felt as firm as the day it was built.

"This thing's in incredible condition," he said.

"Bean!" his father yelled from below. "There's something strange about the way the tide's rising in here. You've got to get out now!"

Bean felt a sharp tug on the rope.

"Come on, Ab. Grab something an' let's go."

Ab tiptoed across the deck toward the nearest skeleton. "Just a minute. They'll believe us if we show them this guy's sword."

"I thought *I* was the crazy one," said Bean, his apprehension rising at Ab's uncustomary boldness. "Didn't you hear what my dad said?"

"I heard." She approached the skeleton quietly, as if afraid of waking it, and dropped to one knee. "This will just take a second."

"Abigail Peterson!" came her father's stern voice. "You get down here this instant! The tide's rising too fast!"

"Just a second!" Ab called. She took firm hold of the sword hilt, then drew it slowly from the scabbard, careful not to disturb the bones of the long-dead pirate. Triumphantly, she jumped to her feet and brandished the sword in the air. "Got it!"

Bean felt another mighty tug on his rope. "Good. Now let's get outta here."

They ran back down the gangplank as carelessly as if it had been a mile wide, then bounded down the stairs, with Bean in the lead. Just as he landed on the last step, it gave way beneath his feet. Without warning, an outcropping of rock near the top of the steps burst apart, giving way to an icy torrent of water that cascaded down on them.

"It's a booby trap!" Bean cried.

23
REVENGE OF THE WIDOWMAKER

IN THE WIDOWMAKER, the men were knocked off their feet by the force of the water spewing from the tiny doorway. For several seconds, it was each man for himself as they struggled to keep their heads above water and get their feet under them. Then, as abruptly as it had begun, the water stopped.

Mr. Peterson was the first to get to his feet. Seeing that Wruggles was floundering, he pulled him quickly to his knees, then rushed toward the door. "Ab!" he cried, his voice strained with fear.

"She's over here," said someone behind him. Turning, Mr. Peterson saw Tiny Martin, who had been thrown against the far wall of the cave like a rag doll, struggling to his feet with Ab's limp form in his arms.

Ab's dad ran through the knee-deep water, tripping and falling several times, until he was standing in front of Tiny, who held Ab as gently as if she were a wounded bird.

"She's okay, I think," said Tiny as he passed her carefully to her father. "She's breathin', anyway."

At that moment, Ab started coughing up lungfuls of seawater. She gagged on the salty brine and threw up.

"That's a good sign," said Wruggles.

Meanwhile, Captain Carver, who had given his flashlight to Bean, was groping frantically about, searching for his son. "I can't find Bean!" he cried. "Does anybody see him?"

"I'm out here, Dad" came the groggy reply from the mouth of the cave, where the force of the out-rushing water had nearly swept him into the Reach. Thinking quickly, Hutch Swenson had grabbed Bean's belt with a boat hook as he washed past.

Captain Carver sank to his knees like a man who had lost all his strength and said a brief prayer of thanks.

"Where's Spooky?" said Ab as soon as she was able to speak. Her father tenderly placed her on her feet.

"Spook!" Bean called, freeing himself from the boat hook.

"Spook!" Ab yelled almost simultaneously.

From somewhere in the darkness above, there was a groan.

Tiny Martin, the only one who had managed to hold onto his flashlight during the chaos, turned its rapidly weakening beam upward. There, straddling a slim outcropping of stone as if it were a bucking bronco, was Spooky. He was dazed. "What the heck happened?" he said, massaging his injured shoulder. "I feel like I been flushed down a toilet."

Spooky had described the experience perfectly. Despite the tumult of emotions that gripped each member of the search party, everyone began to laugh.

"It was a booby trap," said Bean as his father and Tiny helped Spooky down from the ledge. "The bottom step was rigged like a lever. I guess Ab an' me weren't heavy enough to trip it on the way up, or maybe it was just froze up after all this time, but when we come down one right after the other, we hit hard enough to set 'er off."

"It was meant to drown whoever come pokin' around, that's for sure," Wruggles observed. "Pretty good job of that, I'd say."

Captain Carver took Tiny's flashlight and shined it toward the little door, which was now halfway submerged in the rising tide. "I don't know," he said. "Whoever designed it didn't intend for anybody to live through it."

Bean was unsettled by the concern in his father's voice. "Whaddaya mean? You think there's more?"

"I think we'd better get out of here, pronto," the captain replied. "Everybody get back in the boat. Quick!"

Ab didn't seem to be listening. A quick sweep of the flashlight showed her rummaging blindly around in the rising water. "Wait. We can't go yet."

"Ab, now!" her father commanded.

"But—"

"No arguments," said her father. He grabbed her around the waist with one arm, then lifted her off her feet as if she weighed nothing at all and carried her to the mouth of the cave.

Spooky was wasting no time wading to safety in Tiny Martin's substantial wake. But halfway across the cave, he stepped on something. "Ow! What's that?"

"Never mind, Spook," said Captain Carver from the mouth of the cave. He lifted Ab and Bean into the boat. "Come on."

Whatever Spooky had stepped on, he had heard it scrape across the cave floor. He knew it was metal. Bending quickly, he reached into the rising water and ran the flat of his hand across the bottom until he found the offending object. Even in the darkness he could tell what it was. "A sword!" he said, plunging through the water toward safety.

Tiny had helped everyone else into the boat and was standing up to his chest in the frigid water, waiting to give Spooky a hand. "Come on, Spook!" he urged. "This whole place could come crashin' down any minute."

From the boat, Hutch trained the beam of the last remaining flashlight on Spooky as Tiny gripped him under the arms. In his hands, sure enough, was a sword. Ab grabbed it from him and handed to her father. "We found that in the cave," she said excitedly.

Tiny Martin, meanwhile, was just about to lift Spooky into the boat when from somewhere deep inside the cave came a deep, foreboding rumble. Tiny froze, holding Spooky over his head.

"Get in the boat!" Captain Carver bellowed. He was reaching out to take Spooky from Tiny's hands when a mighty flood of water gushed from the little door with ten times the force of the previous deluge. It was followed by an avalanche of stones. Once more, Tiny was knocked off his feet. This time, though, he'd been standing on the narrow granite lip separating the cave from the deep waters of the Reach. In the rising water, there was nothing left to stand on. He was swept under.

"Tiny can't swim!" Wruggles cried as the boat, pummeled by the outrushing water, smashed with a sickening thud against the nearest and smallest of the Orphans.

Somehow the big man, only his arms visible above the flood like the sturdy branches of a submerged tree, managed to hold Spooky aloft long enough for the men in the boat to grab him and pull him aboard.

"Tiny!" Wruggles hollered. "Hutch, get that light down here!"

Hutch Swenson had his hands full trying to keep the swirling waters from crushing the launch against the Orphans. He had surrendered the flashlight to Ab, who promptly shined it over the side.

Thinking quickly, Captain Carver grabbed a rope and tied a thick knot in the end of it. The other end he handed to Wruggles. "Tie that off," he ordered and, without another word, jumped overboard with the knotted end in his hands.

"Dad!" Bean cried reflexively.

For what seemed like minutes, as the roiling waters subsided, there was no sign of life in the impenetrable deep. The feeble beam of Ab's flashlight showed only the first few feet of rope, disappearing into the darkness.

Wruggles hadn't had time to tie off his end of the rope before Captain Carver jumped into the water, and now he and Mr. Peterson were holding onto it for all they were worth. Then, suddenly, it went limp. Frantically, they pulled it aboard. There was nothing at the other end.

"Give it to me," said Bean. "I'm goin' in!"

"No, you ain't," Wruggles snapped. "You stay put." Just to make sure, he gripped Bean firmly by the collar and held him fast.

"But I gotta—"

Bean's protest wasn't out of his mouth when Ab cried out. "Look! There he is!"

Captain Carver burst to the surface, gulping for air. With one hand he reached for the gunwale; his other arm gripped Tiny Martin by the neck.

Wruggles, turning Bean loose, grabbed the captain's hand. Mr. Peterson and Hutch Swenson—knowing that the boat was no longer in peril—bent over the side and grabbed the limp form of Tiny Martin by the armpits, then pulled his head and shoulders clear of the water.

Relieved of his burden, Captain Carver seized the gunwale with his free hand and hung there, catching his breath. "Get him aboard," he sputtered.

Between them, Wruggles, Mr. Peterson, Hutch Swenson, Bean, Ab, and Spooky managed to pull Tiny Martin's immense, waterlogged bulk into the boat and lay him flat on the floor. "Anybody know CPR?" said Wruggles helplessly.

"I do," said Ab, pushing her way through the little knot of men. She kneeled beside Tiny and firmly but gently tilted his head back. She clamped the thumb of her left hand over his lower jaw to hold his tongue in place, then took a deep breath, sealed his mouth with her own, and blew as hard as she could. Nothing happened.

"Dad, push on his chest, like this!" She crossed her hands and pushed at the air.

Her father knew what to do. He straddled the big man, placed his hands just below the sternum, and began pushing rhythmically. "Go on," he said, though he could feel no heartbeat in the massive chest and sensed that the situation was hopeless.

Once again, Ab released a lung full of breath into Tiny's mouth. Then another. And another. She was beginning to feel desperate, and she was getting dizzy and starting to hyperventilate. But she didn't stop. "Push harder, Dad," she commanded.

He pushed harder.

"He's gone," said Wruggles with resignation. He patted Ab's shoulder. "He's gone."

Ab didn't waste time replying. Instead she took one last deep breath and, feeling on the verge of passing out, emptied her lungs into Tiny's gaping mouth.

She had just removed her lips and fallen backward in a swoon when a little geyser of water erupted from Tiny's throat. Instantly, Mr. Peterson turned him on his side so the water could drain out. And drain it did, as Tiny coughed, choked, and sputtered. It took a full two minutes for his lungs to empty themselves. By that time, Wruggles and Peterson, their hearts swelling with relief, had pulled Captain Carver aboard and wrapped him in a coarse woolen blanket they'd found stowed in the cuddy.

At last, Tiny propped himself up on one elbow and, wiping the last dribble of seawater from his chin with the back of his hand, looked at Ab. "Best kiss I ever had," he said with a grin.

The tension broke like a cheap balloon, and everyone laughed the nervous laughter that often follows near disaster.

On the ride across the Reach to Link Dyer's wharf, Bean and Ab told everyone what they had found in the cave.

"A whole ship?" Wruggles asked, his credulity stretched to the limit. "How'd it get in there?"

Ab related the story of the *Destiny,* the *Privilege,* and the *Dauntless* as told her by Mrs. Prinderby, concluding: "The captain of the *Dauntless* heard a tremendous explosion. That must have something to do with it."

"It's not as far-fetched as it may sound," said Captain Carver. "Some pirates are known to have gone to great lengths to safeguard their treasure. My guess is there was a natural cleft in the shoreline back in those days, one big enough to hold the ship. I'm not sure how, but Twing could have put in there and somehow—perhaps with explosives, like Ab says—caused a landslide that concealed the ship without crushing it. If we could find a map of the coastline from those days, it might tell us something."

Shivering and soaked to the skin, the members of the search party climbed onto the float at Link Dyer's wharf.

"Listen up, everybody," said Wruggles. "I don't want anyone breathin' a word of what's happened tonight. Not until I can get some state police over here to look into this business of the kidnappin's."

Agreeing to this, the adult members of the search party clambered into an assortment of trucks and cars and prepared to drive to their homes to warm up, dry out, and think about how closely they had avoided a terrible tragedy—one planned by a pirate two hundred years ago.

"Let me say good night to Ab," said Bean when his father told him to hop into the truck.

"Okay," said his father, starting the engine. "But don't drag it out. I want to get home."

Mr. Peterson overheard the exchange and, with a nod, gave Ab permission to say good night.

"What was your idea, anyway?" Bean asked when they were out of earshot of the others.

"It didn't work," said Ab. "But we found the ship!"

"But what did you think was gonna happen?"

"I thought if we got word out that we'd found the treasure, the Black Moriah would show up and try to stop us from getting it. I figured, with all those men there, they'd just grab him, I guess. Then, when we found the door and the stairs, things just seemed to take off all by themselves."

"Not bad," said Bean with an approving pat on Ab's shoulder.

"For a girl?"

"I didn't say that," Bean defended himself. He fell silent for a minute. Ab knew the look in his eyes. "What are you thinking?"

"I got an idea," said Bean under his breath and, in a hurried whisper, told her what it was.

Later that night Bean and Spooky, warm and full of hot chicken soup and peanut butter and potato chip sandwiches, watched from the darkened window of the tree house and waited for the light to go off in the Carvers' bedroom window. When it did, they counted off fifteen long minutes, then climbed down the ladder and hurried off into the foggy night.

Once more the boys made their way to the rear of the Moses Webster House. Once more they waited. This time there was no storm, just the quiet, enfolding arms of the fog.

"You gonna tell me what this is all about?" Spooky asked as he crawled under the cover of the forsythia bush.

"You'll see," said Bean, his eyes fixed keenly on Daltry Lawson's bedroom window. "Any minute now."

It wasn't any minute, though. Two hours dragged slowly by.

Spooky glanced at his watch. "It's one-thirty."

"Just a little while longer," said Bean. He hadn't anticipated this long a wait. Maybe he was wrong about Lawson. Maybe it was a stupid plan. Or maybe Ab hadn't been able to do her part.

By two o'clock, with Spooky getting increasingly restless, Bean began to give up hope. The idea of slipping into his warm sleeping bag back in the tree house had an almost hypnotic appeal. "Okay," he said. "Bad idea. Let's go."

He had just gotten to his knees when the window of Daltry Lawson's room rattled ever so slightly. It wasn't the wind this time. There was none.

Bean grabbed Spooky by the arm and pulled him back into the shadows under the forsythia bush. "Shh!" he said, his chest tightening with suspense. "This is it."

There was no mistaking the furtive figure of a man climbing out the window and dropping softly to the ground. Nor was there any mistaking the fact that it was Daltry Lawson.

"You were right!" said Spooky, whispering sharply into Bean's ear. "He can walk."

"He can do more than walk," Bean replied.

As if to prove Bean's words, Lawson loped down the backyard in the direction of Indian Creek—passing not five feet from where the boys crouched in hiding—and disappeared into the fog.

"Good work, Ab," said Bean to himself. "Let's go," he said to Spooky. "We gotta keep 'im in sight without lettin' 'im know we're followin'."

"Take your shoes off," said Spooky, kicking off his sneakers.

Bean did the same and, shoes in hand, the boys followed Lawson into the fog, padding soundlessly through the wet grass with soaking socks.

Fortunately, Lawson seemed to have no suspicion that he wasn't alone on the road that night. He walked quickly and was careful to make as little sound as possible, but he kept to the middle of the road, and the boys had little difficulty keeping him in sight.

Once Bean was certain that Lawson was headed for the Widowmaker, he decided to take a shortcut, along the path that skirted Armbrust Hill, then over the bridge at the Race. They slipped their sneakers on.

"You think he's goin' up to the Widowmaker?" said Spooky, jogging to keep up with Bean as they made their way along the seldom used, overgrown path.

"I *know* that's where he's goin'. That wheelchair was just part of his disguise," said Bean. "No one would suspect a guy in a wheelchair of bein' the Black Moriah."

Spooky absorbed this information in silence. "So," he said finally, "he rents the minisub from Captain Kittredge and brings it out here to look for the treasure. Then the sub gets away from 'im, and we find it. So he has to think of another plan, and he figures he'll scare people off Pogus Point by pretendin' to be the Black Moriah."

Bean took up the thread from there. "So he shows up as a crippled guest at the Moses Webster House, an' gets a convenient room on the first floor—"

"So he can sneak out an' be the Black Moriah," said Spooky. "Pretty good idea. But why ain't he dressed up like the Black Moriah tonight?"

Bean thought he knew the answer to that. "'Cause he's in a hurry."

"Why?"

"Me an' Ab had a plan," Bean explained. "She was s'posed to get within earshot of his room an', when she was sure he could hear, but she could make it seem like she didn't know he could hear, she pretended to be on the phone talkin' to me 'bout findin' the treasure at the Widowmaker."

"But you didn't find it," Spooky objected. "Not exactly."

"He don't have to know that," said Bean. "All he knows is what he thinks he heard Ab tell me on the phone, which was all the truth up to where me an' her got on the ship. After that, we kinda made things up."

"Like what?"

"She was s'posed to say how we found the treasure, but the door was too small for Dad and the rest of 'em to get in an' bring it out. And that they'd be comin' up again first thing in the mornin' with tools an' things to widen the door an' get the treasure."

"So you figured Lawson would go up tonight an' take one final stab at gettin' the treasure."

"That's the plan," said Bean. "Worked like a charm."

Spooky almost laughed with admiration. "That Ab's some ol' smart."

"Whaddaya mean, Ab?" said Bean, halting in his tracks. "It was my idea."

"Oh, sure it was," Spooky replied mockingly. "Sure it was."

"It was!"

"Sure, whatever you say."

Bean saw there was no convincing his companion that he was the mastermind behind the scheme, so in frustration he jogged on. "We gotta get there before he does."

Atop the familiar cliff overlooking the Widowmaker, the boys hid themselves beneath the boughs of a wind-bent spruce tree and waited. They didn't have to wait long. No sooner had they settled themselves in the shielding nest of darkness than they heard the scuffling sound of footsteps on the path. Withdrawing deeper into the shadows, they watched Lawson emerge from the mists and, guided by a flashlight, make his way toward the slag heap where, earlier, Bean had seen the Black Moriah disappear.

Bean tapped Spooky on the knee and motioned him to follow.

To make as little noise as possible, the boys again took off their shoes. They emerged from hiding, bent low to avoid being seen as they pursued Lawson through the maze of slag. Losing sight of him for a moment, they rounded a corner just in time to see him disappear through a hidden cavity in the rocks. As quietly as possible, they made their way to the opening and poked their heads inside.

For a brief second, Lawson's flashlight afforded enough light so they could make out a set of steps carved in the stone, the same steps they'd seen on the far side of the wet dock the morning they'd found the minisub. Then the light switched off.

"It's the wet dock," Spooky whispered. "What's he doin' down there?"

Bean wasn't sure. He'd expected Lawson to go to the Widowmaker.

They waited in befuddled silence for a minute until Bean's short supply of patience ran out. "I'm goin' in," he decided. "You wait here an' I'll holler if I need you."

Spooky was more than happy to wait there. But just as Bean was about to enter the cave, he was snared in the sharp halo of Lawson's flashlight and stood frozen like a deer in the headlights.

"Got ya!" Lawson snapped, jumping suddenly from the cave. The boys' legs turned to lead with astonishment, so he had no trouble grabbing them both by their collars. "What are you doing following me?"

"We . . . we . . . we . . . ," Bean stuttered, but words failed him.

Spooky was at no such loss for words. "Let me go!" he cried, trying to free himself from Lawson's determined grasp. Lawson shook him violently. "You stay right here. Tell me what you're doing following me."

At last Bean recovered his tongue. "What are you doin' skulkin' around when you're s'posed to be in a wheelchair?"

That comment earned Bean a shaking of his own. "That's my business," Lawson snapped. "And it doesn't answer my question. You kids have been getting in the way all along. You're going to ruin everything. Now, I've got just the place for you. Get down there." He shined his light down the hole.

"Not so fast," said a voice behind them.

A strong pair of arms seemed to come from nowhere and seized Lawson by the back of the neck. In shock, he released his hold on the boys.

"Hold 'im good an' tight, Tiny," said Constable Wruggles.

Bean looked up in a combination of relief and amazement at the sight of the constable and Tiny Martin. "What're you doin' here?"

"Savin' your necks, I'd say," Wruggles replied. It was at that moment Bean saw that the constable had drawn his gun and was training it on the dumbfounded Lawson. "Ab called an' told me what you was up to. Seems you had a good plan, to a point."

"You're going to ruin everything!" Lawson replied, wriggling fiercely. But his efforts to free himself from Tiny's vicelike grip were in vain.

"That's the idea," said Wruggles calmly.

"You don't understand," Lawson complained.

"Let's see what I don't understand," said Wruggles, taking Lawson's flashlight from him and shining it in his eyes. "You made yourself out to be a cripple"—he ran the light briefly over Lawson's legs—"which you ain't. You come lurkin' 'round the Widowmaker when you figured it was your last chance to get at the treasure—"

"Treasure?" Lawson snapped. "I don't care about any treasure."

"Sure you don't," said Wruggles. "An' I'm the Wonderful Witch of the West. Tiny, give the man a little squeeze, will you? He talks too much."

Lawson squealed pitifully as Tiny applied more pressure to the back of his neck. "You don't understand," Lawson whined.

"Well, I guess you'll have plenty of time to tell me all about it down in the jail cell. Bring 'im along, Tiny."

With a thrust of his mighty arm, Tiny pushed Lawson ahead of him, and the rest fell in behind for the walk down the hill.

"Hold on," said Bean as they were about to descend the path. "Give me the flashlight for a second, will you?"

Wruggles gave him the flashlight, and Bean shined it among the trees until he found what he was looking for. "There it is!" he said as the beam fell on his father's video camera. He removed it from the crotch of the tree and inspected it briefly. "I hope this fog didn't pooch it."

"What's that doin' here?" Wruggles asked, looking over his shoulder.

"I'll tell you 'bout it later," said Bean. "Spook, get our sneakers, will ya?"

Spooky trudged off in his soggy socks to grope blindly among the bushes.

The rest were waiting when, all of a sudden, they heard a hissing sound. "That sounds like a snake!" said Wruggles." Watch where you step." But the words weren't out of his mouth when they were overwhelmed by the fetid stench of rotting flesh. Wruggles started to speak. "What the heck . . . ?"

Before he knew what happened, he received a sharp blow to the back of the head. He went limp and fell with a thud. The last thing he was aware of was the gun being sharply wrenched from his holster.

24
ONE MORE SURPRISE

BEAN FELT HIMSELF SEIZED by angry hands, and some kind of cloth was clamped over his mouth. A sweet, medicinal smell made him nauseated, and for a few seconds he held his breath, but the battle was useless. A moment later he succumbed to the chloroform as his world collapsed in dizzying darkness.

Tiny Martin, disoriented by the sudden turn of events, released his grip on Lawson's neck and Lawson collapsed to the ground. Tiny was trying to figure what to do next when he felt a sharp nudge in the hollow of his back, which he rightly assumed to be Wruggles's gun. He held up his hands.

When Bean came to, it was so pitch dark he thought he'd lost his sight, and his head ached. He groaned.

"Well, sounds like we're all here finally," said Tiny Martin's distinctive voice somewhere in the darkness.

From the sound, Bean deduced they were in a fairly confined space. "What happened?" he moaned. "Where are we?"

"Powder bunker," said Tiny. "I never even knew it was here 'til I brought you down."

Bean's head was reeling. "Brought me down? You put me in here?"

"Me, too," said Wruggles groggily from nearby.

"Didn't have much choice with that gun in my back," said Tiny apologetically. "Took a coupla trips to get the three of you, then he shut me in an' locked the door."

Bean assumed the third person he referred to was Spooky. "Spook?" he said.

"Last I seen've him, he was diggin' around in the bushes tryin' to find your sneakers," Tiny explained. "Don't seem like the Black Moriah knew about 'im, so I didn't say nothin'."

"Then who else is in here?" said Bean.

"Lawson," said Wruggles. "He's in the corner, sleepin' like a baby."

Bean protested. "But if he's in here, then—"

"Who's out there paradin' around as the Black Moriah?" said Wruggles. "Good question. Me and Tiny was cogitatin' on that when you come 'round."

"This doesn't make no sense," said Bean, massaging his head with both hands as if to stimulate his brain. "I was sure Lawson was the Black Moriah."

"Me, too," said Wruggles. "Made all the sense in the world when Ab explained what you was up to. 'Specially when I saw 'im crawl outta his bedroom window tonight."

"You were there?" said Bean, more than a little alarmed that neither he nor Spooky had been aware of the presence of someone who took up as much real estate as Wruggles.

"Me an' Tiny both," said Wruggles. Bean was doubly impressed. "But looks like we gotta do some rethinkin'."

"Well, if Lawson ain't the Black Moriah, and he ain't interested in the treasure, who is he, an' why was he pretendin' to be confined to a wheelchair?" Bean inquired of the darkness.

"Guess he'll have to answer that himself, assumin' he ever comes to," Wruggles offered.

"Question now is, how're we gonna get outta this place?"

Bean ran his hand along the smooth stone floor and wall. "Must be where he kept Ab."

"Ayuh," Tiny agreed. "Poor kid."

Bean couldn't imagine being locked away in this dark, dank hole for six hours, let alone six days. He was suddenly overcome with compassion for what Ab had been through, and with anger for whoever had put her through it.

All at once a raspy, metallic sound filled the bunker. The men instantly fell silent as the heavy iron door swung eerily on its rusty hinges, carving a faint rectangle of light in the darkness. In the dim light was the vague outline of a person.

For a man of his size, Tiny acted with surprising agility. No sooner had the door swung halfway open than he had sprung from the floor and seized the visitor in the vise of his arms.

"Hey!" said the intruder.

"Spook!" Bean cried. He stumbled to his feet and lunged toward the door.

"Well, you sure ain't who we was expectin'," said Tiny, releasing his hold on the boy.

Spooky sputtered a little as he caught his breath. "You fellas sure make it hard on a hero."

"What're you doin' here?" said Bean.

"You want me to leave?" Spooky replied stoically. "I didn't know I was crashin' a party."

"You never looked better," said the constable as he struggled to his feet. "Even though I can't exactly see you."

Bean's mind was racing. "Quick! We gotta get out and find 'im."

"Find whom?" said Spooky cryptically, emphasizing his correct use of the pronoun. "Anyone in particular?"

"The Black Moriah, you idiot," said Bean. "He's gettin' away while we're sittin' here flappin' our jaws."

"Flap all you want," said Spooky with unusual calm. "His hauntin' days are pretty much over, I'd say."

"You're makin' more noise an' less sense," sniped Wruggles.

"What're you talkin' about?" Bean demanded.

"I seen who it was," said Spooky casually. "And if you gentlemen would care to follow me back to the Moses Webster House, I think I can sort this little matter out to everyone's satisfaction."

"He's been hit on the head," Tiny opined.

"How did you see who it was?" Bean wanted to know.

"Simple," said Spooky, reveling in the sensation he'd caused. "I stayed put in the bushes while the Black Moriah was havin' Tiny lug you guys off. Didn't see how gettin' myself discovered would help much.

"When he come out alone after the last trip, he took off his disguise. That's how I seen . . . saw . . . who it was.

"He headed off down the hill, an' I come in here. The door wasn't held by nothin' but a bolt, so I just slipped it. By the way, Constable Wruggles, here's your gun."

Wruggles fumbled for the weapon in the darkness and fastened it in his holster. "Don't have bullets in it anyway," he said.

"Don't have no bullets!" said Tiny.

"Too dangerous," Wruggles explained.

"Wish I'd've known that when he stuck it in my back. I'd've made 'im eat it."

"How'd you get the gun?" asked Bean. "I s'pose you wrestled it from 'im."

"Nope. He just chucked it into the puckerbrush. Almost hit me with it. Oh, I've got your video camera, too, Bean. I think Tiny stepped on it."

Bean's heart sank. His father had saved for months to buy that camera and hadn't even had a chance to use it yet.

"Now, if everybody's ready, why don't we get goin'?" said Spooky. "I got a plan."

"We're s'posed to follow you?" said Wruggles in disbelief. "Ain't that a little like the blind followin' the blind?"

Spooky didn't lose his composure. "Well, let me see. You guys managed to get yourself locked up, an' I set you free. You lost your gun, an' I got it back. You lost the video camera, an' I found it."

Tiny had to agree. "You know, he's got a pretty good point."

"I ain't goin' anywhere 'til you tell me who it is we're after," Bean said adamantly.

"Then I guess you'll just have to stay here," Spooky retorted. "You want me to bring you some milk and cookies tomorrow after the Black Moriah's in jail?"

Obviously Bean had no choice in the matter. Part of him wanted to strangle Spooky, but another part wanted to give him a big hug. He suppressed both urges. "Well, if that's the way you want to do it, let's get on with it." He held out his hand. "Give me the camera."

"Can't," said Spooky. "It's evidence."

Bean's head hurt too much to argue any further.

"What about Lawson?" Tiny reminded them. "I ain't gonna carry him all the way back to town."

After they stepped from the powder bunker, Wruggles shut the door and slipped the bolt. "He'll do right where he is 'til mornin'."

The former captives followed their unlikely savior back to the surface.

Along the way, the men were frustrated in their attempts to find out what Spooky was up to. "You'll see" was all he'd say.

When they arrived at the Moses Webster House, all was dark and quiet. "Let's go in an' get comfy in the living room," Spooky suggested, as if they'd just returned from a pleasant tramp through the countryside. Wruggles looked at Tiny, Tiny looked at Bean, Bean looked at Wruggles, and they all looked at Spooky as if he'd just grown another head.

Wruggles stated the obvious. "We'll wake people up."

"Them that's asleep will stay asleep, an' them that's awake will stay awake, I should imagine," Spooky philosophized. "Long as we don't make a racket."

Having followed him this far, Bean and the men resolved they might as well see it through. As softly as possible, they made their way into the house, then through the kitchen and into the living room.

Wruggles whispered sharply. "What now?"

"Now I'm gonna go upstairs an' tell folks there's a fire," said Spooky.

"You'll do no such thing!" Wruggles objected. "You're even crazier'n I thought you was."

"I ain't gonna tell *everyone*," Spooky explained. "Just wait here." He placed the video camera on a doily in the middle of the coffee table.

"I oughta have my head examined," said Wruggles as Spooky disappeared on his errand. "Between stoppin' the ferry an' sneakin' into people's houses in the middle of the night, my job's gonna be worth about two cents." It occurred to him that having his head examined was exactly what he'd do as soon as the medical center opened in the morning. Whatever the Black Moriah had hit him with, he felt as if it had loosened some of the wiring in his brain.

The pendulum of the grandfather clock in the corner of the room sliced off half a minute or so in perfect seconds. Bean and the men stood scratching their heads and murmuring in befuddlement as they waited for whatever was going to happen next.

They hadn't long to wait. Soon, the agitated shuffling of feet could be heard on the floor above. Moments later the Prinderbys, still in their pajamas, were herded down the stairs and into the living room.

Everyone stared at one another in mutual amazement.

"How did you get . . . ," Professor Prinderby exclaimed, then suddenly corrected himself. "What are you gentlemen doing here?"

Wruggles was about to say, darned if I know, but Spooky spoke. "He was in the tub when I knocked on the door. Wasn't you, Professor?"

"What of it?" snapped the professor. "I trust there's no law against cleanliness. What's all this about a fire?"

"I've left all my things upstairs," said Mrs. Prinderby, clearly confused. "All my important things."

"Mighty funny time of night to be takin' a bath, ain't it?" Spooky said placidly. "You musta been some ol' dirty." He sniffed the air theatrically. "I don't think you soaked quite long enough this time, though."

When the professor turned on Wruggles, little remained of his harmless, scholarly demeanor. "What is the meaning of all this, Constable? Do you intend to let this undersized Neanderthal ramble on endlessly, or is it your job to get us to safety, *if* there's a fire." He took a hasty survey of the house. "Which I doubt," he added. "In which case, I would like to prefer charges against the boy this instant."

Bean could contain himself no longer. "You think *he's* the Black Moriah?"

Wruggles laughed in spite of himself. "Oh, come on, Bean. Even Spook's got more sense than that."

"I beg your pardon?" said the professor, his backbone suddenly stiffened in indignation. "Am I going to have to add libel to the charges?"

"What's he saying, Harold?" said Mrs. Prinderby. "You're not the Black Moriah, you're Harold Prinderby. The boy's been into chemicals of some kind."

"I was up at the wet dock tonight, Professor," Spooky continued. He was having a hard time keeping a straight face and sounding serious. "I saw everything, 'specially when you took off the disguise."

All at once the professor looked like a caged animal. His shoulders slumped and his eyes shot warily from side to side. "The boy's raving mad," he said, though his voice betrayed his unease.

Bean sensed the change in the professor, and suddenly everything came into blinding focus. "You *are* the Black Moriah!" Bean said. All at once he, too, detected the faint smell of rotted fish that soap had failed to wash away.

"Be careful, boy," the professor snapped. "You're saying things you'll regret."

"But he didn't steal the minisub," Wruggles objected. His head hurt worse than ever as he tried to catch up to what was going on.

"No," said Bean. "That was Lawson. We'll get his story tomorrow." Bean moved directly in front of the professor. "*You're* the one who kidnapped Ab, aren't you?"

The professor cringed visibly; nevertheless he protested. "I have no idea what you're talking about. Constable," he said, looking over Bean's head, "if you allow these miscreants to continue, I shall have you up on charges of abusing your office."

"I saw you," said Spooky, unshaken by Prinderby's threats.

Prinderby turned on him, his eyes flashing venom. "You! Who are you! Who's going to take the word of a little . . . of you against me? You have no proof!"

Unfortunate Mrs. Prinderby was driven to distraction. "Proof of what, dear? What are these people talking about? I don't understand."

While she was speaking, Spooky went to the table and picked up the video camera.

"If it's proof you want," he said, "I got it all right here."

"What's that?" Prinderby demanded.

"A video camera," said Spooky. "You remember smackin' Wruggles on the back of the head? I got it all right here." He patted the camera.

Bean was about to remind Spooky there had been no cassette in the camera, but at the same second he realized what his friend was up to and just cleared his throat instead.

Spooky continued. "You remember when you slapped the chloroform over Bean's mouth? I got it all right here." Again he patted the camera. "It's *all* right here. *Includin'* when you come outta the cave an' took off your disguise."

Bean was amazed. Could Spooky pull off this bluff?

The professor slouched a little lower, as if he wanted to tuck his head into his shoulders and disappear.

"There is no fire," said Mrs. Prinderby, taking in the surroundings through her sleepy brain. "Harold, this has been a very cruel joke. Send these men away. I want to go back to bed."

Spooky went confidently to the cabinet in the corner and opened it, revealing a little-used television. He turned on the VCR and, shielding the action with his body, removed a video cassette from a rack of movies. He slipped the cover off and, turning around, held the tape up for all to see. "How 'bout if we have a little show?" he said, slipping the tape into the VCR. "Who wants popcorn?"

Don't push your luck, Bean thought, but he didn't say anything.

"You couldn't have gotten any pictures with that," said the professor. "It was too dark."

It was Bean's turn for a flash of inspiration. "It has a night vision lens," he interrupted. "My father uses it on night rescues." That inspiration was followed by another. "You know all about night vision lenses, don't you, Professor? That's what you used to see in the dark when you played the Black Moriah. Push 'play,'" said Bean. "Let's get this over with once an' for all."

At last the professor was beaten. "No!" he cried weakly, sinking to the floor. "No . . . no more. I confess."

Bean stole a glance at Spooky and gave him a subtle thumbs-up.

"You do?" said Wruggles in disbelief. Then he remembered he wasn't just a witness to this confusing little drama; he was the constable. "I mean, why don't we all sit down an' you just tell us the whole story. An' don't forget, we got your doin's on tape." He gave Spooky an official-looking nod of approval. "So we won't take any beatin' around the bush." Wruggles read the prisoner his rights. He'd always wanted to do that.

"Harold," said Mrs. Prinderby, kneeling beside her beleaguered husband. "Have you been a naughty boy?"

They say confession is good for the soul. If that's true, Professor Prinderby's soul was in pretty good shape by the time he'd finished telling his story.

By late the next morning, for the second time that summer, the exploits of Bean, Ab, and Spooky had electrified the town. From the pool hall to the post office, the Paper Store, Irma Louise's House of Beauty, the fish factory, the lobstermen's co-op, and numerous eating establishments, hardly a sentence was spoken that didn't have something to do with their latest adventure.

Stumpy Budrow leaned forward a little further in his seat at the Port o' Call hardware store. "Now, let me get this straight," he said. He found the story so incredible that he figured his hearing aid must have been acting up. "This professor fella was the Black Moriah?"

"That's right," said Drew Meescham as he rearranged the candy in the iron skillet atop the cold woodstove. "To scare folks off Pogus Point."

"So he could look for the treasure?"

"Not exactly," Drew explained patiently. "That is, it turns out he wasn't so much interested in the treasure for gettin' rich, like you or I would, he just wanted to prove something to his buddies in the academic community."

"Ayuh," said Stumpy doubtfully. This is the part he wasn't too clear about.

Seeing his confusion, Marty Martin leaned closer to the old man. "It's like this, Stumpy," he said. He held up his fingers and ticked them off one at a time as he made his points. "There was these two p'rfessors, see? An' they both were studyin' pirates on the Maine coast. One've 'em said there wasn't no such person as Abnezar Twing—that he was just made up, like Robin Hood or something. Got that?"

Stumpy nodded. "An' one of 'em was this Peterby or whatever you call it."

"Prinderby," Drew said loudly. "Prin-der-by."

"That's what I said," said Stumpy, cupping his hand by his ear. "And the other one was this Lawson character."

"That's right," said Martin. "But that ain't his real name. It's Steerforth." He continued with his story. "Anyway, this Steerforth fella was the one who said there wasn't no such person as Twing. Prinderby said there was. Well, they had lots of arguments and debates or whatever you call it in some kind of archaeology journal no one's ever heard of, an' I guess over time things got pretty hot between 'em."

Stumpy wanted to get his facts straight. "But they was both up to the Moses Webster House. How come they didn't recognize each other?"

"They never met," Drew explained for the third or fourth time. "Steerforth knew who Prinderby was, of course, 'cause he wasn't makin' any effort to hide the fact. But Steerforth used a false name."

"Anyway," Martin interrupted with a look at Drew that said, are you gonna let me tell my story or not? "Steerforth gets wind that Prinderby's found some papers up in Halifax that prove Twing was real, and not only that but he might've buried a treasure somewhere. Something about a code or a poem. I ain't too clear on that myself. But them kids figured it out somehow."

"Smart kids, they are," said Stumpy.

Everyone agreed with a nod. "So, anyhow, this Steerforth fella, who's a marine archaeologist, heard that Prinderby was on his way out here to do some research. Puttin' two an' two together, Steerforth figures it's got something to do with Twing. So he rents a minisub from Captain Kittredge an' comes out here on the sly an' keeps an eye on Prinderby. Seems Steerforth was worried 'bout what'd happen to his reputation if Prinderby was proved right, so he figured he'd try to find the treasure first. Even if it proved him wrong, he'd get the credit for findin' it at least. Or if Prinderby was wrong, Steerforth'd be there to say 'I told you so.'"

Stumpy shook his head. "Hard to believe they went to all that trouble just to make a point."

Drew wasn't so sure. "I've heard you an' Mouse Philbrook get some heated up over politics, Stump," he said. "You go pretty far out on a limb to prove a point."

"That's different," said Stumpy. "Mouse is a Democrat. He needs talkin' to."

The old men laughed.

The scene was much the same at Irma Louise's House of Beauty. "What's the word I'm lookin' for?" said Irma Louise as she rubbed some foul-smelling chemicals into Maisy Hitchcock's blue hair. Then she remembered. "Chutzpah! That's it. Chutzpah. That's what them kids got."

"Chutzpah?" Maisy echoed. "What's that mean?"

"Means nerve. Gumption," explained Ophelia Brazeel, who was sitting near the window leafing through a magazine without looking at it.

"Oh," said Maisy. "I see. Why, yes. They certainly have that by the bucketful." She shook her head. "So, it was Professor Prinderby who kidnapped Abigail Peterson and put her in the powder bunker?"

"That's right," said Irma, massaging a little too vigorously.

"And there never was any film in that video camera?" said Maisy, so astonished she forgot to say ouch.

"Never was," said Irma.

"And it was Steerforth who kidnapped Captain Kittredge and locked him in his own submarine?" said Ophelia.

"All this kidnapping, " said Maisy. "You'd think a couple of professors would have more sense than that, wouldn't you? I mean, what are they teaching at the universities these days?"

"Makes you wonder, don't it?" said Ophelia.

"But why was Steerforth pretending to be cripple?" Maisy asked.

"So no one'd suspect what he was up to," Irma explained. "If people are lookin' for a kidnapper, they ain't likely to suspect someone in a wheelchair, are they? Amazin' thing is, Prinderby never knew this Steerforth was onto him. Didn't even know they was both hidin' their victims in the same place—that powder bunker and the float dock, or whatever they call it, are right side by side."

"Them kids figured it out though," said Ophelia, putting down one magazine and picking up another. "Wicked clever they are."

"Wicked clever," Maisy agreed.

A group of teenagers was gathered on their customary rocks up at the quarry, and they were so caught up in the adventures of Bean and Ab that the girls almost forgot to flirt with the boys, and the boys almost forgot to show off for the girls.

"What about the treasure?" said Rodney Walker, flipping his hair out of his eyes with a jerk of his head. "They ain't just gonna leave it there, are they? We oughtta go get it."

"Right," said Kyle Littlefield sarcastically. "Half the town almost gets themselves killed out there—includin' Cap'n Carver, who was a navy Seal—an' you're gonna walk in an' take the treasure, are you? I'll come to the funeral, if I'm not too busy."

The girls all laughed. Kyle Littlefield was the cutest boy in school and the captain of the basketball team. He even played the guitar. Hot stuff.

Kyle continued. "They're bringin' army engineers over to figure out how to get in there. Besides, Wruggles has the place sealed off."

"Bean and Ab are some good at figurin' out mysteries, ain't they?" said Rodney, wanting to change the subject.

"Way I hear it," said Pam Philbrook, "Spooky's the one who got that professor to confess."

"Ain't as dumb as he looks," said Kyle. This was high praise indeed coming from the most popular boy on the island. He rolled over on his stomach. "He's my cousin, you know."

No one thought it a good idea to mention that, on the island, almost everyone was Spooky's cousin, one way or another.

Steerforth was not talkative. Hunched over the little folding table at the municipal building where Constable Wruggles had his office, he seemed less troubled about being charged with kidnapping Captain

216

Kittredge than by the fact that Professor Prinderby had proved the exis-
tence of Abnezar Twing.

"It's those meddling children," he snapped. "Just my luck to take a
room at the Moses Webster House, among a hornets' nest of pint-sized
Sherlock Holmeses."

Wruggles considered this. "Seems the only one you got to blame is
yourself." He popped his suspenders with his thumbs. "You never would've
had all this trouble if you an' Prinderby had just gone in cahoots with each
other. If you'd've just told everyone what you had in mind, the town
would've turned out to help."

"First," snapped Steerforth, "I'd never have gone in cahoots, as you
say, with that prig Prinderby. But I don't expect someone of your mentality
to understand. Besides," he continued, "why should I? I had a perfectly
good copy of the map and the poem—which he'd been foolish enough to
let a mutual friend make a scan of. Who needed Prinderby?"

Wruggles let the insult roll off his back.

"Second, it should be obvious, even to someone such as yourself, that
having a town full of hicks stomping around up there would surely have
destroyed valuable evidence. Archaeology is a meticulous, studious affair.
Even I credit Prinderby with having the sense to try to scare you all away,
although I think this whole business of resurrecting the Black Moriah was
sophomoric, at best. Still, I thought I'd choke that night those kids came in
and said the Black Moriah had been seen again. Made me drop my newspaper. I'd kept Prinderby in sight all evening, so I knew it couldn't have
been him. Just for a second or so, I began to wonder if I was wrong about
the old imbecile."

"Well, long as we're here waitin' for the sheriff to come on the next
boat," said Wruggles, "why don't you just tell me how that sub got away
from you in the first place."

Steerforth laughed with no good humor. "Early that morning, I had
been out in the Reach, watching Prinderby through the periscope. He
hadn't a clue I was there.

"He disappeared from view among the slag heaps above the cliff, so I
put into the wet dock. In my hurry to find out what he was up to, I didn't
tie up the sub. I just left it there. I'd forgotten the tide was going out.

When I got back—after a fruitless search for Prinderby, I might add—it was gone. Apparently the tide had pulled it out into the Reach. Then the incoming tide must have pushed it into Indian Creek, where that wretched little boy found it."

"So you tried to steal it back the night after the storm," Wruggles hypothesized.

"Well, of course," Steerforth snapped irritably. "I had to keep an eye on Prinderby. I knew he was playing at being the Black Moriah, which told me he thought he was on to something. Curse those children."

"Thing I don't understand 'bout that," said Wruggles, "is why you'd kidnap Kittredge an' keep 'im in the sub. Didn't do you much good that way, did it?"

Steerforth was scornful. "I *detained* him because he surprised me when I was trying to get the sub off the barge. What was I supposed to do, bang him over the head? Sounds like the kind of thing that ignoramus Prinderby would have done. Still, I couldn't have him blabbing all over town now, could I? So I . . . borrowed him." Steerforth's head sank into his shoulders. "As for keeping him in the sub, the sneaky old devil sabotaged it after we were in the wet dock. It was useless to me. I trust you will note in your official report that I took care of him. I assure you, I had every intention of releasing him once I got the better of Prinderby . . . one way or the other."

Wruggles took all this in philosophically. "Well," he said at last, "I guess the judge is gonna find you an entertainin' character."

One mystery remained. Ab, who had slept through the professor's confession, was determined to be the one to figure it out. She spent several hours that day poking around in the attic and was just about to give up the search in frustration when she found what she was looking for—two little speakers attached to a wireless receiver taped to the rafters above the ceiling over the tower room. "That's how he did it!" she proclaimed.

This discovery promoted a search of the Prinderbys' belongings, during which Wruggles found a portable control panel, a wireless transceiver, and headphones tucked in the professor's precious briefcase. "With this little outfit," said Wruggles, "he could set himself up anywhere within five hundred feet of the house an' hear the goin's-on in the tower. Then, with this microphone, he pretended to be a ghost, tryin' to scare you kids off the trail."

"That's what he was doin' up at the bandstand that night. He wasn't listenin' to CDs. He was listenin' to the seance!" said Spooky.

"It was quite a little setup, actually," Ab explained. "He controlled the thumping on the walls, that wicked awful stink, everything, right there from the bandstand."

"How'd he do that?" Spooky asked. Clearly the professor was a man of hidden talents.

"A little motorized thumper thing," Ab replied, keenly aware how girlish the description sounded. She tried to shape the device with her hands, but it didn't help. "Like a mallet hooked up to a little motor; it just tunked the rafters whenever he pushed a button."

Spooky could accept that. "But what about the smell?"

"A CO_2 cartridge hooked up to the same switch," said Ab. "I found that, too. He had the same chemicals in an aerosol can that he carried with him when he was pretending to be the Black Moriah. That's where that sickening smell came from."

"That explains that hissing sound we'd hear whenever he showed up."

"He used the same chemicals they use in science class every year to stink up the school." She hadn't taken that class yet, so she didn't know what the chemicals were. She waved her hand in front of her nose. "Stinks awful."

"He also hid electrodes under the rug, which were connected to a battery under a loose floorboard in the closet," said Bean. "That's how everyone felt that charge of static electricity during the seance."

"That don't make sense," said Spooky. "Carpets don't conduct electricity."

Ab smiled and held up a spray bottle. "It does if it's been sprayed with water—just enough to be damp."

"The positive and negative ions filled the air with static electricity." Mr. Peterson explained. "Quite an elaborate setup."

Wruggles was thoughtful. "I feel sorry for Mrs. Prinderby," he said. "Her own husband usin' her superstitions like that to try to make everyone think they were talkin' to the dead."

"Ambition is a lot like love," said Mrs. Carver that night when everyone was gathered at the Moses Webster House for a celebratory dinner. "It makes folks do strange things."

They'd been talking about the Prinderbys, how the professor had risked everything to try to prove himself right, and how his wife—completely baffled by all that had happened—had already vowed to stand by him no matter what.

In the end, just before two state policemen carted him off to the mainland for his arraignment, Professor Prinderby had asked to speak to Bean and Ab and their parents. It had been a tense meeting, but he said he was sorry for all he had done and begged for their forgiveness.

"I don't know what came over me," said the professor, on the verge of tears. "I've behaved disgracefully, and I put people in danger. I never meant it to—"

"He never meant to hurt anyone," said Mrs. Prinderby, patting her husband on the head.

The professor was unable to speak, but he nodded emphatically. When he finally gained control of himself, he looked sheepishly at Ab. "I never intended you any harm. Honestly. I don't know what came over me. It's just that, you children were always just one step behind me. There seemed nothing I could do to shake you off my trail." He raised the same woeful eyes to Ab's parents. "I was beside myself, seeing what you were going through."

"Not enough to tell us our daughter was alive!" Mrs. Peterson snapped, tears welling in her eyes.

Prinderby hung his head. "No," he confessed. "I was blinded by my ambition. I justified my actions to myself, convincing myself that if only I could find the treasure before the memorial service, I could have released her, and no one would have been the wiser.

"But when the day of the memorial service came, and I was no closer to finding Twing's treasure, I had no choice but to let her go."

"But you figured if she was found on Lane's Island," said Bean, "that would throw people off the trail."

Prinderby nodded miserably. Ab almost felt sorry for him. Then she remembered all he had put her parents through and realized he had earned whatever punishment he would get.

"Time to go," said Wruggles.

"One more thing," said the professor. He produced a manila folder from his briefcase and placed it carefully on the table. "I want to leave these with you," he said, sliding the envelope to Bean. "These are copies of Twing's personal papers. Perhaps you'd care to read them." He looked sadly at the little bundle of papers as Bean withdrew them from the folder. "I know it doesn't make up for . . . . That's my life's work," he said softly. He began to cry again, and the officers led him away.

Mrs. Prinderby followed close behind, carrying her overstuffed satchel of mysterious objects. "If only I could get through to Anabel," she said cheerfully. "I'm sure she has a lot to say. Tonight, I shall consult the stars."

Two days later, a package arrived at the Moses Webster House for Professor Prinderby. The return address was the Royal Bureau of Prisons, London, England. After consulting with Constable Wruggles, the Proverbs received permission to open the folder. Everyone gathered for the occasion.

Mr. Proverb pushed the folder across the table to Bean, Ab, and Spooky. "I think the honor should be yours," he said graciously.

Ab asked for a knife.

"Heck with a knife," said Spooky. Grabbing the envelope from her, he ripped it open with his teeth before anyone had time to protest. He withdrew a thin sheaf of papers from the folder and tossed it to his companions. "Have at it," he said with satisfaction.

Bean began to read the records aloud, but the flowery, old-fashioned handwriting proved too much for him. He surrendered the chore to Ab, who read the nine pages from first to last. It was the record of the trial of Abnezar Twing, as well as a copy of his last will and testament, which his poor wife apparently never received. When Ab had finished, everyone sat looking at one another.

"Then he didn't go down with the *Privilege*," said Bean. "He was captured in a pub in Halifax an' sent to England to stand trial."

"So it would appear," said Captain Carver. "And somewhere between his capture and his execution, he wrote the poem and got it to his wife, hoping she'd find the treasure."

"But even if she had found it," said Ab with concern, "she'd have tripped the booby trap. She would have drowned!"

"There must be a clue we're missin'," said Bean. "Something that told her to avoid that first step. If we hadn't stepped on that, we'd've been in an' out with no trouble."

They reread the record, but found no hint of a warning about the first step. What they did find, though, among Professor Prinderby's papers, was a love letter from Anabel Twing to "her red-haired love."

"That's curious," said Mrs. Carver. "Let me see the trial record again." Ab handed it to her, and everyone watched in silence as she read. "Aha!" she said at last. "I think we've solved that little mystery. Here's a description of Twing from the court reporter: 'Abnezar Twing flinched not as the litany of foul deeds attributed to him were spoken solemnly by the judge. Nor did he cringe when, at trial's end, his sentence was read: Death by hanging for crimes against the Crown. Asked by his lordship the judge if he wished to say anything in his own behalf, he only ran his fingers through his thick black hair and said, "You carry out your sentences, your lordship, and I shall carry out mine."'"

Mrs. Carver put down the paper and cast a knowing glance at Ab, who said, "But Anabel's letter was to a red-haired—"

"Oh, my goodness!" said Mrs. Peterson, her eyes widening with understanding.

"What?" said Spooky, who didn't get the point. "What?"

"Apparently," Mrs. Carver explained, "Anabel hadn't been entirely faithful to her husband while he was away at sea."

"You mean, she—"

Mrs. Carver nodded. "Evidently, Abnezar found out about his wife's indiscretions and—"

"He didn't *want* 'er to know about the first step!" Bean said. "He didn't want 'er to come out of there alive!"

"How horrible!" said Ab.

"He thought he'd have his vengeance from beyond the grave," said Mrs. Proverb. "How dreadful."

"He was a dreadful man," said Mrs. Carver. "Not that it justifies his wife's unfaithfulness, but just look at how he poisoned the crew of the *Destiny* after they'd gone to all that work to help him hide the ship."

"He gave them all a drink of poisoned rum," said Ab, recalling the passage from the confession. "Then he left them to die, sealing the little door behind him.

"But the *Privilege* never returned to pick him up, as planned. So he had to hitch a ride on a fishing schooner back to Halifax, where he found out the *Privilege* had gone down in the storm. Then he was captured."

The phone rang in the hall, and Mr. Proverb rose to answer it. A few seconds later, he returned. "It's for you, Captain Carver," he said. "Someone with the Army Corps of Engineers."

The conversation that followed was muffled, and those gathered around the table could make out only a word here and there. When Captain Carver hung up and returned to the table, all eyes were anxiously on him. He sat down.

"The army engineers say they're baffled. There's no way they can figure to get back in the cave without setting off a landslide that will bring the whole thing tumbling down, destroying the ship in the process. He says his hat's off to Abnezar Twing."

Spooky didn't like that. "So it's just gotta stay in there? Treasure an' all?"

"For the time being," said Captain Carver. "Maybe someday engineers will come up with a way of getting in, but for now . . ." He shrugged his shoulders. "The man did say he found a map among the oceanographic archives that explained how Twing got the ship in there." Captain Carver got a napkin and drew a diagram as everyone pressed around. "Like I 'd thought, there was a natural cleft in the shoreline, like this, big enough and deep enough so Twing could sail the ship right in. The cleft was wide at the bottom, but the sides almost came together at the top." He added an inverted V to his diagram. "There were high cliffs on either side of the cleft, here and here." He added dotted lines to indicate where the cliff tops had been. "He sealed off the entrance with the masts of the ship and other trees cut down for the purpose, then blew the tops of the cliffs away with explosives. They caused an avalanche that wedged huge stones in the top of the funnel and tumbled down to the ocean in a pile that, eventually, covered the wall of masts and trees he'd created. Of course, he'd already built the little door and the steps, as well as the booby trap."

"That's something else I don't understand," said Constable Wruggles. "How'd that booby trap work? You said the first step set 'er off."

"You've got to hand it to Twing," said Captain Carver. "He was one heck of an engineer. He rigged it so whoever was in the tunnel would drown instantly."

"And he thought he knew just who that was going to be," said Ab with a shudder of disgust. "Anabel."

"He sure didn't think it would be you two," said Captain Carver. "Anyway, he built a reservoir that was filled by rainwater over the course of a year or two. He probably left an opening on one side and dammed it with boards, or rocks, or both. Somehow he rigged a trigger mechanism, so the dam would give way when weight was applied to the first step. The supports caved in and the whole assembly tumbled down the stairwell— followed by all that water. When the water was released, the supports gave way, and a few tons of loose boulders crashed down and filled the tunnel."

"Murder an' burial, all at once," said Wruggles, shaking his head.

"But the door was so small," said Ab. "It was all Bean and I could do to get through it. How could all those pirates have used it?"

"People were a lot smaller in those days," Mr. Proverb explained. "A man Bean's size would have been about average. Someone my size, or Captain Carver's size, would have been considered a giant."

"Or my size," said Tiny Martin.

"No, Tiny," said Wruggles. "You'd've been considered an immovable object."

Everyone laughed. In the silence that followed, the big clock in the living room could be heard ticking off the time.

Mr. Proverb rubbed his belly with satisfaction. "I told you there was a logical explanation for everything."

Captain Carver finished his coffee. "And so ends the mystery of the Black Moriah," he said, putting down his cup.

And so it had.

Bean and Ab were down at the public landing early the next morning to say farewell to Captain Kittredge.

"Well, you got that nasty business all sorted out," said the captain as he climbed into the sub.

"We couldn't've done it without you," said Bean.

"Me?" Kittredge laughed. "I don't see how my getting myself kidnapped was much help."

"I wasn't talkin' about that," said Bean. "Dad says you saved my life when I was caught in the submarine."

Kittredge smiled. "Glad I could help." He reached down into the sub and flipped a switch. The thrusters whined to life.

"Captain?" said Bean. "You're an engineer, right?"

"I am. Why do you ask?"

"Do you think those army engineers are right 'bout there bein' no way to get to the treasure?"

A curious smile crept to the corners of Kittredge's mouth. "Well, those fellas are awfully good at what they do."

"But?" said Bean hopefully.

"But so was ol' Twing," Kittredge replied. "I doubt he'd have arranged things in such a way that he couldn't get at the ship, or the treasure, in the event someone tripped his booby trap."

Ab seized on the captain's meaning. "There's another way in!"

Again Kittredge just smiled. "I'd best be off." He untied the bow line and tossed it onto the dock. "I'd look for a keystone, if I were you."

"Keystone?" said Bean.

Kittredge crossed his arms and leaned on the rim of the conning tower. "As I see it, Twing didn't go to all the trouble of hiding that ship just so he'd have a place to hide his treasure, assuming there *is* any. He could have dug a hole anywhere for that. No, I'd say he meant the *Destiny* to sail again. That means he engineered a way to get it out. To my way of thinking, that means there's a keystone somewhere."

"What is a keystone?" asked Ab.

"I know that," said Bean. "It's the stone at the top of an arch that holds the other stones in place."

"Bingo!" said Kittredge.

This made no sense to Ab. "But they say he blew off the top of the cliffs and the stones just fell into place."

Kittredge held up a contrary finger. "Fell into place the way he *wanted* them to," he said. "My guess is he and his men set some stones in place before the explosion—a sort of frame or foundation that all that rubble would come to rest on." Kittredge stood up so his head and chest were above the conning tower. "That's what I'd have done, anyway. Ah! Here's my ride."

The kids had been so involved in the conversation that they hadn't even noticed the Coast Guard launch until it nudged the float.

"Captain Kittredge?" said a seaman as he jumped to the float with the painter in this hand.

"That's me," said Kittredge.

Bean and Ab watched as Kittredge maneuvered the little sub into place behind the launch and lines were tied between the vessels for the trip across the bay. By the time preparations were concluded, Kittredge was in the launch and the kids were waving good-bye.

"But how do we find the keystone?" Ab called.

"Study your literature," Kittredge called cryptically. He'd spent the previous night reading Prinderby's copy of Twing's poem, and he'd discovered a final clue. But he was an old man, with plenty of adventures of his own. This one belonged to the kids, and he'd let them figure it out.

"Mark my words," he said, raising his voice to be heard over the deep-throated gurgle of the launch's engine. "Twing meant the *Destiny* to sail again. And some day, it will!"

"And someday," the captain added to himself as he waved a final farewell, "those two will be the ones to unravel the last piece of your puzzle, Captain Twing." Kittredge smiled, gave a little salute, and took up the slack on the line as *Jellybean* fell obediently into place in the launch's wake. "Some day," he said.

But before that day, Bean and Ab would have lots of other riddles to solve. In fact, at that very moment in another part of the world, a mystery was already unfolding that would involve Bean and Ab in a most unexpected way.

Author's Note

Although he didn't take part in Bean and Ab's fictitious adventure of the Black Moriah, Captain Kittredge really does exist. Retired to the little village of South Thomaston on the coast of Maine, after an illustrious career in the navy, the captain has built numerous minisubs, which now ply the oceans of the world for purposes of research and recreation. Now in his eighties, the captain has taken up flying a one-man ultralight that he also built himself.

Proving that fact can often be stranger than fiction, the Black Moriah, though exaggerated for purposes of this story, actually existed on Vinalhaven Island in Penobscot Bay, Maine. There are a number of conflicting accounts of this dreadful apparition, which began haunting the darkened byways of the island in the early years of the twentieth century. People generally agree on a few points, however. First, the Black Moriah appeared only to women, often following them on their way home late at night. Second, a foul smell always accompanied the materializations. Lastly, no one ever found out who, or what, the Black Moriah was. Nor does anyone seem to know where the name Black Moriah came from, or what it means. The last reported sighting was in 1937.

Abnezar Twing is based on the real-life pirate Captain Edward Nelson. His story was told in Edward Rowe Snow's *Unsolved Mysteries of Sea and Shore* (published in 1962), from which I drew a great deal of inspiration. Snow's account is reprinted below, with the gracious permission of the author's daughter, to whom I am indebted.

Edward Rowe Snow writes:

I discovered that many years ago, on the Cushing side of the Saint George River, settlers are said to have found what they considered was an artificial underground cave with a subterranean passageway right down to the water's edge. My informant told me that some years ago an author, Aubigne Lermond Packard, who made an intensive study of the entire area, was convinced that pirates did bury treasure somewhere along the banks of the river, probably at or near the cave.

On the other hand, a long talk which I had on April 1, 1963, with Clarence Dyer of Tenants Harbor gave me the opinion that few present residents of the area believe the treasure is buried in the region of the cave.

Wholly different from anything that the Indians might have constructed, the cave was assumed by many to have been dug out by pirates. Later called the Pirate's Cellar, the cave was probably the headquarters where the pirates met and divided their spoils. Some local historians always thought that the treasure was secreted inside the cave. Nothing was ever found of value in the cave, however, and scores of treasure hunters have dug in the general vicinity unsuccessfully.

The only pirate ever actually known to have been in the area was Captain Edward Nelson, a native of Charlottetown, Prince Edward Island. Nelson was the son of a well-to-do islander. Every fall after the year 1819, when the lad was seven, the boy's father sent Edward down to Halifax aboard a ship with a load of fruit and produce for the market there.

Unfortunately, the elder Nelson did not realize just what social activities were possible at Halifax during the week the schooner was being unloaded. When Edward was nineteen, Mr. Nelson made his son captain of the schooner, not an unusual promotion in those days. However, Edward's interest in the night life at Halifax, where he was away from parental restrictions, became greater with his assumption of complete authority on the schooner, now the scene of lively parties and dances.

Edward married a local girl in Charlottetown, and by her had two daughters. They built a house not far from his father's residence, and Edward was given a substantial section of the Nelson estate at the time.

Meanwhile, the annual fruit and produce evening parties at Halifax soon became the talk of the city. News of these eventually reached Prince Edward Island, with the dancing and drinking sprees reported in great detail to the patriarch of the family. When he found out that Edward was spending considerable time in the company of young ladies of questionable reputation, Mr. Nelson was shocked. He was particularly grieved by the wording of one document which has been preserved. It stated that Edward was 'very wild and drank and intrigued with the girls in an extravagant manner.'

The day of reckoning came, a family quarrel resulted, and Edward and his father parted company. It was discovered that Edward had squandered a good portion of the receipts of the last voyage, and because of this the farewells were particularly bitter. He never saw his mother or father again.

Through the assistance of one of his male associates at the evening parties, Nelson obtained a position as lieutenant in the Nova Scotia Fensibles at Halifax. Moving there, he left his wife and children in Charlottetown to live on the rents they collected from the property Edward now owned.

At Halifax, he met a Scotsman named Ansel Morrison in whose company he was often seen. Then both men suddenly vanished, and Halifax saw them no more.

The two men had become pirates!

Capturing a trim 'little New York battleship' which carried ten guns, they quickly got together a crew of fifty ruffians and joined the brotherhood of pirates. They began by treating their captives well but soon had a reputation for showing them little mercy.

Their first important capture was a trim brig belonging to a Mr. Hill of Rotherhithe, England. Putting aboard a prize crew, they sailed the vessel down to New York where they sold both her and the cargo for a tidy profit.

A cruise to the West Indies followed. Here, in the space of two years, seventeen ships from Holland and England were captured. By this time Nelson and Morrison had become depraved savages. Their methods of torturing the sailors and passengers were diabolical, but they would usually save the lives of the prettiest ladies aboard for their own purposes . . . (when they concluded their despicable entertainment, they disposed of their victims) by the simple expedient of throwing them overboard.

One day they landed on the island of Saint Kitts, where they plundered and set afire two Dutch plantations, murdering the men and slaves. (The women they kidnapped).

Voyaging back toward Nova Scotia, they captured no less than ten more vessels, all of which they sailed into New York where the ships were sold for handsome profits. On several occasions the pirates would sail to the Saint Georges River, where they would go ashore at several locations and relax, far from the cares of piracy.

After more successful voyages, [Nelson was a very wealthy man, and] Morrison was not far behind. . . .

By this time, both men were actually tiring of their life of looting and carousing, and while off the coast of Brazil they suddenly agreed to end their partnership and leave the sea forever. It was arranged that each should go his separate way. Morrison stated that he wished to return to Aberdeen, Scotland, which he had left twenty years before, while Nelson now admitted that he was anxious to resume his relationship with his wife and children, whom he had not seen for many years.

A discussion was held on board the pirate vessel concerning the plan of action for Edward. It was decided that the pirates would sail to the Saint Georges River where Nelson's treasure would be unloaded and buried. The pirate vessel then would proceed to Charlottetown to put Nelson ashore, after which Morrison and the other pirates would sail across to Scotland.

As they approached New York, however, Nelson decided to go ashore. He made arrangements to purchase a country estate, whose owners had perished in a shipwreck. Soon he rejoined his companions aboard the ship, and they sailed for Maine. Reaching Portland, they paid off the entire crew with the exception of fourteen men who were needed to handle the vessel.

Then they sailed back to the Saint Georges River and unloaded the bulk of Nelson's fortune. Six men put the treasure in the long boat, and after carrying it ashore where they dug a great hole and buried the loot, Nelson carefully identifying the location on a map he drew in the lower left corner of a chart. The sound of six shots was heard by those aboard the pirate craft, and when Nelson returned to the beach he was alone.

"The others ran away," Nelson stated unabashed, and the sailors realized that he had wished no living witnesses to the burial of his treasure.

Always a careful man, Nelson had kept out [a substantial amount] of his loot, and it was still aboard when the remnants of the pirate band sailed away from the Saint Georges River forever. A storm came up that night which increased in violence before morning, and the ten men were unable to control their vessel. Soon the craft was wallowing in the trough of the seas, and the men abandoned all hope of escaping.

Crashing ashore on a small island some distance from Charlottetown, the ship went to pieces. Although seven of the pirates drowned, including Morrison, Nelson and two others escaped. Morrison's treasure went down with the ship, but Nelson managed to retrieve his remaining wealth. Unfortunately, the chart with his map on it had been reduced to a mass of pulp by the salt water and was worthless.

Making his way overland with his two assistants, Nelson decided it would be wise to [give them a few thousand dollars] each and get them off the island before revealing himself to his wife and family. The three men hired a rig and made their way to Charlottetown, where they stayed at an inn.

Soon the weekly boat to the mainland took the two pirates away. Nelson then left the inn and hired a team to take him home. He was warmly received by his incredulous wife, who introduced him to his two daughters. She then told him that both his father and mother had passed away.